Harry Partch

Contemporary Music Studies

A series of books edited by Peter Nelson and Nigel Osborne, University of Edinburgh, UK

Please see the back of this book for other titles in the Contemporary Music Studies series

Harry Partch
An Anthology of Critical Perspectives

edited by
David Dunn

harwood academic publishers
Australia • Canada • France • Germany • India
Japan • Luxembourg • Malaysia • The Netherlands
Russia • Singapore • Switzerland

Amsteldijk 166
1st Floor
1079 LH Amsterdam
The Netherlands

British Library Cataloguing in Publication Data
Harry Partch: an anthology of critical perspectives—
    (Contemporary music studies; v. 19)
    1. Partch, Harry, 1901–1974—Criticism and interpretation
    I. Dunn, David
    780.9'2

    ISBN   90-5755-065-2

Cover illustration: Harry Partch in the late 1960s.

Music

CONTENTS

INTRODUCTION TO THE SERIES

The rapid expansion and diversification of contemporary music is explored in this international series of books for contemporary musicians. Leading experts and practitioners present composition today in all aspects—its techniques, aesthetics and technology, and its relationships with other disciplines and currents of thought—as well as using the series to communicate actual musical materials.

The series also features monographs on significant twentieth-century composers not extensively documented in the existing literature.

Nigel Osborne

ACKNOWLEDGMENTS

During the complilation of this anthology I have benefited greatly from the assistance of several individuals. In addition to the various contributors, I would like to thank the late Kenneth Gaburo and Lingua Press for allowing access to its substantial Partch archive, Danlee Mitchell for his cooperation in providing a variety of materials and personal support over many years, and Betty Freeman for permission to select from her photographic documentation of Partch.

I also wish to acknowledge the following for allowing me to publish articles:
Latin American Music Review for permission to reprint "Harry Partch: Verses in Preparation for *Delusion of the Fury*" by Paul Earls. It was first published in the *Anuario interamericano de investigación musical / Yearbook for inter-American musical research*, Volume III, 1967.
Perspectives of New Music for permission to reprint "Beyond Harry Partch" by Ben Johnston, published in Volume 22, nos. 1 & 2 (Fall–Winter 1983 / Spring–Summer 1984): 223–232.
Percussive Notes Research Edition for permission to reprint "In Search of Partch's *Bewitched*" by Kenneth Gaburo, published in Volume 23, no. 3, March, 1985, Percussive Arts Society, Urbana, Illinois.
The Harry Partch Foundation for permission to print "The Rhythmic Motivations of *Castor and Pollux* and *Even Wild Horses*" and "The Umbilical Cord Still Vibrates" by Harry Partch. These articles and the photographs on pages 109–123 are copyright © The Harry Partch Foundation and are used by permission.

LIST OF PLATES

PREFACE

The work of composer Harry Partch remains surprisingly controversial, even these many years after his death. While many of his supporters would claim that this is a testament to his creative originality, his detractors will probably take delight in the general failure of Partch's musical and theoretical contributions to penetrate the institutional status quo of the American musical establishment. His most vehement critics have generally seen his work as either trivial or heretical. His most passionate devotees have elevated him to the dubious status of prophet. In my opinion, neither view does justice to the man or his music.

It has been my intention, in the editing of this anthology, to walk a middle line which reflects upon the significance of Partch's work while respecting the inclusive nature of his philosophical assumptions. Rather than resolving the inherent complexities of the work, this collection of critical perspectives emphasizes the often extraordinary contradictions surrounding, and deeply embedded within, the man and his work. It is my contention that these very contradictions account for the vitality that his life and music exuded.

These essays have been principally chosen for their diversity in order to represent the spectrum of serious opinions, past and present, which demonstrate the heterodox complexity of Partch's contributions. Many of these statements (Rasch, Hackbarth, and Earls) are self-explanatory in that they continue an academic tradition of theoretical scholarship. Others (Johnston, Brant, and Harrison) combine historical and theoretical insights with personal recollections. The remaining works (Dunn, Barkin, and Gaburo) are intentionally problematic in their attempt to combine subjective scholarship and philosophical insights through text quotation, typographic juxtaposition, and collage. While the Gaburo essay articulates a profound understanding of the philosophical basis of Partch's concept of *corporeality* through encoding its content deeply into the expressive language and format, the Barkin piece evolves a complex *play* of language out of the direct physical act of listening to Partch's music. The result not only captures the complex and contradictory nature of the sounds but also much of Partch's eccentric personality as well.

The collection is organized into three categories derived from Partch's own self-descriptive language: "This is my trinity: sound–magic, visual beauty, experience–ritual." This is by no means a rigorous attempt to categorize the contents of each paper. It is merely suggestive of general topic areas for organizational convenience. Three of the essays have appeared elsewhere. They are here reprinted in order to give them a new forum. Each presents a statement of continuing interest that expresses the variety of opinions and observations surrounding the Partch legacy. The two essays by Partch have been included because it seemed appropriate to assert his voice within the context of so many others.

I have purposefully chosen to not duplicate what is available elsewhere, specifically Partch's own theoretical testament, *Genesis of a Music*. The reader is advised that Partch's book is, in many ways, prerequisite reading for this volume of *commentary*. Likewise, there is a general avoidance of biographical data that is readily available from several reference sources.

David Dunn

Introduction

REFLECTIONS, MEMORIES AND OTHER VOICES

A Dialogue between David Dunn and Danlee Mitchell

Danlee Mitchell has been the musician closest to Partch. As his primary assistant for many years until his death, and as the principle inheritor of the Partch tradition, he has kept the ideas alive through performance of the music and the teaching of its theoretical basis. David Dunn is an experimental composer and philosopher who was an associate of Partch and performer of his works.

The following dialogue was recorded at San Diego State University, where Mitchell is a member of the music faculty, on April 4, 1987. The additional commentary is excerpted from statements by Partch himself (left column) and from those by various composers, critics, and supporters (right column). The resultant heterophony not only attempts to highlight many of the contrasting aspects of Partch's work but, more fundamentally, to reflect upon how these dichotomies are a deeper expression of the man and the historical issues and confusions which he embodied.

Everything in my nature protests against the idea of one so called authority or a jury of 'authorities,' adjudging what is 'bad,' 'good,' or 'best.' Creative work and ideas must, in the end, compete in the broad, dynamic, and comparatively timeless area of human affairs. What the prophets—real or alleged—say is of transient importance.[1]

DD: What impressed me the most about going through all of Harry's writings and correspondence was how, as he got progressively older, he kept getting more deeply depressed about the view other composers and critics had of his work. People would take one element and build a whole theoretical construct out of that. Was that your experience of him?

DM: Yes, that's very perceptive. Harry would often say, "they're just taking one little part of my work and using that to evaluate me when they don't understand the totality of what I stand for." I heard that many times.

DD: There are certainly a lot of his position statement, such as in *Genesis of a Music*, which are a formal description of his point of view. Was there a

For all its complexity and immensity, I can't help feeling that Harry Partch's music, like that of Charles Ives, is less well jelled than the sounds put forth by many a lesser but more stylized contemporary composer. For me, at least, the visual and pragmatic beauty of his unique instruments is more important—they are totally fulfilled and wholly original,

---

[1] Harry Partch, quoted by J. David Bowen, *Music Between the Keys*, **HiFi/Stereo Review**, February, 1961.

I've been drawn to ancient Greek ideas for the simple reason that they do not hesitate to touch basic questions in an art sense. A mother murders her son. I would not dare depict anything of the sort if it were my idea. A mother murders her son, or a father is tricked into a cannibalistic eating of his children, but this is Greek drama, and acceptable even in Meridian, Mississippi. Or perhaps especially in Meridian, Mississippi.[2]

more informal expression, that came out of working with him over so many years, which conveyed to you a sense of how he felt that his concept of total integration was compromised?

DM: Do you mean, how was it compromised by his critics and detractors?

DD: Yes, and by his supporters.

DM: I was a product of normal, Western academic instruction. From my earliest association with Harry he introduced me to a variety of other cultures. One thing he really admired about ancient Greek theatre was its overall integrated approach where musicians weren't just musicians, and dancers weren't just dancers. There was a total immersion by practitioners of theatre into stagecraft. He thought that this had been lost in the gradual evolution toward abstraction in Western music. He wanted to return to it. He probably made his first bold step into integrated theatre in *The Bewitched*. I don't think that you can really say that any of his works before that were totally integrated in terms of performance. Many of his earlier works, however, lend themselves to a totally integrated production in hindsight. For instance, Barstow and *U.S. Highball* were produced after Harry's death in an integrated manner where the musicians acted out the whole piece theatrically. One of the essential ideas of Partch's integrated theatre was that the musicians should be totally involved in the visual and theatrical aspects of performance. I feel that *The Bewitched* was the first time that he was really able to experiment with this because it was designed into the piece. Of course, the first two productions never got this because the choreographers couldn't understand how to deal with musicians and, during the 1950's, we musicans were way too inhibited to let ourselves go.

Harry also stated that the sound of his music was itself physical. I can't quite buy this. I think he was a

whereas the music is maybe two-thirds baked, full of undigested 19th century stuff. Not so the visuals! They are astonishingly beautiful, these Partch creations. Partch himself is California at its zany best.[3]

What Mr. Partch seems not to realize is that however accurate an instrument may be persuaded to be, the pitch of the voice is actually always a curve, not a fixed point.[4]

Partch's ideas are more interesting than his exposition was convincing.[6]

The scores themselves do not help at all; they are simply cryptic notes, or cryptic ratios.[5]

---

[2] Harry Partch, untitled lecture at the University of Oregon, 1964; *MS Lingua Press*.

[3] Edward Tatnall Canby, *Audio*, August, 1972.

[4] Henry Cowell, review of *Genesis of a Music*, in *The Saturday Review*, November 26, 1949.

[5] Harry Partch, *Manual: On the Maintenance and Repairs of—And the Musical and Attitudinal Techniques for — Some Putative Musical Instruments*, 1963; MS *Lingua Press*.

[6] Marjory M. Fisher, *San Francisco News*, February 10, 1932.

I start with something that I can't describe very well. It's a result of impressions, experiences—a lifetime of experience—and I would add that the verbal element is always, with me, as important as the sound element. More recently, I would say there is a third element which is just as important as these two, and that is the visual element. That's more recent in my life, but the verbal element was always there, from the time I was 14 and I began writing music. The verbal element, the music element, the visual element—I suppose it all boils down to the human element. The musical idea comes first, but I think almost simultaneously of instruments.[8]

I have something that even Johann *Sempervirens* Bach couldn't count on: phonograph records.[9]

little bit off-base and not thinking too comprehensively about what he was saying. If you look at his works, they require an overall integrated approach where you just don't have musicians in the pit, dancers just dancing, or actors just acting like in a 19th century grand opera. It isn't just the music having a physical quality that constitutes Partch's concept of corporeality.

DD: In this statement that he made about his music being physical, was he specifically referring to the notes in the score and the sounds of the instruments?

DM: I don't know. Harry would have to be quizzed on this statement.

DD: In the performance of pieces like *Petals*, for instance, he doesn't specify a theatrical aspect, per se. Did he demand a physical presence from the performers that was theatrical?

DM: No. *Petals* was a study piece. Whenever Harry wrote a major work he would always write a study piece for it. The study piece for *The Bewitched* is called *Sonata Dementia*. As I recall, he wrote it in sonata allegro form in three movements. He just used the piece to study the musical material and never intended for it to be performed.

DD: Was it ever performed?

DM: Not to my knowledge. He wrote another curious piece while he was in Wisconsin. There was some criticism amongst the faculty at the University of Wisconsin, so Harry wrote a piece in strict Renaissance canon in order to demonstrate to the academicians that he could write any of their fodder. At the time he was supported by the English department. I don't think he really intended for some of his pieces to be performed in public. They were performed in private. We did perform *Petals* in public because it's a good abstract piece.

Only an examination of the score could detect whether any organized system of composition is involved. After the first novelty wears off one is inclined to doubt that there is much real creative force or originality to Partch's innovations.[7]

All his opposition came from the Music school…One faculty member suggested his instruments be smashed…they were scared of Partch, had never seen the likes of him before. But don't worry. They've forgotten all about Partch. Everything is quiet and peaceful since he's gone.[10]

[7] Albert Goldberg, *Los Angeles Times*, October 17, 1954.

[8] Harry Partch, from an interview by Peter Jacobi, *The Strange Realm of Harry Partch, **The Music Magazine***, July, 1962.

[9] Harry Partch, quoted by J. David Bowen, *Music Between the Keys, **HiFi/Stereo Review***, February, 1961.

[10] Marshall Glasier, letter to ***Daily Cardinal***, Madison, Wisconsin, September 29, 1948.

DD: This brings up an interesting issue. It suggests to me that Harry conceived the music separately as an abstract idea and then attempted to integrate the various aspects toward his corporeal ideal. He must have thought about them as separate elements and then tried to find a way to integrate them rather then conceiving the whole.

DM: That's a good point because he did issue all of his music on records. If they were totally integrated in terms of visuals, music, and drama, why issue them on records? He probably did want his music to stand by itself if the other corporeal aspects failed in production.

DD: Personally I don't think it's always true that the music is capable of sustaining interest when separated out. A lot of the music in *Revelation in the Courthouse Park*, for instance, is not completely successful on its own, nor do I think it was intended to be.

It is not only difficult to define my theater concepts as a whole—it is impossible. Even if one of them is adequately pinned down for the moment the next will very likely fail to fit into the prescribed mold.[11]

DM: *Revelation* is a good example. A recording of *Revelation* does not give you very much of the total impact. *The Bewitched*, though, does stand on its own as a recording. *Delusion of the Fury* does have some weak moments but it also stands fairly well on recording.

There is not going to be anything halfway about this production, it's either going to be the biggest success or the biggest failure we've ever had.[13]

DD: One of the problems with Partch's theoretical writings is that the concept of corporeality leaves open any rigorous definition.

DM: That's true. Many people misinterpret Harry's ideas. They want the playing of the music to be a sufficient definition. To me that is not the case. Just playing the music is not being corporeal. You might as well just go play a Beethoven sonata. To perform Harry's music corporeally, you have to have a total theatre situation and only certain of his works have this potential. If you perform *Castor and Pollux* as just a concert piece, it's not corporeality.

Finally, they are not, and never can be, concert music.[12]

Partch seems to take a new philosophical approach. He attempts to recreate the emotion superimposed upon the reality. In other words, he portrays the three levels of: reality, the emotional acceptance of reality,

DD: Do you mean that a large percentage of Partch's work doesn't fit within his own class of ideas referred to as corporeality?

Another statement that was quoted to

[11] Harry Partch, program notes to *Water! Water!*, 1962; MS *Lingua Press*.

[12] Harry Partch, program notes to *Water! Water!*, 1962; MS *Lingua Press*.

[13] Arch Lauterer, comment about the Mills College production of *Oedipus*, quoted in the *San Francisco Chronicle*, March 9, 1952.

me—I am a bridge between Varese and Cage. Well! What to say? I've been totally isolated from contemporary music my entire life. Not a single contemporary composer has influenced me in the slightest degree. My influences are very easy to state— Chinese lullabys, and Chinese music, live, when I was very young. American Indian rituals, live, when I was very young. Christian hymns, African rituals and Oriental drama on records before 1920.[15]

There is at least one factor which my various theater concepts have in common; they tend to *include*, not exclude, and therefore to encompass a fairly wide latitude of human experience. They do not exclude—for example—"bad material" simply because it is thought to be "bad". Gymnastics are not excluded from dance; the half-conscious rituals of experience—an exhibition of gymnasts, or an insane basketball game—are not excluded from musical

DM: If you perform his pieces as concert pieces than they are not corporeal. Many of his pieces do have the potential for visual and dramatic integration as corporeal theatre. *Barstow, U.S. Highball*, and *Castor and Pollux* all have this potential while *The Bewitched* had it specifically engineered into it. In the one performance that *Revelation in the Courthouse Park* had, the musicians were not really integrated corporeally into the dramatic situation. We have to see if this is possible in a new production. *Revelation* served to cathartically work out some psychological problems for Harry and he didn't really do any indepth thinking about how to bring the musicians into the whole. There is nothing in the score itself to suggest this and during the performance the musicians and instruments were on each side of the stage. The dramatic action went on in the center. In the next piece after that, *Water! Water!*, he tried to make up for this by having the instruments assume dramatic characters. They would even be moved around on stage.

DD: Did it work?

DM: It had a few problems. That was his only commissioned work and he wrote it under a time limit. It put him under too much pressure and didn't allow him to stand back from the work with sufficient perspective. I haven't thought about *Water! Water!* for over twenty years.

DD: The reason I'm asking this question about the lack of a definitive description for the concept of corporeality, as Harry put it forth, has to do with an intuition that I have about him as a fairly heroic figure. Within the course of twentieth century music he seems to have attempted a redirecting of its course in a way which is typical of a larger evolutionary pattern of development. This is known as the "draw back to leap forward" scenario in systems theory. The evolutionary trajectory becomes too constrained and specialized along certain lines of development and cannot continue to evolve. Forms stagnate or break apart. An example of this in music would be what happened with tonality in the context of the atonal and dodecaphonic schools of composition. 19th century tonality became too

and the deeper appreciative emotion. That is a tenuous idea to put into words, and the music expresses it far more clearly.[14]

No other composer, not Arnold Schoenberg, or John Cage, has threatened the institutional routine of music so fundamentally as Partch.[16]

---

[14] William K. Archer, *Daily Cardinal*, Madison, Wisconsin, October 11, 1946.

[15] Harry Partch, letter to William M. Bowen, October 11, 1967; MS *Lingua Press*.

[16] Peter Yates, *"Genesis of a Music"*, **High Fidelity**, July, 1968.

concepts. The key of C and the dominant seventh chord are not excluded, nor old jokes, nor nonsense, nor hobos, nor commonplace tunes, if the overall dynamic, dramatic, or satiric purpose demands them. And as for the nineteenth century cliche—well, he frequently fills the role of a long-lost friend, a consoler, a beloved and trusted comforter.[17]

The forms that imagination may devise transform the primitive sound generation ideas into vehicles for new and exciting adventures, and the act of transforming in itself, like a fire by a stream, is an antidote to this age, a transcendence of its materials. And it is a small reaching back, through many thousands of years, to the first men who wished to find meaning for their lives through art.[18]

constraining and broke open into new organizing principles. Partch was another example of this attempt to break apart the constraints, only his way of doing this was to pull back as far as he could into ancient models.

DM: Particularly ancient Greek models but also African and Indonesian.

DD: Yes, attempting to step outside of the Western frame. While he was not unique in doing that he was certainly one of the first composers to give that serious credibility and comprehensive attention.

DM: He really tried to implement it.

DD: In that sense, I associate his concept of corporeality with some aspect of a 'primal' identity. He was trying to suggest a function for art within Western society that's integrated in ways similar to a tribal culture. Such cultures often do not have words for art. It is integrated as a continuous component of the social and religious fabric. It's part of the general cosmology and philosophy which integrate all aspects of life within that social order. To desire that level of integration and then try to place it within a culture where art is often a commercial commodity, is a difficult concept. I don't think he knew how to do it. There is a contradiction throughout his work in that for all his discussion of corporeality, it remained a highly abstract concept. It appears to have been an ideal that he aspired to while remaining very confused as to how to achieve it. What I think he meant by corporeality was something at the source of the malaise which plagues twentieth century Western culture. Corporeality was his word for everything that is lacking and thereby prevents the embracing of our full human potential. He obviously had some strong intuitions about what was missing and tried to articulate this through his creative work. He was trying to discover something we had left behind in our scientific advance into materialism and industrialism. I think he intuited that it had something to do with our assumed dissociation

Unlike the ruck of critics and theorists of music, Partch examines the core of music: tones, notation, instruments, composition.[19]

Cloud Chamber Music begins as a depressed reaction to a false clarion, but then seizes American Indian incentives as a reinvigorating antidote. The future is, in a certain sense, the past. We are not to be saved by science fiction become fact but rather by ancient myths and ritual, which retain intact the dignity of human life as an inseparable part of nature.[20]

---

[17] Harry Partch, program notes to *Water! Water!*, 1962; MS **Lingua Press**.

[18] Harry Partch, *Some New and Old Thoughts After and Before The Bewitched*, 1958; MS **Lingua Press**.

[19] Keith McGary, **Antioch Review**, Fall, 1949.

[20] Ben Johnston, *Harry Partch's Cloud Chamber Music*; included in this edition.

To be aware of this time and place, and the desideratum of the individual's significance in the face of the machine, is one thing. But nothing could be more futile or downright idiotic than to *express* this age. Or any other age. The prime obligation of the artist is to transcend his age, there to see it in terms of the eternal mysteries, to use its materials at the same time that he transforms them into magic. What this age needs more than anything else is an effective antidote. And if the contemporary artist could actually be present in any other age it is probable that he would feel the same about it.[21]

Purity is rampant. Given progressively antiseptic departments there is no place else to go— pure music, pure chance, pure art, pure dialogue in the theater. Entirely apart from the obvious need for crossfertilization

between mind and body since the 17th century. Because of his historical location there was no way of really understanding how to do this reintegration. It remained a fairly abstract idea.

DM: As far as implementing it and making it an alive thing within our culture, he knew that this was contradictory.

DD: For him the body was another abstract concept because of what he left out, namely politics and economics as the social body. It's the mirror of academia. I think his obsessive railing against the academy was demonstrative of how locked into that model he was.

DM: That's a very good evaluation of Harry. He knew that he was in the Western world and that his ideas wouldn't become a part of the fabric of how we live. He felt that everything in our culture was dead from the neck on down. He blamed Christianity for negating the body. His whole creative approach was a release from his frustration with living in Western culture. It was his psychological safety valve as a statement against the society that he lived in and despised. All the satisfaction he wanted in his life was to be given a chance to be a reflection of what we are, what we had lost, and what we might become.

DD: Do you feel that his major driving desire was to not be specialized? Even if he failed at being whole, he could claim, at least to himself, that he made the effort.

DM: Yes, and he lived it in his own private world. He was not a specialized person. He was an instrument builder, theorist, composer, intellectual, and deeply emotional person.

DD: Do you think that he wanted to have more influence than he had?

Corporealism was a theory that Partch lived. It is a vehement protest against what he considered the negation of the body and the bodily in our society.[22]

He was opposed to our culture as he found it, and if he was undoubtedly first a dropout, he never relinquished the role of reformer, even in the actions and attitudes of his old age. He saw our social conditions as those of an advanced stage of decay, and looked to earlier and more "primitive" cultures not with nostalgia but with hope and exhortation.[23]

Although he has never had any direct influence in shaping American music, Partch has influenced those who are now influential.[24]

---

[21] Harry Partch, *Some New and Old Thoughts After and Before The Bewitched*, 1958; MS **Lingua Press**.

[22] Ben Johnston, *The Corporealism of Harry Partch*, **Perspectives of New Music**, Spring-Summer, 1975.

[23] Ben Johnston, *Harry Partch's Cloud Chamber Music*; included in this edition.

[24] Arthur Woodbury, **Source**, vol. 1, no. 2, July, 1967.

among the creative arts there are the same needs of invigoration beyond the arts. Music and physics are certainly related studies, yet aside from an occasional adventure into electronic music there is little or no recognition of a crossfertilization need, either by music professors or the what-was-good-enough-for-Bach-is-good-enough-for-me physics professors.[25]

The imaginative man ponders all his experience, not just some of it. He doesn't relegate disturbing, or confusing, or ineffable experience to a dusty subshelf in his brain and continue his little pattern of existence as though his ear had never been twitched.[26]

Religious rituals with a strong sexual element are not unknown to our culture, nor sex rituals with a strong religious element. (I assume that the mobbing of young male singers by semi-hysterical women is recognizable as a sex ritual for a godhead.)[27]

DM: He knew that he wasn't accepted and that what he had to offer wasn't attractive to most of the general culture. He felt very much alone but he was happy in his own world. He only drank to calm himself down and not to drown out unhappiness with his creative world. He drank because he was so excited in the afternoon. Otherwise his brain would not calm down enough to allow him to have a nice peaceful evening.

DD: I have sensed, for a long time, that Harry pushed toward a more complex identity for our humanness. If corporeality was his attempt to reembrace everything from the neck down then this not only implies a physical being but also a sexual one.

DM: He defined immaturity as the rejection of experience. He expected a mature person to try and embrace all of the experiences in life. He drew the line at experiences which were detrimental to a person's health in that he did not support the drug culture, but in terms of intellectual and physical experiences that could enlarge one's life, he felt that a mature person did not reject an experience that came into their life on arbitrary moral or intellectual grounds. Concerning sexuality, Harry would have preferred a bisexual society where everybody physically loved each other. His fantasy was much closer to ancient Greece.

DD: So he was a proponent of the polymorphous perverse.

DM: Right.

DD: My interest has also been in seeing Partch within the context of 20th century philosophical thought. He was an intellectual by any standard. He was involved with scholarship and a thinking perspective on the world. At the same time, he wanted to see that as just part of a larger experiential wholeness. I think he was an instigator for what now seems visible as an archaic revival. We certainly seem to be living through a major historical bifurcation where the underlying epistemological assumptions of Western civilization are being radically transformed. Such

A Californian musician called a few days ago and is working on the relation between words and music. He has made and is making other musical instruments which do not go beyond the range of the speaking voice but within that range make a music possible which employs very minute intervals. He speaks (does not sing or chant) to this instrument. He only introduces melody when he sings vowels without any relation to words. I hope to bring to London with me the zither we use with Dulac's music and you might try this method of getting variety. He has been given a fellowship by an American institution to create these instruments and to

---

[25] Harry Partch, *Symposium*, **Arts in Society**, vol. 2, no. 3.

[26] Harry Partch, letter to Jacques Barzun, April 4, 1956; MS **Lingua Press**.

[27] Harry Partch, *REVEL: a Composer's Statement*, (1961?); MS **Lingua Press**.

There is the ancient tradition of probing, of a lonely, lonely searching—looking for contemporary answers to ancient questions; I like to think that the same kind of searching illuminated the Renaissance, and ancient Greece and the T'ang Dynasty of China.[28]

Forgetting all about 2000 years of Christian civilization, for a moment, I would call my music Dionysian and dithyrambic, even though what might be considered the opposite character is also present at times. But I believe spiritually and materially, in ranging over the whole history and pre-history of man, through work and divination.[31]

I care a great deal about an age or ages that have been discovered through digging and presuming and learning. But I care even more for the divination of an ancient spirit of which I *know* nothing.[32]

transformations appear to be periodic in the sense that they have occurred previously. Certainly it happened during Hellenistic Greece and again during the Renaissance in Europe. The Renaissance was a pulling back into old models as the Medieval world-view came apart in the face of mercantilism. It was an embracing of classical models in order to find new forms through which the intelligensia could reshape the culture. We appear to be undergoing a similar transition in the sense that science has begun to move away from the Cartesian dichotomy which has diminished the value of direct experience. Simultaneously we seem to be involved in the evolution of a planetary culture. Partch seems to have intuited both of these in wanting to create a globally based music which articulated a reaching back into archaic modes of experience.

DM: He was intuitive of this. He saw what was in the ancient world and what might possibly be coming. He didn't read on these concepts which you are discussing but he was an intuitive mirror that looked both forwards and backwards. He had a large overall view and cultural intuition which he tried to incorporate into his work. That's precisely how he evaluated himself.

DD: Part of this shift from the Medieval worldview into the Renaissance was the existence of transitional figures. Certainly many of the thinkers that are now seen as the creators of the scientific paradigm were not rationally moving in that direction. In fact, most of them were stuck between worlds. Newton, for instance, was a practicing alchemist. They straddled between a modern scientific view and Medieval Scholasticism or the Hermetic tradition in the form of occult science. One of the major ingredients in occult philosophy is the concept of a participatory consciousness. From this point of view you can't separate out mind, body, and environment. There are significant pathways of pattern and interaction that link all of these. They saw the universe as a whole which is participatory and alive. Much of this tradition is very ancient and can be traced back to

make musical settings for my *King Oedipus*. I shall give him an introduction to Dulac. We cannot however use him in our work at present, he is on his way to Spain to perfect his discovery: it is still, I think, immature. He is very young, and very simple.[29]

Partch doesn't defend his music, but he defends his principles.[30]

The first composer of outstanding creative gifts to turn the scientific spirit of inquiry to the matter of music's materials, rather than to content himself merely with

---

[28] Harry Partch, *Palace Lecture*; MS *Lingua Press*.

[29] William Butler Yeats, letter to Margot Collis, November 17, 1934.

[30] *The Wisconsin Journal*, February 23, 1947.

[31] Harry Partch, untitled lecture at the University of Illinois, March 24, 1957; MS *Lingua Press*.

[32] Harry Partch, notes for BMI brochure, 1968.

These instruments have been developed, built and rebuilt, over what seems to me now like a long sucession of generations—actually, it has been only about forty years. They may seem unusual, but if they do, this is because I am a profound traditionalist. And if this seems like an odd statement, it is perhaps because my traditions are rather ancient.[34]

In musical magic, the roots can be seen with greater clarity in the simpler instruments, from simpler ages. Already, in the nineteenth century, when the freshened visions of the Renaissance had dissipated, the profession of music was removed some few degrees from the magic of nature.[35]

My direction, as it finally evolved, was more the result of lonely daydreaming than of revolt.[36]

ancient Egypt or to Pythagorean number mysticism. What's fascinating about Partch is that much of this is present in his work. There are clues which link it to this continuity of an Hermetic tradition. Certainly his tuning system is full of a kind of Pythagorean number mysticism but also the things we have referred to in his general philosophy. The experiential emphasis is very aligned with many of the European pagan traditions. This was also repressed by the Christian church. I personally think that the sound of his work is often evocative of some sort of daemonic impulse. There is this incredible somatic concern embraced by both the Hermetic tradition and Harry's work. Besides the music, did he ever speak of anything in private that might support this?

DM: When I met Harry he was 55 years old. He was an avid reader and knew the English language inside out. Who knows what Harry read before I met him. He had an uncanny ability to remember what he read in great detail. His mind was very efficient at assimilating data and then correlating it. At the time that I knew him, his library did not have books on Medieval or Renaissance art and philosophy but he knew a great deal about these things. He was also interested in the pre-Greek periods of mankind, including the names of tribes and their philosophies. Even though he was historically sophisticated, he didn't keep a library of this material. Throughout his life he never really had the resources to store books so he would go to a public library to do his research.

DD: What about his personal beliefs?

DM: Harry was not a religious person. He did not believe in extraterrestrial divinities. Nor did he believe in the Christian heaven and hell. These were questions that were just too big. His questions were more along human lines.

the slick mastering of current techniques. In any other field he would be appointed head of a department set up for research into the crucial subject he has opened up.[33]

It is a pity that the size and fragility of Mr. Partch's instruments prevent them from being transported easily. It is also a pity, in a way that his art is absolutely unique. Unlike more traditional forms of music, it will probably die with its creator, never to be heard again.[37]

I happen to know that it costs one foundation $1,200 a year to

---

[33] Peggy Glanville-Hicks, quoted by J. David Bowen, *Music Between the Keys*, *HiFi/Stereo Review*, February, 1961.

[34] Harry Partch, *Palace Lecture*; MS *Lingua Press*.

[35] Harry Partch, *Some Old and New Thoughts After and Before The Bewitched*, 1958; MS *Lingua Press*.

[36] Harry Partch, letter to David Bowen, October 3, 1960; MS *Lingua Press*.

[37] Winthrop Sargent, *Musical Events*, *The New Yorker*, September 21, 1968.

DD: What about his relationship to nature?

DM: He was primarily an urban person. Even though he had been a hobo, he was a man of the cities. Despite his lonely life, he was very tribal and his ensembles were part of that. He could live very simply and didn't need a great array of materialism around him. He loved nature but he wasn't actively engaged with it, in the sense of hiking or mountain climbing.

If you want to look at Harry clinically, he had two personalities. He had a personality that was very loving and sociable and, at the same time, he had a personality that had a lot of frustrations in it. You could even call it slightly demonic. Most of the time he was highly sociable except when he felt that his work was being compromised. But he did have this darker side that was very frustrated. I think that his music reflected this other personality at times. Under certain stimuli or stress he would revert to this darker aspect. He may have used his music to bring this to a sonic expression. You can see this in *Delusion of the Fury* and *Revelation in the Courthouse Park*. The latter work has a lot of psychological inspirations such as his frustration with his mother. There are sections that are completely built upon his invoking a particular state of being that is cathartic. These are the dream walking scenes of Sonny and Mom. Sonny is King Pentheus and Mom is Agave.

When I first knew him he told me that, if one had problems, what they should do is make the sign of the goat and then state the problem followed by an incantation: "Get behind thee." I didn't know what the sign of the goat was. He never demonstrated it. This was said to me in a very rational manner. I did hear him one time when he invoked this incantation. He was upset by something and he did this consciously. He didn't realize that I was around and was surprised when he came out of the room he was in to discover that I hadn't left. So I guess that I did experience Harry having a metaphysical frame of reference that he didn't allude to in public. If you know that this is true then you can see it in his creative output. I see it very clearly in *Revelation*.

Perception is a sand flea. It can light only for a moment. Another moment must provide its own flea.[38]

maintain a young man who is working with great knowledge and fervor at musical composition based on new scales and instruments. Well, at the institution where he works are whole attics filled with discarded tests once part of a great piece of educational research. Counting all the wasted typing and man-hours of drudgery, one attic's worth would keep the musician in funds for ten years. Double his grant and he might achieve his results in less time, certainly with less wear and tear. The great obstacle to this obvious improvement is that the educational tests were tangible, undeniable "facts," though useless; whereas a piece of strange music or even an instrument bristling with stops and keys seems dubious, insubstantial, hardly fit for listing in an Annual Report.[39]

With the possible exception of Varese, there was no one so strikingly bard-like in manner. He exuded

---

[38] Harry Partch, *Some Old and New Thoughts After and Before The Bewitched*, 1958; MS **Lingua Press**.

[39] Jacques Barzun, *Distrust of Brains*, **Books and the Arts**, January 6, 1945.

There are perhaps a few areas where the exercises of freedom, in an individual pattern and philosophy, does not make its holder suspect. But the creative artist, to the extent that he is obliged to fly in the face of time-honored usages, acquires that shade of anarchism appropriate to his flight. And after several decades of weathering, he begins to have the strange patina of the recidivist, the unregenerate criminal.[41]

It is painful to pursue this. I do not consider the jukebox joint a very desirable place for a "ritual," and I wouldn't even try to get there "without misunderstanding," whatever that means.[42]

DD: Do you have any ideas about where he picked this up?

DM: I have no idea. At the time I was very suspicious of the metaphysical aspects of people's lives. I probably inhibited him from discussing it further.

DD: You wouldn't speculate as to whether this was something superstitious that he picked up from his hobo days, or was it something more directly associated with occult practice?

DM: I don't know. You can also see some of this in *The Bewitched*.

DD: I think it's also present in a piece like **Barstow**. There's that passage where he sets the graffitti line, "Jesus was God in the flesh." He treats it in a manner that has two sides. It reminds me of the ancient god Abraxas who was two-faced. Partch sets it first as a psuedo-hymn and then its reiterated in this very dark, mocking articulation.

DM: He felt that Christianity was a very oppressive force and also projects this in his *Hymns to Dionysius* in **Revelation**. The subtitle for **Revelation in the Courthouse Park** is *After the Bacchae of Euripides*. These hymns are set in the style of old Protestant hymns but are very demonic in their overall musical effect. I do think that Harry's music reflects both of his personalities. There really are moments that express this demonic voice.

DD: Do you think that this was present very early or did it evolve much later?

DM: It was certainly there when I first met him. I saw it very clearly when we were rehearsing *Revelation*. I immediately recognized this in the music.

DD: My experience of Partch was that this was an unconscious and intuitive process. It was a very dissociative state of mind that he entered at times. The wisdom, as did most of his haunting, grotesquely gripping music. One could not help the feeling down deep inside that ultimately, Partch was a kind of closet warlock.[40]

He apparently has a private frame of reference, a personal semantics...there is little if anything in his music that would cause a listener to do more than cock an amused ear.[43]

---

[40] Heuwell Tircuit, *The Wizard of Modern Music,* **San Francisco Sunday Examiner**, September 22, 1974.

[41] Harry Partch, untitled lecture at Columbia University, April 9, 1959; MS **Lingua Press**.

[42] Harry Partch, letter to David Hall, June 6, 1967; MS **Lingua Press**.

[43] Harold Rogers, *Exotically Weird Music from Harry Partch,* **Christian Science Monitor**, July 6, 1957.

two sides of his personality were not well integrated. It seems that the kind of thing that he was trying to heal, by what he was trying to embrace and creatively express, was a deeper kind of split that resided within his own psychological makeup. Do you have any sense of how aware these two different personalities were of each other?

DM: I never spoke to him about it.

DD: I knew this other aspect of his personality quite well. He seemed very good at keeping it out of public view. Do you think that he tried to hide it?

Another element of contemporary life which cries for an antidote is the labor-saver, the miracle button, which does virtually everything, increasingly and progressively, the miracle dial of electronics. And in this category should be included services which the artist has forgotten how to do for himself. Labor is saved, and a value is lost in the process.[44]

DM: He tried to control it. When something became too unbearable, it would just come out. It would run its course and then he would go back into his normal social identity.

DD: Did he ever compose while in this darker state of mind?

DM: No, but he tapped in on it for inspiration. He was always rational while composing. He always composed in the morning in isolation, sometimes for many months.

DD: It almost seems that the music itself was the process of communication between these distinct personalities.

DM: I think you could say that.

I remember when living dangerously was the individual's choice rather than the government's policy.[45]

DD: As a description of desires, intellectual interests, and emotional compulsions, the music was demonstrative of what he wanted to see in the world in terms of a healing of the lack of integration within the Western psyche. At the same time it was an internal process of healing that same lack of integration within himself. He was a carrier of the disease which he accused our culture of. He could not have been so attuned to the illness that permeated the specialization of Western culture if he had not felt that profoundly within his own makeup.

Philosophically, I would call my music Western, if I have to

DM: That is in essence the creative and psychological world of Harry Partch. He was using music to

I doubt that Partch will be disturbed when I say that his work is now clearly where it should be, nearer the jukebox than the symphony; that his music conveys the extreme rhythmic intensity, which the eye cannot easily grasp, of popular American dance, as when one tries to watch a roomful of dancers in near-anarchic rhythmic commotion, always controlled by the same beat. He has liberated music from the vestigial minuet, the expectation of precise forms, formalities, and structure by definite repetition, into a continuous ongoing and a translucent texture without back or bottom which one can hear through, so that the silence audibly behind the earlier *Verses* become progressively more resonant, until it is no longer even an enclosure, as with Ruggles or Ives, or even an interpenetrating difference, as with Webern and Cage, but a participating sound, as it occasionally

---

[44] Harry Partch, letter to William M. Bowen, October 11, 1967; MS *Lingua Press*.

[45] Harry Partch, misc. notes; MS **Lingua Press**.

place it. The initial response of many people is that it is "Oriental," but there have been many Orientals in my audience here in California and none of them who has bothered to express himself considers it "Oriental." In fact, the bewilderment of many Orientals is easily equal to the bewilderment of many Caucasians.[47]

Thinking only of the good of our souls, we do not need, right at this moment, more machines. We will undoubtedly *get* more machines, but we don't need them. What we need is a good strong antidote for the machines we've already got.[48]

Based upon what I have seen, I would say

exorcise his own lack of health. He was using music in a very organic way.

DD: This attempt to pull back and reintegrate pre-Western and non-Western forms is from a very Western perspective. That's a major issue in ethnography. Any ethnography which attempts a description of another culture is also a description of the anthropologist's culture. I don't think we ever step outside of that. Partch was representative of an act of desperation where an attempt is made to find other models from which new organizing principles can be constructed. In that sense I see him as a premonition of an archaic revival. At this point we are so desperate because of the incredible state of disequilibrium that our culture finds itself in and how this disequilibrium has been spread to other cultures in the world.

The other way of looking at this is that something new is on the horizon. The disequilibrium might possibly represent the manifestations of change toward a new order whose structure is not yet comprehensible. We can try to discern a pattern but prophecy is not very successful. I think Harry's work was not merely an attempt to step outside of Western traditions. He was someone locked within a Western perspective trying to find clues to help push a culture in a transformative direction. The metaphor for that is the evolution of a planetary culture in which our relationship to technology is redefined. Harry certainly railed against the machine modalities that we are being locked into. He rejected industrialism and scientific materialism and was looking for clues as to how to step outside of these epistemologies.

DM: I don't see too many other composers attempting to do that.

DD: Someone like Boulez is representative of the continuation of the European model no matter how much he tries to be otherwise. His is a very 19th century perspective. That brings up another issue. Obviously Partch was a tonal composer and that

becomes with Schoenberg.[46]

It follows that in Partch's works a positive and a negative aspect exist simultaneously. The positive aspect is the rebirth of (pre-Christian) vitality; the negative element is the presence of the mechanized modern world that threatens this instinctive life. Partch neatly epitomizes this dual concept by describing many of his works as 'satyrs'; they are satires in the modern sense on the present, but they also re-invoke the satyrs who were the source of man's potency. So it isn't a simple case of white against black: not a churlish lament against our industrial civilization, but an emotional (rather than intellectual or scientific) desire that industry's power should serve the ends of life, not death.[49]

It (*And On the Seventh Day Petals*

---

[46] Peter Yates, *Art and Architecture*, July, 1966.

[47] Harry Partch, misc. notes; MS *Lingua Press*.

[48] Harry Partch, untitled lecture at Columbia University, April 9, 1959; MS *Lingua Press*.

[49] Wilfrid Mellers, *An American Aboriginal, Tempo*, Spring, 1963.

that the deliberate beguiling of youth into the academic "modern idiom" is worse than an assault on the street. Both are malevolent, but the second is honest.[50]

The trouble with Schoenberg was that he never appreciated simplicity as a necessary tool.[51]

Monoliths belong in stone—one stone, one monolith at a time—all innocent of conspiracy. The truly creative art

carries with it certain kinds of philosophical dichotomies at issue in the 20th century. Certain philosophical views, which want to see the arts within a context of social function, have regarded the rejection of tonality as a necessary step toward a socially engaged music. Schoenberg was seen as a rejection of 19th century ruling class values. Tonality was associated with these bourgeois values and a worldview that was seen to be locked into capitalist agendas. From that perspective, Partch would be regarded as a reactionary. So, is there a different way of looking at tonality which is more ancient that is implied by Partch's concept of corporeality?

DM: I think his tuning system was something which he happened to stumble upon. He embraced that and integrated it with his philosophical points of view. He realized that he was living in an equal tempered mainstream. With his new tuning system he placed himself in a position of extreme opposition to any system of equal temperament. You can have equal temperament systems with 200 notes per octave and have pretty good intonation but he particularly considered twelve to be very oppressive. He felt that he was rectifying the tonal inadequacies of Western music.

DD: But doesn't that imply something that is physically based and some sort of organic wholeness which has been lost?

DM: We don't have a very clear picture of pre-Christian theory. Perhaps he thought that he was reviving some of the holistic properties of that period. I think that he thought of his tuning system as a return to a more holistic ground. In his book, *Genesis of a Music*, he assigns metaphysical and psychological attributes to various intervals in the chapter called *The One Footed Bride*. That chapter is a mystery to me.

DD: He felt that there was some sort of physical mapping for tonality that was objective.

Fell on Petaluma) is so much more demanding than a work of similar size and difficulty—say, *Structures* by Boulez—that I'm not sure those who appreciate that type of complication can come near estimating this; they would be trapped in the superficials of rhythm and beat and, in many cases, lack ears trained to distinguish the diversity.[52]

As is usually the case with microtonal music, the novel excitements of the color do not, in the long run, compensate for the losses which the rigid limitations of microtonality impose.[53]

In a home in Santa Barbara lies an organ which accommodates forty tones to the

---

[50] Harry Partch, letter to William Wilder, September 3, 1957; MS *Lingua Press*.

[51] Harry Partch, quoted by Heuwell Tircuit, *The Wizard of Modern Music, San Francisco Sunday Examiner*, September 22, 1974.

[52] Peter Yates, *Arts and Architecture*, July, 1966.

[53] Alfred Frankenstein, *High Fidelity*, March, 1954.

must break out of the monolith, especially an art so egregiously and repetitively commercial as that of music. And the act of breaking out is both an anguish and an anodyne. Such is my testimony.[54]

DM: He describes, "intervals of suspense" and "intervals of power." That's material for a long scientific investigation of what he may have meant. I never spoke to him about that aspect of his theory. There's alot of questions that died with Harry. No one knew what questions to ask. It's taken this many years to begin to sort through what he was all about.

octave, a product of some young neglected genius who will probably be a bearded angel before he hears even the first public whisperings of his ideas rising from the earth.[55]

---

[54] Harry Partch, record notes to *And On the Seventh Day Petals Fell on Petaluma*, **Composer's Recordings Inc.**, (CRI 213 USD), 1967.

[55] Noel Heath Taylor, **Pacific Coast Musician**, April 16, 1938.

Part I

SOUND–MAGIC

1

THE RHYTHMIC MOTIVATIONS OF *CASTOR AND POLLUX* AND *EVEN WILD HORSES*

Harry Partch

"Do you write classical or popular?" This is a frequent question, when I say I am a composer. We can be amused by the oversimplification, yet it indicates—among simple people—a profound feeling of a basic difference. Yes, a dichotomy—and in my opinion an annoyingly unhealthy one too. The generally unspoken contempt of the one for the other is palpable, even though one may hear: "Some of my best friends are jazz musicians," or "Ditto-ditto-ditto—play in the symphony."

When I answer the simple question with a stumbling "Neither, I write my *own* music," I directly convey my status as a rebel, but also indirectly admit that I am groping around for something *human* to hang onto. I don't *like* to be alone either. Spiritually—that is, by the standard of serious probing into the history and esthetics of music, and also by the standard of belief which goes its way with little hope or expectation of financial reward—I belong to the "classicals." Yet by the touchstone of human needs of this age I find myself looking upon the "populars" across the gully with frank admiration. O, I am *critical*—of technique of composition, performance, *and* concept. I can single out, almost never, a single composition or performance that I would like to hold onto for the rest of my life, in the way that I like to hold onto a certain Brahms trio. Nevertheless, the essence of the sum total adds up to *strength*.

What is the difference? The "classicals" carry on the tradition—if not the spirit—of musical insight, of a profound and subtle nature. The moods, the messages, run the various gamuts of intellect and emotion. The trouble with this is that the whole profession tends to become rarefied, to become something only for those *in the know*. And when the cognoscenti constitute the general staff of a culture, as they do in serious music in this country, it is time for those who think for themselves to start a revolution, or get out.

Let's talk about the disease itself. The disease is a loss of contact with this time and this place. The preoccupation with musical Europe of preceding ages by the "classicals" effectively blinds them to anything so mundane as this time and place. And in describing the situation in these terms it becomes fairly easy to high-light the differences between the two cultures, co-existing on two sides of a chasm.

By my own definition of the "classical" attitude, it would seem that this side of the chasm has everything, yet there is at least one quality that is singularly lacking—a quality which spontaneously gains acceptance because it fills a need of this time and place, and it will be profitable to leave the subject of the degradation of values by the industrial era to the political economists and the social scientists, at least for the present. Let us be realists, yes—even optimists, in that we must and will proceed with what we have—a situation that exists, rather than lapse into an enchanted dream about a world where music critics get salaries paid to them for writing sense.

I spoke of one singular quality the "populars" have (if I seem to confound "popular," "Dixieland," "jazz," "progressive jazz," it is because of the recogni-tion—in my simple mind—of the fact that they are all on the same side of the gully). I do not refer to the limited harmonies they use, which are infinitely boring, nor to the average subject-matter—God forbid! nor to the delivery of words, which is often fresh, often natural, often *human*, even in moans, nor even to the instrumenta-tion and individual performance on instruments, which is frequently exciting. For the particular purpose of the point I am making, and of the motivations behind *Castor and Pollux* and *Even Wild Horses* I refer to the potentialities of its rhythms, and its only half-conscious attitude towards its rhythms.

One is attracted to what stimulates his imagination, his spirit of adventure, his inherent creative desire—something we *all* have in common. As I have said—the harmonies suggest no possibility for development, the themes seldom, and the factor of the delivery of words in *Even Wild Horses* (*Castor and Pollux* involves no text) is a minor one. The rhythmic practices of the "populars" are the crux. After I have sat through a couple of hours with a good band in a night club, these are a source of both fascination and annoyance. Fascination because the music tends to fulfill a basic need—of both the naive and the sophisticated; annoyance because it goes endlessly on its way, with a strict, limited bong-bong-bong, almost always without retard or acceleration, almost always without subtle nuance or elaboration (except within the framework of that steady bong-bong), and almost always *with* the tawdriest kind of melodic utterance, however intriguing the instrumentation and delivery may be.

We can analyze these factors further. The steady, undeviating beat is a fea-ture of all or nearly all primitive musical cultures. It sometimes proceeds for hours, to the point of stupid hypnosis—and *stupid* is to my mind *the* adjective. Yet within the frame of a limited objective, perhaps *even this*—this that annoys my susceptibil-ities so greatly—is one of the sources of the strength I seek! I am at least willing, in *Castor and Pollux,* so to postulate. Further, with "classical" music in mind, the matter of accents within the timed bong-bong is a *different* factor. In a sense, the flinging of every tone into the air in a time relation to another tone flung into the air is an accent. Some are stronger than others, and, when the percussive department is considered, the comparison between the strong and the weak (not called accents at all) is very striking.

A percussive sound is one in which the tonal envelope is initially wide, a sudden impact, which quickly—or slowly—diminishes, and, obviously, the rhythmic character of popular music is primarily determined by its percussion—only secondarily by its various winds (unless they are used in a percussive manner).

The expectation of a regular (or implied) beat in nearly all "classical" music, old or contemporary, frequently becomes, in "popular" music, an expectation of an *accent* only *halfway* through the beat, or *one-third* or *two-thirds* through the beat, or *one-fourth* or *three-fourths*, or even *two-fifths* or *three-fifths* through the beat— this last not notated but strongly felt. Much of the time these fractional "accents" are part of a running pattern—not always accented. This essay is no primer of the African musical influence, but it must contain a simple statement of African musical character, and at least mention in passing that of the "inferior" peoples of Europe, particularly the gypsies. That the African sense of rhythmic subtlety has degenerated, in the course of its evolution from tribal ceremony to Cuban ritual to Hollywood night club, requires no laboring, it seems to me. Its history is of little present concern to me, because I see in its developed forms—rumba, conga, samba— seeds for stimulating expansion and *strength*. And I like to build at least somewhat on the cognition of those around me. Even those who don't like rumbas, congas, sambas, have this cognition; they can't avoid it. This, then, becomes the rhythmic motivation behind **Even Wild Horses**. I will *put back*, if I can, the nuance and subtlety that the trans-atlantic crossing and two or three centuries have dissipated. Yes, and more, too—the insight and profundity of our European tradition in "classical" music.

I realize that I am not the first to undertake this kind of hybrid realization—or revitalization. Again, I am uninterested in history. Right here I am only concerned with this effort, to bring the attitudes I admire—the serious "classical" attitudes, both in music and dance (I call both **Castor and Pollux** and **Even Wild Horses** dance music)—into some rapport with an obvious need of this time and place, with what is to my mind admirable and strong. Yes, it has been done before, but it has never been done in a scale *different* from that used in popular music, nor with a strong and varied percussion department of *new* instruments, not one of which is to be found in a night club, and—frankly—more like those on the banks of the Congo (or in a Balinese temple) than on the Harlem River.

Because I use a 43-tone-to-the-octave scale, and because I use new instruments, which I myself have built, the sounds and harmonies of the two dance compositions under discussion are—I think—uniquely my own. Only the rhythms suggest—I repeat, *suggest*—some recognition of present-day musical experience. I imagine that any dogmatic drummer who is a technical master of rumba, conga, and samba, would like to make me the central figure of an auto-da-fé, with my own Bass Marimba supplying the faggots, for my effrontery in using these names for this music.

So be it. Having efficiently antagonized "classical" musicians for thirty years, why should I leave undemolished the other possible bridges leading out of my lonely isolation? Still, I really do not expect this result; I wish that most "seriously" trained musicians had the open-mindedness toward new techniques that I have frequently found in jazz musicians.

But to get back to the first of the rhythmic elements, the one I questioningly admire, the steady—or steadily implied—bong-bong-bong. In *Castor and Pollux*, I preserved this steady beat for 16 minutes with the intention of making it sufficiently varied and interesting in subsidiary rhythm and beat (it is in alternate measures of 4 and 5 beats, and 3 and 4 beats), and by melodic and harmonic elaboration and contrapuntal accumulation, that it would not only be bearable but—if my postulate is correct—give it a *strength* it would not otherwise possess. *Castor and Pollux* is entirely percussive—even plucked strings are essentially so, although the Kithara tone dies slowly—and *Even Wild Horses* is mostly percussive; the only singing tones are by the Adapted Viola and Chromelodeon. Even the voice in musical speech should be mostly percussive.

In order to effect the kind of sum total of the parts—rhythmic and tonal—that I envisioned—*enauralized*—for *Castor and Pollux*, it was necessary to repeat phrases frequently, which in the playing of the pairs of instruments may seem musically pointless. Yet this helps in gaining familiarity with the themes, and on each second hearing—in the sum total—the juxtapositions cause each single repetition to be heard under entirely different musical conditions (the steady beat excepted). The work is constituted, in a sense, of a series of coincidences, of carefully calculated, musical "double exposures," as climaxes to series of "single exposures."

My elaborations upon the basic samba, rumba, conga, ñañiga percussive patterns in *Even Wild Horses* are mostly too complex for interesting, or even bearable, verbalization, and—of course—words give no idea of the emotional effect. Something besides the brain of a good musician has to vibrate in order to provide this. I have carried the *samba* through on the straight, traditional 4/4, but here and there it is interspersed with a few measures of fast 13/16 time—that is, 3/16ths of the 4/4 beat are left out, in continuous passages. The *rumba* is kept on the traditional 4/4 only when the viola is silent. With the viola singing—obviously a solo—the measure pattern is alternate 3/4–4/4, which gives a somewhat Hindu *seven* character to the Cuban dance form.

The *ñañiga* I have notated as 2/4, rather than 6/8, because it is conceived as a straight 2 against 3 throughout the first fast section—Bass Marimba against the ñañiga Wood Block and Cymbal. The *conga* has a deleted beat in the second and fourth measures, but those two missed beats are added to the sixth measure, making it 5. Thus, the measure beat-pattern is 4–3–4–3–4–5, but the strongly characteristic conga beat is always present, as traditionally, in alternate measures. The scenes that I call *Afro-Chinese Minuet* and *Tahitian Dance* possess the implied elements; it would be futile to try to pin these down to experiences that the average American knows as well as rumba, conga.

These are dance forms—of a folk nature—yet this music is not folk music, it is art music written for interpretive dance techniques. I have written no choreography, but I feel sure that this music *can* be danced, and I would like nothing better than to inspire some inquisitive dancer, who feels that this exposition makes a little sense here and there, to undertake it. Does an interpretive dance *have* to have a story? It *does* have to have some implied dramatic sequence; it *does* have to grow and develop from related tensions, and these, I think, the music supplies, without story, although I am sure a story that fits it could be invented. The modern folk spectacle of a ballroom full of people doing a samba is quite an experience—without inherent dynamic sequence. Here again, there is the strength of this time and place, the immediacy, the rhythmic actuality.

Also (in the compositions under discussion), the dance forms are not maintained (the rumba excepted) throughout, but are metamorphosed, developed, into something very different from their starting moods—the minuet and the ñañiga become radically different. Thus, too, the dance should develop and evolve, assuming dramatic and dynamic significance in the process.

Fragments of voice are written into the five final scenes of **Even Wild Horses** —extracted from Rimbaud's **A Season In Hell**. Where do these fit into the rhythmic motivations? There is a reason deeper than the sheer animalistic exhilaration of well-exploded and explosive words. It is to be found in the poet's life and character and in the composer's feeling of affinity.

Rimbaud abandoned literature at an age—19—that has nothing to do with insight and not so terribly much to do with maturity. The insight of his poetry is essentially the attraction, of course, without which the subsequent abandonment would be meaningless. In a few almost-frenzied phrases he explored most of the avenues of spirit attainment, contemplation, escape, conjecture, of most of the poets before him, and since. He poured out innocence, he dwelt on the primitive, the humanness (and doom) of those who transgressed. He "sought out" the rooming houses that the "intractable convict" might have "*consecrated* [italics mine] by his passing." Louise Varèse, one of his translators, speaks of his "mysterious honesty." There is also an expression of insufficiency, of nothingness, "...a face so dead, that perhaps those whom I met *did not see me.*"

To imply that he abandoned literature because of some mystical search for the "meaning of life," in which literature seemed impotent, and not because his greatest effort was ignored by those who alone had the power to perceive, is to imply that he was less than human. If anything, Rimbaud was more than human. When he speaks of the already "intractable" boy poet "locking himself within the coolness of latrines," he suggests an honest humanness, and acceptance of his humanness, which we of the Anglo-Saxon milieu would deny even under extreme torture. Primitive innocence—the child—primitive man. A value lost? Not wholly. Never, so long as man is mortal. This, then, suggests a motivation for a musical wedding of Rimbaud with an elaboration of African and other rhythms.

In reading and re-reading *A Season in Hell*, certain phrases came out of the book and hit me with a musical sock on the pancreas. So, I have taken these out of context, rearranged, juxtaposed them, in a pancreatically musical way. I doubt if the Rimbaud exegetes will forgive me, but I comfort myself with the belief that Rimbaud the Irreverent would.

To end, a slight digression. The titles, both of compositions and of their sections, were affixed spontaneously and light-heartedly—even whimsically. They seemed fitting at the moment of birth, but I feel sure that others, equally or more fittingly, could be substituted with very minor if any effect on the total reaction, especially since this is *movement* music by concept. **Even Wild Horses** what? At one time I knew the answer. Perhaps I still do, but I cannot articulate it.

2

A WORD OR TWO ON THE TUNING OF HARRY PARTCH

Rudolf Rasch

Introduction

The contributions of Harry Partch to the music of the twentieth century are many and manifold. Not the least important are the innovations he carried through in the instrumentation of his music. From the beginning on he worked with musical instruments of his own design (and building), or at least with thoroughly adapted existing instruments. These unique instruments are so well-known nowadays that they need not be described here.

But these new instruments always brought their own, new tunings with them. None of Partch's instruments employs the 'traditional' tuning of Western 19th-and 20th-century music: twelve-tone equal temperament. On the contrary, Partch developed an entirely new theory of tuning and intonation, to be applied to his instruments and the music to be played on them. The tunings of Partch's instruments all fall within one tuning system, a system that we would call an *extended, 11-limit just intonation*. Partch incorporated his tuning system in a broader concept, that of "Monophony", defined: "An organization of musical materials based on the faculty of the human ear to perceive all intervals and to deduce all principles of musical relationship as expansion from unity, 1/1."

Partch developed his ideas about tuning at a time when interest in tuning and microtonal music (with the exception of quarter-tones) was virtually non-existant. His work in this field can be called pioneering without any reservation. Parts Two and Three of *Genesis of a Music* (1947, 2/1974) are rather faithful expositions of these ideas, and I will use them as the bases for my study.

This article is meant to be a short account of Partch's theorizing on tuning in the light of the approaches of our times. At the same time, it may serve as an introduction to this theorizing for the non-initiated reader. To this end I will describe Partch's thinking on the subject as if it still had to be written down; I will not hesitate to use (anachronistic) terms of the 1980s.

Partch invented for his theories about tuning and intonation and his tonal system, a number of new terms or new, variant meanings of already existing terms or combinations of terms. He often capitalized these words (e.g., Otonality, Numerary Nexus, Monophony) and I will do so too, in order to indicate that these terms are Partch's. The first times they appear, they will often be placed within double quotes. Most terms invented by Partch or used in a special sense are explained in a glossary on pp. 68–75 of Partch's book (2/1974). Terms introduced by me or used by me in a special context or meaning are placed within single quotes. Current terminology that is used in rather conspicuous places (e.g., when being defined) is often set in italics, when used for the first time.

Partch was, of course, well aware of the newness of his thinking. This explains, probably, the rather frequent references he made in his book to acoustical and psychoacoustical literature. It is as if he wanted to argue that his intonational proposals made sense from the point of view of perception. Were his text written today, on the one hand he might not have felt the necessity of founding his theories so much in acoustics and psychoacoustics, on the other hand this foundation would have looked entirely different because of the vast progress made in these fields after the Second World War. For these reasons, we will not touch upon the psychophysical implications of his intonational system.

A problem when studying Partch, is the relationship between theory and practice. *Genesis of a Music* presents a well-formed, unitary theory of music and intonation. But the majority of Partch's instruments are percussion (which have sounds with inharmonic overtone structure), or plucked or struck strings (which have sounds with rapid decay). Neither category is very well suited to illustrate or make manifest subtle differences in tuning and intonation. Listening to Partch's music, one is, of course, aware of a certain 'intonational color' but it is difficult, if not impossible, to grasp the intonational details of the Monophony from arpeggios and ruffles.

In order to describe the practical implications of his intonation system, easy access to scores and instruments is a necessary requisite, out of my reach now and here. This article will deal, therefore, exclusively with Partch's theory.

Basic concepts

In the preface to the second edition of *Genesis of a Music* Partch wrote that he "rejected both the intonational system of modern Europe and its concert system." Indeed, he replaced traditional Western tuning and intonation (that is, 12-tone equal temperament) by a system of his own, and he tried to avoid the concept of the traditional tonal and tuning systems as much as possible. Although he succeeded to a remarkable extent in this respect, it still is possible to relate a number of aspects of his music theory with traditional concepts. He himself pointed to these relations in order to clarify his new concepts. We will refer to these relations when, for example, we convert his music notation into a system based on conventional staff notation. These interrelations show, on the one hand, that Partch could not escape being a child of his time and culture, and on the other hand the flexibility of Western musical ways, perhaps realized now more than in Partch's times.

Partch did not work with traditional intervals, neither with their names nor with their qualities. Interval names such as 'major third', 'fifth', etc. were discarded and replaced by *frequency ratios* that expressly and by definition only refer to just or pure realizations: 2/1 (our octave), 5/4 (our major third), 7/4 (our harmonic seventh), etc. A number of ratios, as used by Partch, do have obvious and easy-to-use equivalents in traditional interval names; but a good number of other ones—especially those with factors 7, 11, and/or 13 in numerators or denominator —do not have such equivalents. Numbers used as numerators were called "over-numbers" by Partch, those used as denominators "under-numbers". The use of ratios gave Partch the freedom to explore many intervals not available in the traditional 12-tone, 5-limit tonal system. When Partch used traditional interval names, this was usually to denote a distance on a "7-white, 5-black" piano keyboard.

Ratios were not only used to indicate intervals, but also to indicate individual tones. Tones were—in Partch's view—never really isolated, but always referring to some pitch anchor, the tone with ratio 1/1. Consequently there is no separation of tone and interval systems in Partch's musical thinking. This often means that tones—indicated by ratios—are treated as intervals, or the other way around. (Partch used the word "note" exclusively for the written symbol, and "tone" for everything having to do with pitched sound.)

Partch's tone and tuning systems are based on small-integer number ratios, beginning with the basic ratio 1/1 (unison). The smaller the number involved in the ratios, the more consonant the ratio; the larger the numbers, the more dissonant—says his "First Concept" (p. 87). Partch did not qualify his ratios in classes of more or less consonant or dissonant intervals (as is done in traditional interval theory), but conceived of a continum from perfect consonance (1/1) to "an infinitude of dissonance". Neither did he work out a dissonance measure based on some sort of precise function relating the amount of consonance/dissonance to the magnitudes of the ratio numbers.

The ratio 1/1 is the basic ratio, or the "Prime Unity" of Partch's system. His use of the 2/1 (octave) ratio does not differ essentially from that in traditional Western music: tones with a ratio 2/1 are the same tones, or replicas in different registers. The functioning of the 2/1 contains the seeds for the whole ratio system. Since the factor 2 represent only octaves, it is the odd factors of the numbers in every ratio that determine the 'quality' of the ratio. The traditional Western tone and tuning systems use three such qualities (in Partch's terms: "Identities"), which can be characterized by the numbers 1 (unison, or, for that matter, octave), 3 (perfect fifth), and

5 (major third); 7 (harmonic seventh) is present in highly exceptional cases only. Partch adopted the same set of qualities but extended the series with 9 (whole tone) and 11 (eleventh harmonic) so that his tone system has six Identities. If the numbers are used as numerator of ratios and the ensuing ratios are brought within a 2/1 (octave) range, there arises the following series: 1/1, 3/2, 5/4, 7/4, 9/8, and 11/8. When these ratios are reordered according to their magnitudes, the following 'scale' arises: 1/1, 9/8, 5/4, 11/8, 3/2, and 7/4, corresponding to a fragment of the harmonic series with numbers 8, 9, 10, 11, 12, and 14. In Partch's eyes these tones did not form a scale in the traditional sense, but just had a specific relation-ship to the basic 1/1. These relationships or Identities are characterized by the odd-number components of the ratio. Ratios with different Identities referring to the same basis are said to constitute a "Tonality". This concept of tonality clearly is very different from the traditional concept of tonality.

In the above examples the odd ratio numbers are in the numerators. There-fore they are "over-numbers" and provide an "Odentity" (short for "Over-Identity") of the ratio. Their tonality is an "Otonality" (short for "Over-Tonality"). But odd ratio-numbers may also occur in the denominators of ratios as "under numbers" to provide "Udentity" (short for "Under-Identity"). This is the case with ratios such as 8/9, 4/5, 8/11, 2/3, and 4/7. A series of "Udentities" also forms a tonality, or, more specific: a "Utonality" (short for "Under-Tonality").

In Partch's view ratios had a "Dual Identity" (Concept 2, p. 88): one, the Odentity, determined by the odd-number component of the numerator, and another one, the Udentity, determined by the odd-number component of the denominator. A ratio thus always belongs to two tonalities, an Otonality in accordance with its Odentity, and an Utonality in accordance to its Udentity.

When two or more ratios have different identities on one side ("over" or "under") but the same identity on the other side ("under" or "over"), this constant identity on the other side is called the "Numerary Nexus". To repeat Partch's examples (p. 72): The 8/5 Otonality has the Numerary Nexus 5 and consists of the ratios 1/5, 3/5, 5/5, 7/5, 9/5, 11/5, or, when brought into a single, ascending octave scale: 1/1 (= 5/5), 11/10 (=11/5/2), 6/5 (=2x3/5), 7/5, 8/5, and 9/5. The 5/4 Utonality also has Numerary Nexus 5; it consists of the ratios 5/1, 5/3, 5/5, 5/7, 5/9, and 5/11, or, brought into a single ascending octave scale: 1/1, 10/9, 5/4, 10/7, 5/3, and 20/11.

The 43-tone system

The way Partch constructed a tonal system out of his principles of intonation is quite peculiar. He started with the so-called "Tonality Diamond", which is a two-dimen-sional diagram of ratios. One dimension is the Odentity, the other one the Udentity. Since the dimensions are drawn right- and left-oblique from their base (1/1), the

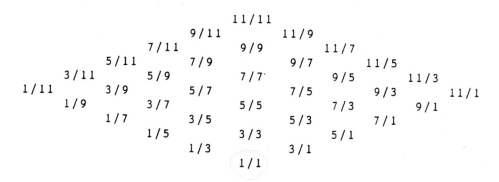

```
                    7/7
          12/7              7/6
     11/7          3/3             14/11
   10/7         11/6      12/11          7/5
 9/7        5/3        11/11      6/5          14/9
8/7     9/6        20/11      11/10      12/9      7/4
 4/3      18/11        5/5        11/9      3/2
   16/11         9/5        10/9      11/8
       8/5          9/9        5/4
          16/9          9/8
                    1/1
```

Primary tonality

Figure 1   Basic composition of the 11-limit Tonality Diamond

diagram gets a diamond-shaped appearance. Figure 1 depicts the 11-limit Tonality Diamond, in a version slightly different from Partch's as in his Diagram 9 (p. 159).

```
                    11/11
          9/11              11/9
     7/11          9/9             11/7
   5/11         7/9        9/7          11/5
 3/11       5/9        7/7        9/5          11/3
1/11     3/9        5/7        7/5        9/3      11/1
 1/9      3/7          5/5        7/3      9/1
   1/7          3/5        5/3        7/1
       1/5          3/3        5/1
          1/3              3/1
                    1/1
```

Figure 2   Partch's Expanded Tonality Diamond

We will call a stripe of the Diamond from lower-left to upper-right a 'row', one from lower-right to upper-left a 'column'. Thus the rows of the Diamond contain the Otonalities, the columns the Utonalities. The vertical centre of the Diamond contains ratios with equal "over" and "under" numbers: unisons or Prime Unities. The ratios left of the centre are smaller than 1/1, and those right of the centre larger than 1/1.

Partch's Tonality Diamond is different from our basic diamond in that all ratios are multiplied or divided by powers of two in such a way that the ratios are in magnitude between 1/1 and 2/1. Moreover, the ratios in one Otonality are ordered in a single ascending sequence, and those in one Utonality in a single descending sequence. Figure 2 contains Partch's version of the 11-limit Tonality Diamond. Since the six ratios in the centre all represent 1/1, and two ratios (3/2 and 4/3) are present twice in the Diamond, the total number of different ratios in the Tonality Diamond is 6×6−5−2 = 29.

Constructing tonal systems from a Tonality Diamond as described has certain consequences that Partch grasped empirically, but which actually reflect certain mathematical properties of the Diamond. Partch's 29-tone Tonality Diamond can be called the *1/1-to-2/1 part of a quasi-Farey system of intonation*. Let me explain this. A *Farey series* is the complete series of non-reducible fractions with ratio numbers not exceeding a predetermined integer. (This integer is called the *order* of the system.) A *Farey system of intonation* (see Rasch, in press) is the series of fractions, taken from a Farey series, with magnitudes from 1/1 to 2/1 and interpreted as intervals or relative pitches. The ratios in Partch's Tonality Diamond make up a Farey system of intonation of order 11 if one excludes the ratios with numbers greater than 11, such as 12/7, 14/11, 16/11, etc. (These fractions would be part of Farey systems of intonations were the order increased to 12, 14, 16, etc.).

Farey systems of intonation have certain properties as a consequence of the arithmetical structure. Several of these properties are also discernable in Partch's Tonality Diamond. First all ratios between neighboring ratios are superparticular ratios, i.e. ratios with a difference of one between numerator and denominator. Examples of these ratios between ratios are 49/48, 64/63, 81/80, 100/99, and 121/120.

Second, the ratios with relatively low numbers have more 'space' around them than those with higher numbers, or, in other words, the superparticular ratios that separate low-number Farey ratios from their neighbors are larger (thus involving lower numbers themselves) than those separating high-number Farey ratios from their neighbors.

This second property of Farey systems of intonation is the cause of a rather uneven spacing of the ratios between 1/1 and 2/1. There are relatively wide gaps especially next to 1/1 and 2/1, but also surrounding ratios such as 3/2, 4/3, and 5/3. Partch felt the need to fill these gaps with other ratios in order to obtain a more even spacing of ratios within the octave. We will discuss these extensions below.

A third property is that the system is symmetrical within the octave, not in terms of the original ratios, but in terms of logarithmic transformations of them, such as carried out when the ratios are converted into cents. The symmetry also exists in terms of the ratios between ratios.

We have jumped immediately into the full system with six Identities, thus providing the full so-called "11-limit", a terminology invented by Partch and now in general use. Partch himself first illustrated the concept of the Tonality Diamond with a *5-limit* Diamond, including only three identities ('1', '3', '5'; pp. 109–118, including Diagram 5 on p. 110). Similar terminology leads to the terms *7-limit, 13-limit*, etc. to denote tonal and tuning systems with factors not greater than 7, 13, etc. There is a 13-limit Tonality Diamond in the 'historical section' of Partch's book (Diagram 28 on p. 454).

It is customary now—especially after Barbour's epoch-making *Tuning and Temperament* of 1951—to describe just-intonation systems in terms of prime factors. Partch's approach is different from the standard one in his treatment of the number 9, which is a separate Identity in Partch's system, but on the '3'-dimension in most modern descriptions. Partch's system is a *four*-dimensional system in our terms, with dimensions '3', '5', '7', and '11'. (Compare this to his *six* Identities.) In accordance with their dimensional description, just intonations can be pictured in dimensional diagrams, including one, two, three, or more dimensions. Every occurrence of a factor 3, 5, 7, etc. means a standard step along the respective dimension. Let us look at Partch's Identities (Odentities) 1/1, 3/2, 5/4, 7/4, 9/8, and 11/8 in this respect. 1/1 is the base, the center of every just-intonation system. The Identities 3/2, 5/4, 7/4, and 11/8 all mean a one-step displacement along the respective dimension, but the Identity 9/8 means a two-step displacement along the 3-dimension (from 1/1 via 3/2 to 9/8). The Udentities 1/1, 4/3, 8/5, 8/7, 16/9, and 16/11 mean similar displacements, but in opposite directions. All other ratios in the system may be described as combinations of the basic ratios. They imply a compound displacement in the diagram, according to their descriptions.

When the number of steps along a certain dimension in a just intonation is equal, wherever this dimension occurs, the just intonation will assume the shape of a rectangle or a (three-, four-, etc. -dimensional) block when pictured. Such a just intonation is now called an *Euler-Fokker genus* because of the contributions of the physicists Leonhard Euler (1739) and Adriaan Fokker (1945) to the developments of these systems (see Rasch 1987). An Euler-Fokker genus with two dimensions may be represented in a two-dimensional (rectangular) tone-grid, one with three dimensions in a three-dimensional (block-shaped) tone-lattice. Euler-Fokker genera are characterized by a listing of the number of steps in each dimension. The number of steps is represented by a repeated mention of the dimension, so that there arise descriptions such as [3 3 5 5], [3 5 7], [3 3 5 5 7 7 11 11], etc.

How does Partch's system fare as an Euler-Fokker genus? When we look at the 11-limit Tonality Diamond, we can call that system an incomplete Euler-Fokker genus, with dimensions of 3, 5, 7, and 11. Since there are series of four fifths (for example, from 16/9 to 4/3, 1/1, 3/2, 9/8), two major thirds (from 8/5 to 1/1, 5/4), two harmonic sevenths (8/7 to 1/1, 7/4), and two eleventh harmonics (16/11 to 1/1, 11/8), the full Euler-Fokker genus would have the factors [3 3 3 3 5 5 7 7 11 11], containing 5×3×3×3 = 135 tones, and would be represented four-dimensionally. But Partch's Tonality Diamond only partially fills the full space of the Euler-Fokker genus, by including only ratios with at most a single factor (other than 2) at either side of the fraction dash, with the exception of 3×3 = 9. Nevertheless we may represent an 11-limit Tonality Diamond as an (incomplete) Euler-Fokker genus; the result is shown in Figure 3.

Since Partch's Tonality Diamond is a quasi-Farey system of intonation, it is bound to have wide gaps around the simplest ratios, such as 1/1, 2/1, 3/2, etc.

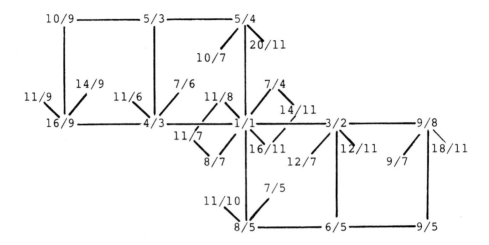

Figure 3   Partch's 29-tone system diagrammed as an incomplete Euler-Fokker genus

Partch filled these gaps with several ratios, in a more or less trial-and-error way, but one that made possible an increase of the number of Tonalities, both Otonalities and Utonalities.

Between 1/1 and 12/11, and between 11/6 and 2/1, four new ratios were inserted; between 7/6 and 6/5, 9/7 and 4/3, 4/3 and 11/8, 16/11 and 3/2, 3/2 and 14/9, and 5/3 and 12/7 one extra ratio was provided. These additions amount to fourteen new ratios, so that the whole system now contains 43 ratios. Partch's system is a *43-tone, 11-limit just intonation*.

The new ratios differ from the ones in the original Diamond in that they may contain more than one Identity above or below the fraction dash, such as 33/32 (3×11/32) and 21/20 (3×7/4×5). But the new ratios are chosen in such a way that the symmetry within the octave is maintained. More often than not, they are *not* the Farey fractions that would appear first between the 'primary' ratios, were the Farey order increased.

The original 11-limit Tonality Diamond contained twelve tonalities only: six Otonalities and six Utonalities. The extensions to the Diamond provide ratios for sixteen more tonalities, eight Otonalities and eight Utonalities. Of these extra tonalities only two are available complete through all their Identities: the 3/2 Otonality (3/2, 15/8, 9/8, 21/16, 27/16, and 33/32) and the 4/3 Utonality (4/3, 16/15, 16/9, 32/21, 32/27, and 64/33).

In his Appendix I Partch continued a tradition dating back to the second half of the seventeenth century: that of providing a list of all intervals which occur somewhere in an intonation system. German tuning theorists such as Werckmeister (1645–1706), Neidhardt (ca. 1680– ca. 1739) and Sorge (1703–1778) all provided lists of that kind, which they called calculi (plural of Latin singular calculus). Partch's Appendix I, "Cents Values of Intervals" is no different from the historic calculi. It provides a listing of no fewer than 340 frequency ratios with the corresponding conversions into cents, probably the largest such table ever produced. The multitude of different ratios is, of course, a consequence of the multi-dimensionality of Partch's Monophonic Fabric. Unfortunately Partch's listing does not include names of tones or pitches which are the boundaries of the listed intervals.

Notation

Partch often refused to write down his music in ordinary, traditional staff notation. His staff notation, usually indicated certain strings or (finger-) keys, as in a tablature or percussion notation; but the notes did not say anything about the sounding pitches. Indeed, at first sight it looks very difficult, if not awkward or impossible, to notate Partch's music on ordinary music staves. However, music in extended 7-and 13-limit just intonations written during the last three decades (by, amongst others, Ben Johnston) has been written down in ordinary staff notation, which has greatly helped in the dissemination of this music.

In order to have more than incidental performances of Partch's music, a transcription in staff notation would be a prerequisite. Therefore, I here propose such a transcription method, based on already available customs, concepts, and methods. This notation system starts with the Pythagorean pitches, which depart from the Prime Unity only by one or more perfect fifths and octaves or, in other words: the *3-limit* pitches. We will write them as ordinary naturals with or without single or double sharps and flats. For example, if 1/1 is called "G", this leads to:

$$16/9: F \quad 4/3: C \quad 1/1: G \quad 3/2: D \quad 9/8: A.$$

If the system is extended with *5-limit* pitches—as in classical just intonation—, these 5-limit pitches are always slightly lower or higher than a 3-limit pitch, since $(5/4) = (81/64) \times (80/81)$. The 5/4 is the the 5-limit ratio, the 81/64 the 3-limit ratio, and the 80/81 the difference between them, an interval known as the *syntonic comma*. Each factor 5 leads the ratio one syntonic comma away from the Pythagorean ratio. Raising a 3-limit pitch by a syntonic comma, i.e. to convert it into a 5-limit pitch, can be indicated by adding a plus-sign (+); lowering it by the same amount by a minus-sign (−). Examples are:

$$10/9: A− \quad 5/3: E− \quad 8/5: E♭+ \quad 6/5: B♭+ \quad 9/5: F+.$$

The new pitches introduced by the *7-limit* always differ from 3-limit (Pythagorean) pitches by the amount of 64/63 (an interval often known as the *septimal comma*), since: $(7/4) = (16/9) \times (63/64)$, in which 7/4 is the 'septimal minor seventh' or 'harmonic seventh', 16/9 the 3-limit minor seventh, and 63/64 a downward septimal comma. The septimal comma can be indicated in notation by a 7 (downward) or an inverted 7: ⟨upward⟩.

Examples are:

$$7/4: \text{F7} \quad 7/6: \text{B}\flat7 \quad 14/9: \text{E}\flat7 \quad 7/5: \text{D}\flat +7.$$

The new pitches of the *11-limit* differ from 3-limit pitches by the amount of what may be called an *undecimal comma*, or the interval 33/32. The interval of the eleventh harmonic (also called the 'Alphorn-Fa') is then described as an enlarged perfect fourth: $(11/8) = (4/3) \times (33/32)$. We propose that the undecimal comma be notated with a pi-like sign π (upward) or an inverted pi (downward): ʊ. Since the size of the undecimal comma is 53.273 cents, it is only slightly larger than the equal-tempered quarter-tone of 50 cents. Examples of notations involving the undecimal comma are:

$$11/8: \text{Cπ} \quad 16/11: \text{Dʊ} \quad 12/11: \text{Aʊ} \quad 11/6: \text{Fπ}$$

(Ben Johnston uses arrows up (↑) and down (↓) for 11th-partial relations, but we do not borrow this custom, since arrows have been used in a multitude of meanings in microtonal notations.)

Although not in Partch's system, we also propose a notation for the new pitches of the 13-limit. The thirteenth harmonic is best derived from the Pythagorean major sixth. It can be said to be equal to such a major sixth flattened by the amount of a *tredecimal comma* of 27/26 or 65.337 cents: $(13/8) = (27/16) \times (26/27)$. The flattening by a tredecimal comma can be indicated by a mirrored B or: <ઘ>, the rising by such a comma by a normal B. Ben Johnston derives the thirteenth partial from the 5-limit minor sixth, which gives a smaller comma, of 26.841 cents: $(13/8) = (8/5) \times (65/64)$. His signs are 13 for a rise by 65/64 and for a similar lowering. An intermediate-size comma, of 43.831 cents, would arise were the thirteenth harmonic derived from the 5-limit major sixth: $(13/8) = (85/3) \times (39/40)$.

When pitches require more than one accidental sign, we propose an order according to increasing limit. In agreement with normal use, we write the accidentals behind the note names in text, before the notes in music. The sharps and flats are always nearest to the notes, than follow the quintal (5-limit), septimal, undecimal, and tredecimal comma. Thus in text, the tredecimal comma comes last, after the note name; in music, the tredecimal comma comes first, before the note symbol.

When pitches are derived from ratios that contain more than one of the factors 3, 5, 7, and 11, the procedure in order to find the appropriate notation is to analyze the ratio into a product of ratios, of which one is a Pythagorean ratio (one with factors 2 and 3 only), while the others are commas (quintal, septimal, undecimal, and/or tredecimal). This analysis is always possible. We give a few examples:

$$(21/20) = (256/243) \times (81/80) \times (63/64) \qquad A\flat + 7$$
$$(11/10) = (256/243) \times (81/80) \times (33/32) \qquad A\flat\pi$$
$$(10/7) = (729/512) \times (80/81) \times (64/53) \qquad C\sharp\angle$$
$$(14/11) = (4/3) \times (63/64) \times (32/33) \qquad c7\mathcal{u}$$
$$(7/5) = (1024/729) \times (81/80) \times (63/64) \qquad D\flat + 7$$

Table I gives notations for all the 43 pitches of Partch's Monophonic Fabric.

Ratio of Tonality	Ratio of Extension	Conversion into cents	Notation
1/1		0.	G
	81/80	21.506	G+
	33/32	53.273	Gπ
	21/20	84.467	A$\flat$+$\angle$
	16/15	111.731	A$\flat$+
12/11		150.637	A$\mathcal{u}$
11/10		165.004	A$\flat\pi$
10/9		182.404	A-
9/8		203.910	A
8/7		231.174	A$\angle$
7/6		266.871	B$\flat$7
	32/27	294.135	B$\flat$
6/5		315.641	B$\flat$+
11/9		347.408	B$\flat\pi$
5/4		386.314	B-
14/11		417.508	C7$\mathcal{u}$
9/7		435.084	B$\angle$
	21/16	470.781	C7
4/3		498.045	C
	27/20	519.551	C+
11/8		551.318	Cπ
7/5		582.512	D$\flat$+7
10/7		617.488	C$\sharp$-$\angle$
16/11		648.682	D$\mathcal{u}$
	40/27	680.449	D-
3/2		701.955	D
	32/21	729.219	D$\angle$
14/9		764.916	E$\flat$7
11/7		782.492	D$\angle\pi$

Table I   (*contd.*)

8/5		813.686	E♭+
18/11		852.592	E𝑢
5/3		884.359	E-
	27/16	905.865	E
12/7		933.129	E∠
7/4		968.826	F7
16/9		996.090	F
9/5		1017.596	F+
20/11		1034.996	F♯-𝑢
11/6		1049.363	Fπ
	15/8	1088.269	F♯-
	40/21	1115.533	F♯-
	64/33	1146.727	G𝑢
	160/81	1178.494	G-
2/1		1200	G

Partch and Fokker

In some ways Partch's music-theorizing resembles that of the Dutch physicist Adriaan Daniël Fokker (1887–1972). Fokker started his musical studies in the 1940s. He built all his musical theories on the basis of tuning and intonation systems, while his tuning systems are all based on the harmonic series. He included the seventh harmonic in most of his theoretical conceptions and discussed the effects of incorporating the eleventh and thirteenth harmonics. Three microtonal instruments were built according to his designs: the small just-intonation 'Euler-organ' (1943), the large 31-tone pipe-organ (1950), and the electronic 31-tone 'archiphone' (1970). So far the parallel between Fokker and Partch can be maintained. But the differences between the two men are much larger, Partch being a musician by vocation and profession, Fokker being a physicist by profession and dealing with music out of interest only.

That the two men knew of each other's existence and activities is apparent from a small correspondence between them in 1946, just between the publication of Fokker's main work *Rekenkundige bespiegeling der muziek* (Arithmetic reflection of music; in Dutch, 1945) and the first edition of Partch's *Genesis of a Music* (1947). The first letter of Fokker to Partch, probably written in February 1946, is not known to me. But Partch's answer of 25 March, and Fokker's reply of 7 May are extant in the Archives of the Teyler Foundation in Haarlem (Netherlands). I quote them in full in the Appendix of this article because they show so perfectly the different approaches to music and intonation of Partch and Fokker. Obviously, there was little mutual understanding; I do not know of any further correspondence. Although Partch's theories could have been of use for Fokker's further intonational research, Fokker seemingly did not study Partch's *Genesis*. On the other hand, there are no references to Fokker's work in the second edition of Partch's *Genesis*.

The mutual contacts and cooperation among American and European microtonalists would have to wait many years in 1946, well until the 1970s and 1980s.

Appendix

1. Letter of Harry Partch to Adriaan Fokker, 25 March 1946, obviously in reply to a letter by Fokker asking for information about Partch's work.

March 25, 1946

Prof. dr. A.D. Fokker
Damstraat 21 rood
Haarlem
Nederland

Dear Prof. Fokker:

Thanks for your kind inquiry. I'm sorry I have no material to send you at the moment. The few articles I have written on my work are far from satisfactory—too general, and my book will not appear until early next year. It is scheduled by the University of Wisconsin Press under the title *Genesis of a Music*.

The system I use has 43 just tones to the octave, with both the 7th and the 11th correct in some fourteen tonalities; the reverse of these intervals is correct for the minor tonalities. I have built three harmoniums with this intonation, two with unusual keyboards and one in which the 43 degrees are spread consecutively over three and a half octaves. I have also built a large instrument with 72 strings that is evolved from the ancient kithara, a harmonic canon with 44 movable bridges and strings, a viola with an elongated neck (played between the knees), and two electric guitars, unfretted, but marked. Not all these instruments were built from the ground up; many were simply adapted.

I am essentially a composer, drawn into these endeavors because of dissatisfaction with an over-industrialized art of music, with all the crystallization that implies. I am primarily interested in the musical and emotional values of spoken inflections; I write no music without either words or voice. I believe we should have genuine consonance if we want it. I feel that temperament is an evil influence, and in expressing the belief I do not overlook the three centuries of music written for tempered instruments.

Intonation is a neglected subject and art, and there are few with whom one can even discuss the matter. I was consequently very happy to have your inquiry.

Yours sincerely,

Harry Partch
Sterling Hall
University of Wisconsin
Madison 6, Wis.
U.S.A.

2. Letter of Adriaan Fokker to Harry Partch, 7 May 1946, in response of Partch's letter of 25 March. The 'rough copy of a letter' which Fokker enclosed, is a 'Letter to the editor' published in Physica.

7th May 1946

Dear Mr. Partch,

I thank you very much for your letter of 26 March. I was interested to read that you proposed to use the harmonic 11th too. This is very much in advance of the time. I should be glad if only the seventh was put in its rightful place.

I should like to know how your 14 tonalities are formed, and also the minor tonalities.

I understand that you are using an equal temperament of 43 normalised one-seventh tones in the octave, equal steps. I think the quality of a temperament, whereby it recommends itself, is given by the degree in which it approximates the just intonation of the intervals which are required in the kind of your music. I am sending you a rough copy of a letter where I define a numerical measure for the degree of perfection. As it stands I confine myself to the intervals of the perfect octave, perfect fifth, perfect third and perfect seventh. The deviation of the perfect ideal is measured, for the temperament of 43, by the number 0.000 023 5, whereas for Janko's temperament of 41 by 0.000 011 16, and for Huygens' temperament of 31 by 0.000 007 38. It is possible that taking the eleventh into account the figures would turn out in favor of the 43-temperament, I did not look after that.

When working with this increased precision, one needs an adequate notation. I found it in a book 200 years old, in the Trattato di Musica of Giuseppe Tartini, Padua, 1751, who advocated a consistent use of the harmonic seventh.

How do you manage to catch and fix on paper the inflections of the living human voice? It is so very difficult to reproduce the fixed calls of the birds, and much more so the delicate shades of the voice?

Who are the few people with whom you in America can discuss these matters? I am trying to persuade composers here to use the beauties of the harmonic seventh. Progress is slow.

With kind regards,

yours truly,
(Adriaan Fokker)

References

Barbour, J. M. *Tuning and temperament*. East Lansing 1951.

Euler, L. *Tentamen novae theoriae musicae*. St. Petersburg 1939.

Fokker, A. D. *Rekenkundige bespiegeling der Muziek*. Gorinchem 1945.

Rasch, R. A. (editor) *Adriaan D. Fokker: Selected musical compositions 1948–1972*. Utrecht: Diapason Press, 1987.

Rasch, R. A. "Farey systems of musical intonation." Accepted for publication in *Contemporary Music Review*.

3

HARRY PARTCH'S *CLOUD CHAMBER MUSIC*

Ben Johnston

The challenge provided by Harry Partch's pitch usages is much stronger than it appears, lost as it is among half a dozen more radical seeming elements in his work. In particular, the impressive array of sculptural new instruments of the plectra and percussion types, whose sound has a strong attack component followed by a relatively sharp decay, obscures rather than dramatizes Partch's pitch designs.

It is not the melodic element that gets short shrift but rather the harmonic. In Partch's art both are overwhelmingly important parameters, along with metrical rhythm. Far from dethroning pitch as a major organizing element in music, as much radical twentieth century music does, Partch gives it a very powerful new lease on life. His microtonal melodies, particularly those so close in sound to spoken language, have attracted much notice, but entirely too little attention has been directed to Partch's return of harmonic practice to a just intonation basis.

Expanded just intonation is not simply a particular scale used in lieu of twelve-tone equal temperament. It is a radical, though by no means new, principle of ordering sounds by systematic use of numerical proportions. The same principle, applied to metrical rhythm, is one of the main elements giving provocative newness to the music of Elliott Carter, or in interesting juxtaposition, to the earlier music of John Cage and Lou Harrison. This practice was pioneered by Henry Cowell and Charles Ives. While this list gives the practice a conspicuously American pedigree, a similar usage occurs in the music of Alban Berg, Stefan Wolpe, and Luigi Nono. With respect to large-scale time divisions the same can be said of Krszysztof Penderecki's music.

In respect to pitch, the proportional system has consistently dominated not only all Western art music before the Baroque era but the music of several major Asiatic culture groups, notably the Indian, the Chinese, and the Arab. While it may once have seemed that Western art music would dominate such cultures, the trend for a long time seems to be aggressively in an opposite direction.

The unique and typically Western aspect to Partch's pitch system is its inclusiveness. He attempts a generalized theory of proportional pitch systems

(Harry Partch, *Genesis of a Music*, DaCapo Press 1973). While I do not feel he achieved this completely, he gave powerful impetus in a direction in which no other Western composer of any stature had moved for centuries.

Partch often claimed not to have any compositional expertise or ability. This was a facet of his self-taught artistic position. He felt defensive against the monolithic establishment of Western European music and its entrenched United States wing. In fact he developed highly original and effective techniques of composition which were, however, so thoroughly integrated into his total artistic effort that he disliked discussing them. But because almost all of his pitch notation is in the form of instrumental tablatures, his work has neither been published nor studied by musicologists. It has so far received too little serious attention from other composers.

Cloud Chamber Music is the eleventh of *Eleven Intrusions*, a set of small-dimensioned pieces, composed by Partch in 1949 and 1950. They were recorded in 1950 at Gualala, California by Partch, my wife Betty and I, and Donald Pippin, with recording engineer Harry Lindgren. Several of these works were later released on records in the album, *Thirty Years of Lyrical and Dramatic Music*, on Gate Five Records, a private label. *Cloud Chamber Music* is among those *Intrusions* released in this recording.

The "Cloud Chambers" referred to in the title are "found objects", the bottoms and tops of pyrex carbouys used in vapor-trail experiments to explore behavior of sub-atomic particles. They were obtained, as cast-offs, from the Radiation Laboratory at the University of California at Berkeley. Partch cut off the tops and bottoms by soaking a string in kerosene, tying it around a carbouy and then lighting it. Upon being chilled by immersion in water, the pyrex broke along the line heated by the burning string.

The bowls were chosen and used specifically because of the pitches which they produce when struck, and thus were integrated into the harmonic fabric of the works in which they are used. Like these, many of Partch's instruments provide a limited selection of pitches rather than a gamut, falling in the tradition of percussion rather than of keyboard instruments.

In an analogous way voices are treated as if they were "found objects" in Partch's compositions. A Partch vocal line is an abstraction, in the sense that it is a heightened manner of speech. But especially as performed by him, such lines are uncannily accurate transliterations of natural speech. The use of this technique in characterization is far closer to legitimate theater tradition than to lyric theater or opera.

The use of the voice in *Cloud Chamber Music* is in imitation of American Indian chant. Partch uses the Zuñi *Cancion de los Muchachos*, a chant which he heard himself as a boy in New Mexico. Partch has spoken of his recollection of the Indians of the Southwest as a tattered remnant. Something of his concern and compassion is here evident.

The music begins with a carillon on the cloud chamber bowls and quickly settles into a mournful lament set for adapted viola and guitar with kithara and marimba accompaniment. Resonant chords on the kithara supported by chimes from the bowls and diamond marimba back up the dialogue between the two principals.

After several phrases the diamond marimba introduces an accelerated tempo, ushering in the bass marimba and viola, which present the *Cancion* in a defiantly affimative mood. This leads to a dance-like passage for the two marimbas, followed by a second presentation of the *Cancion*, this time by solo male voice, a part intended for Partch himself in the original version. The dance-like duo again intervenes, following which the viola and a chorus of all the musicians sing the *Cancion* accompanied by all the instruments except the kithara, whose player now takes up an Indian deer-hoof rattle.

This climaxes in a cadenza for cloud chamber bowls after which the ensemble expresses its aroused state in guttural vocalization, culminating in a shout of solidarity.

The "scenario" is thus relatively simple and clear: the outburst of cloud chamber bowls first inspires a lament led by the violist, who then, aroused by the high-pitched marimba's insistent beat, presents the magical *Cancion*, first instrumentally, then vocally (on the recording this vocal part is taken, unhappily, by the guitar), alternating with the lively marimba duo. Then the whole ensemble joins in, with the ritual deer-hoof rattle, provoking another outburst of the bowls, which this time arouses defiance and group fusion. Bearing in mind the origin of the bowls in the atomic energy program and the role of the Southwest in that development, Partch's exhortation to the downtrodden is not hard to read. His music is seldom even this far from direct verbal and theatrical meaning, resting solidly as it does on corporeal aims.

It is of significance that Partch cast himself, an aging man, in the role of inciter, with the viola, by far the most "traditional" of his instruments from a Western musical viewpoint, as the agent undergoing the change first. The lower solo voice drops down a fourth from the G pentatonic scale to the C pentatonic (with four common tones), only to be answered by the more youthful ensemble in the higher scale, again dramatizing the difference in roles as well as ranges of voice.

Partch persistently saw himself as an inciter of youth, having little hope for the flexibility or perceptiveness of older, more culturally fixed people. He was opposed to our culture as he found it, and if he was undoubtedly first a dropout, he never relinquished the role of reformer, even in the actions and attitudes of his old age. He saw our social conditions as those of an advanced stage of decay, and looked to earlier and more "primitive" cultures not with nostalgia but with hope and exhortation.

Cloud Chamber Music begins as a depressed reaction to a false clarion, but then seizes American Indian incentives as a reinvigorating antidote. The future is, in a certain sense, the past. We are not to be saved by science fiction become fact but rather by ancient myths and rituals, which retain intact the dignity of human life as an inseparable part of nature.

The musical means Partch uses are in a fascinating way an illustration of this same allegory. Beginning with the "nature sound" of the found object, the instruments weave a microtonally chromatic web out of materials related to their sonorities, only to be elbowed aside by the resurgence of elements simpler not in a "natural" but in a cultural context, aligning not only the instruments (a late flower of civilization) but also the voices, a primal material of music. At the end the mood is one of battle, and the microtones are subordinate to the easily perceived and sung pentatonic scale, serving as its aura and support.

In translating Partch's tablature notation into something approximating "ordinary" notation, I have used accidentals I devised for my own use in presenting ratio-scale derived music. In such notation, uninflected notes refer to C major just intonation (tonic, dominant, and subdominant triads tuned in 4:5:6 ratios). ♯ and ♭ raise and lower respectively, by a ratio of 25/24 (ca. 70 cents). + and -raise and lower, respectively, by a syntonic comma 81/80 (ca. 21.5 cents). L and ⌐ raise and lower, respectively, by the ratio 36/35 (ca. 49 cents). ↑ and ↓ raise and lower, respectively, by the ratio 33/32 (ca. 53 cents). The following combinations occur

$$\#, \#\!\#, \flat, \flat\flat, \#\flat, \#\!\#\flat, \flat\flat, \flat\flat\#, \#\!\#\overline{\flat}, \flat\flat, \#\!\#\overline{\flat}, \overline{\flat}, \flat\flat, \uparrow, \uparrow\uparrow, \downarrow, \downarrow\downarrow.$$

Partch's theory of harmony categorizes pitches in tonalities of two kinds: otonalities, corresponding to major chords, and utonalities, corresponding to minor chords. In Partch the term "tonality" does not refer to a scale, and not at all to a system of progressions. The ratios of an otonality stand in the ratio 4: 5: 6: 7: 9: 11 (referring to partials of a single overtone series). The utonality is the inverse of this, referring to the same partials of an "undertone" series. Thus 1/1 otonality consists of the ratios 1/1, 5/4, 3/2, 7/4, 9/8, 11/8, or C, E, G, B♭, D, F↑-. The 1/1 utonality consists of 1/1, 8/5, 4/3, 8/7, 16/9, 16/11 or C, A♭, F, DL-, B♭-, G↓. Note that the 1, 5, and 3 identities of these two tonalities do not give parallel major and minor of C, but rather C major and F minor. In traditional tonality the tonic and its fifth are the focus of inversion rather than simply the tonic. Partch uses only the tonic, though he does not call it that. It is also interesting to note that in 1/1 otonality all the denominators of the ratios are powers of 2, while in 1/1 utonality all the numerators of the ratios are powers of 2. In Partch's terminology 2 is the numerary nexus of each of these tonalities. In all otonalities, the *numerary nexus* is in the denominator while in all utonalities it is in the numerator.

By letting 1/1 serve as each of the identities in an otonality and in an utonality, Partch generates what he calls a tonality diamond:

$$\frac{11}{8}$$

$$\frac{9}{8} \qquad \frac{11}{10}$$

$$\frac{7}{4} \qquad \frac{9}{5} \qquad \frac{11}{6}$$

$$\frac{3}{2} \qquad \frac{7}{5} \qquad \frac{3}{2} \qquad \frac{11}{7}$$

$$\frac{5}{4} \qquad \frac{6}{5} \qquad \frac{7}{6} \qquad \frac{9}{7} \qquad \frac{11}{9}$$

$$\frac{1}{1} \qquad \frac{1}{1} \qquad \frac{1}{1} \qquad \frac{1}{1} \qquad \frac{1}{1} \qquad \frac{1}{1}$$

$$\frac{8}{5} \qquad \frac{5}{3} \qquad \frac{12}{7} \qquad \frac{14}{9} \qquad \frac{18}{11}$$

$$\frac{4}{3} \qquad \frac{10}{7} \qquad \frac{4}{3} \qquad \frac{14}{11}$$

$$\frac{8}{7} \qquad \frac{10}{9} \qquad \frac{12}{11}$$

$$\frac{16}{9} \qquad \frac{20}{11}$$

$$\frac{16}{11}$$

C↑

A+   A↓♭

F♭+   F+   F↑

D   D♭   D   D↑♮

B   B♭   B♭   BL   B↑♭-

G   G   G   G   G   G

E♭   E   EL   E♭   E↓+

C   C♯   C   C↓+

AL   A   A↓+

F   F♯↓+

D↓

When "evened out" with a few "secondary ratios" which add missing identities to some of the incomplete tonalities as well as filling in scale gaps, this selection is the basis of Partch's 43-tone scale:

$\frac{1}{1}$	$\frac{81}{80}$	$\frac{33}{32}$	$\frac{21}{20}$	$\frac{16}{15}$	$\frac{12}{11}$	$\frac{11}{10}$	$\frac{10}{9}$	$\frac{9}{8}$	$\frac{8}{7}$	$\frac{7}{6}$	$\frac{32}{27}$	$\frac{6}{5}$	$\frac{11}{9}$
G	G+	G↑	A♭+	A♭	A↓+	A♭↑	A	A+	AL	B♭	B♭-	B♭	B♭-↑

$\frac{5}{4}$	$\frac{14}{11}$	$\frac{9}{7}$	$\frac{21}{16}$	$\frac{4}{3}$	$\frac{27}{20}$	$\frac{11}{8}$	$\frac{7}{5}$	$\frac{10}{7}$	$\frac{16}{11}$	$\frac{40}{27}$	$\frac{3}{2}$	$\frac{32}{21}$	$\frac{14}{9}$	$\frac{11}{7}$
B	C↓+	BL	C↑+	C	C+	C↑	D♭	C♯	D↓	D-	D	D♯-	E♭	D♯↑

$\frac{8}{5}$	$\frac{18}{11}$	$\frac{5}{3}$	$\frac{27}{16}$	$\frac{12}{7}$	$\frac{16}{9}$	$\frac{9}{5}$	$\frac{20}{11}$	$\frac{11}{6}$	$\frac{15}{8}$	$\frac{40}{21}$	$\frac{64}{33}$	$\frac{160}{81}$	$\frac{2}{1}$
E♭	E↓+	E	E+	EL	F↑+	F	F+	F♯+↓	F↑	F♯+	F♯	G↓	G- G

The tonality diamond is the basis of design of the diamond marimba, the blocks of which are arranged in raked tiers, with 11/8 (C↑) at the top and 16/11 (D↓) at the bottom, so that a glissando stroke descending from right to left gives an otonality and a glissando stroke descending from left to right gives an utonality.

The bass marimba, by contrast, has only eleven blocks, arranged from low (cello C) to high (7/6 below middle C). The notes are 4/3, 3/2, 5/3, 1/1, 8/7, 16/11, 8/5, 16/9, 11/6, 9/8, 7/6, or C, D, E, G-, AL, D↓, Eb, F, F↑, A+, Bb.

The adapted viola has an elongated neck, and is pitched an octave below the violin. It is performed gamba-style, held between the knees.

The adapted guitar in this piece has strings tuned at the unison (1/1 or G-). It is stopped with a plastic rod, Hawaiian style.

The kithara has twelve banks of six strings each ranged parallel, vertically. Each bank is a hexachord. Bank 1 is AL overtonality, minus the eleven identity. Bank 2 is C↑ utonality. Bank 3 is F otonality. Bank 4 is A+ utonality. Bank 5 is D↓ otonality. Bank 6 is F↑+ utonality minus the eleven identity. Bank 7 is C otonality. Bank 8 is G utonality. Bank 9 is Eb otonality. Bank 10 is B utonality. Bank 11 is G- otonality minus the eleven identity. Bank 12 is D utonality minus the 9 and 11 identities. Bank 1 and bank 12, against the arms of the kithara, are equipped with plastic rods between the strings and resonators, for creating glissandi.

The pitch content of the bell-like cloud chamber bowls is complex. I have determined what seems to me the predominant pitch of each bowl, but I doubt if these are the pitches Partch heard, since the tonalities do not always match. He did designate such found objects by pitch, though not in his score. His practice was to integrate them into the sound fabric harmonically. But given my interpretation the four bowls used in this piece comprise the 5, 3, 7 and 9 identities of D∠—otonality. This, plus the complex penumbra of tones surrounding it, is the opening sonority created by the cloud chamber bowl flourish at the opening of the piece.

The tension and melancholy of the opening duet is achieved by the use of the higher (7, 9, 11 and in a few cases even 15 and 21 identities) of the tonalities, largely without their triadic (1, 5, 3) identities. When these identities are subordinated to the simpler one and grouped around a simple scale structure, as they are once the *Cancion* is introduced, the effect is exuberant and strong.

The melodic style of the lament imitates the glides of spoken inflection. Partch frequently "drops off" a note to a neighboring tone before moving to the next important melodic tone. He mixes tonalities sometimes, as earlier twentieth century composers often mix triads and sevenths in "pile-up" combinations with multiple pitch references. His use of non-harmonic dissonances is perhaps a little freer than in common practice period style, but is essentially similar both in procedure and in effect. The chord tones cohere because of their smoother blend.

An analysis of the tonalities and non-harmonic tones yields the following insights: Note the way successive tonalities are usually related by common tones, either actual or implied (as missing members of a tonality). Seldom does Partch use "unrelated" successions of tonalities. The melodic lines follow stepwise designs basically, but one must remember the presence of almost four times as many notes per octave, so that the variety of "step" sizes varies considerably. Much of the expressive power of the music rests in this aspect of the melodies. In other works Partch calls for these inflections for voice, usually with a spoken quality. Here the viola and guitar imitate this vocal "intoning".

Cloud Chamber Music lacks the rhythmic complexity of many of Partch's works. Even in those works such as **The Bewitched**, where complications of meter abound, the effect is dance-like, never "ametrical". Similarly, even in complex microtonal melodic passages accompanied by relatively dissonant combinations of higher identities of superimposed tonalities, Partch's music never sounds atonal, but rather tonal in a totally new way.

Cloud Chamber Music is a work in which the simple and the complex meet in an expressive way. Partch has made their meeting "part of the plot".

4

DAPHNE OF THE DUNES: THE RELATIONSHIP OF DRAMA AND MUSIC

Glenn Hackbarth

Although perhaps overshadowed by academic writings about his theories relating to pitch and intonation, Harry Partch's investigations into the general nature and meaning of musical expression were also of considerable originality and consumed a large portion of his creative thought. What he saw was a Western culture whose music had become increasingly abstract; a mass expression,[1] whose emphasis on the mental and spiritual transcended reality and conveyed no real or direct meaning to the listener. During the early portion of his career, Partch's ideas gradually coalesced into a stance which was in direct opposition to these qualities. He believed that, above all, music should be corporeal. It must represent the intimate expression of the individual, and it must ultimately be emotionally tactile, communicating to the listener in a vital and tangible manner.

To create this sense of communication Partch relied heavily on visual representations and, especially, on the voice. About the latter he wrote: *It is intimate; one voice and one instrument is the ideal; a few more are admissible, but nothing approaching a mass of participants, either of voices or instruments, which inevitably produces the mass in spirit, or Abstraction.*[2] In this and other respects his affinity to the Greek drama, which he viewed as one of the few successful mergers of vocal drama and music, is quite evident.

But the inclusion of words does not in itself necessarily render a composition corporeal. It is most important that the words succeed in conveying meaning. In most of the existing vocal repertoire Partch felt that the voice had been employed essentially as an instrument, and in that sense had become merely another instrument of the abstract orchestra. It succeeded only in conveying the stylistic qualities

---

[1] By this Partch did not mean that abstract music was the music of the masses but rather a concept in which the identity of the individual was subordinated to that of the collective mass.

[2] Harry Partch, *Genesis of a Music*, 2d ed. (New York: Da Capo Press, 1974), p. 61.

of the music; not the meaning. To divorce itself from the abstract, the voice must first seek to present the spoken rhythms inherent in language and it must do so in a smooth and natural manner.

Considering his views of the verbal and its relationship to musical drama, it is of little surprise that the vocal element would constitute an important factor in Partch's music. The majority of his compositions—*Barstow, U.S. Highball, Oedipus, The Bewitched*, and *Delusion of the Fury*, among others—utilize the voice extensively and often in varied and traditionally unusual contexts.

But a work need not include verbal elements to qualify as corporeal. The action of the drama could conceivably be carried by visual actions alone. *Daphne of the Dunes* is a clear example of this genre. Written by Partch in 1967 as music to a dance-drama based on the myth of Daphne and Apollo, the visual action is so clear in its implications, the story of Daphne and Apollo so universal in its conception, that the drama succeeds in dance as effectively as if it were being spoken or sung.

Although it maintains the appearance of one of Partch's more extensive later works, *Daphne of the Dunes* actually has its origin in a composition written almost ten years before: *Windsong*, composed in 1958 as the sound track to a film produced by Madeline Tourtelot. Partch states in *Genesis of a Music* that *Windsong* was "re-written in 1967, without substantial change . . ."[3] and further qualifies the close relationship between these two works in the preface of *Daphne of the Dunes* where he writes "A re-copying of the score composed for the film *Windsong* in 1958,"[4] adding that the music was to retain its 1958 copyright under the title of the earlier composition.

Indeed, a comparison of *Windsong* and *Daphne of the Dunes* reveals that the differences are extremely minute. In various locations Partch added or deleted several measures, but there are no major revisions or structural reorganizations of the material. Even the minor additions to the score are usually repetitions of material already existing in near proximity, suggesting only a re-evaluation of the macro-rhythm by a composer freed from the more rigid timing constraints necessary to coordinate music and film.[5]

The other primary bond which exists between these two works is the drama, succinctly described by Partch in the preface to *Daphne of the Dunes*.

> The subject of the film, made by Madeline Tourtelot in 1957, is the story of Daphne and Apollo, transposed from ancient Greece to the dunes of a Lake Michigan summer art colony.

---

[3] *Ibid.*, p. 472.

[4] Partch, "Daphne of the Dunes," unpublished holograph score, p. 1.

[5] The only changes in instrumentation were the addition of the Gourd Tree and the Blue Rainbow, both built after *Windsong* was written.

In the myth, or at least the Roman version of it, the god Apollo is enamored of Daphne, virgin daughter of a river god. Apollo pursues her. This is most natural—it is what he knows how to do. The story makes no sense whatever unless one remembers that almost any virgin, either male or female, automatically resists seduction, however beautiful or otherwise desirable the would-be lover. Apollo pursues, and Daphne calls on her father river god for help. At the crucial moment—when she is only an inch away from becoming a non-virgin—her father changes her into a green laurel tree. Apollo, both appalled and frustrated—with arms clasping the rough bark of a tree—, nevertheless regains his sexual sobriety, and decrees that thenceforth all victors in any area of competition are to be crowned with green laurel leaves.

The story is at least some indication of the Greek sex ethic. But the film Windsong deals in fact with the Puritan American sex ethic, and Madeline Tourtelot, in a stroke nothing less than brilliant, turns the virgin American Daphne into a white, bare-limbed, dead tree at the top of a sand dune.

This, of course, has an even more devastating effect on Apollo. His reaction is shock, disbelief in the world he has always known, and a sudden, immediate decision. Split. The idea of crowning someone with a dead tree never even occurs to him, naturally.[6]

Although the realization in *Windsong* by Partch and Tourtelot adheres to this basic sequence of events, the action between Daphne and Apollo is prolonged and intensified through frequent symbolic allusions to the plot. Daphne is represented symbolically by relatively stable objects of nature: sand, grass, trees, and poplar leaves. As, in the ensuing drama, Daphne's sexual innocence begins to dissipate, so does the stability of most of these elements. The sand slowly erodes. Leaves and branches gradually drop from the trees ultimately leaving the desolate skeleton at the film's conclusion. These events are periodically interrupted by two other symbolic actions: gulls flying in pursuit of food, and snakes struggling in the sand. The end product is a complex web of activity in which several different representations of the same drama are in continual interaction.

While Partch explicitly stated that the re-writing of *Windsong* was not an afterthought but a possibility that he envisioned when working on the soundtrack,[7] he was also aware of the problems which would be created by the absence of these symbolic representations. Ultimately, the majority were left for the prospective choreographer to solve, Partch providing only minimal indications in the score of *Daphne of the Dunes* relating to the basic action and the following suggestions in the preface:

The two dancers, Daphne and Apollo, need not be, should not be, on stage constantly. I feel that moving shadows, effected by rotating a prism before the light of a slide projector, or possible moving colored lights, should substitute for the male-female nature symbols.

---

[6] Partch, "Daphne of the Dunes," p. 1.

[7] *Ibid.*, p. 2.

> *The climactic scene is a difficult problem of staging, but certainly not unsolvable. The dead tree must somehow become magically present, in the spot where Daphne the dancer is last seen, and Apollo must be seen in headlong flight. Thereafter, lights, shadows, should return.*[8]

Despite the visual differences which would inevitably exist between *Windsong* and a staged production of the dance, *Daphne of the Dunes* is heavily in debt to the sequential action of the original film for its musical structure. The score of *Windsong* reflects not only a careful synchronization of the music with the film, but, more significant, an attempt by Partch to achieve a close integration of musical materials and visual drama through the use of musical themes or motives to represent the various characters, types of dramatic action, and symbolic allusions.

The opening section of the work functions dramatically to establish the setting and initiate the introduction of the characters. In the film this action is first confined to shots of a flowing river and the music is fashioned to be appropriately turbulent. Partch employs only percussion instruments—the Cloud-Chamber Bowls, Spoils of War, Gourd Tree, Diamond Marimba, Bamboo Marimba, and Bass Marimba—placing them into a rhythmically aggressive context in which constant sixteenths articulated in groups of five at a brisk tempo dominate the texture. A parallel feeling of turbulence is also evident in his organization of pitch. Through an abundant use of polytonal structures and extensive chromaticism, Partch creates a texture which frequently lacks a strong sense of tonal stability.

The primary motive of this section (R1) is found in the Diamond Marimba at the very beginning of the piece. It consists of an ostinato pattern which projects the 1 and 5 identities of a 16/9 otonality (the main pitch center of the work) with 12/11 and 8/7 functioning as upper and lower neighbors to 10/9. While this tonality receives the initial support of the 16/9 cone gong of the Gourd Tree, it is presented over a 3/2 pedal in the Bass Marimba. The tonal incompatibility of 3/2 and 16/9 (neither are found together in any otonality or utonality of the 11-limit system) generates a polytonal atmosphere which is typical of this section and the work as a whole.[9]

---

[8] *Ibid.*

[9] All examples generally observe the format of placing Partch's original tablature notation immediately above a transcribed part for each instrument. Since conventional notation fails to adequately express the expanded pitch resources of Partch's system, a system of pitch diacritics developed by Ben Johnston has been adopted. To arrive at the various accidentals employed to represent the ratios, the following procedure was observed: All naturalized (or uninflected) pitches represent ratios in C major just intonation in which the tonic, subdominant, and dominant triads have been tuned in 4:5:6 proportions. A # or ♭ raises or lowers a pitch, respectively, by the ratio of 25/24, a + or -raises or lowers by the ratio of 81/80, a ∟ or ⅂ raises or lowers by the ratio of 36/35, and a ↑ or ↓ raises or lowers by the ratio of 33/32. In addition, the various symbols must at times be employed in combination to accurately represent a given ratio.

Example 1

From a dramatic perspective, the symbolic ramifications are quite clear. As the work progresses, 16/9 emerges as a pitch center associated with Apollo. Similarly, 3/2 becomes the frequent domain of Daphne. The tonal conflict which exists between these two centers at the opening of the work provides a clear fore-shadowing of the dramatic conflict between Daphne and Apollo during the re-mainder of the drama.

A secondary motive associated with the river setting (R2) is presented by the Diamond Marimba in measure 17. Visually this theme corresponds to shots of a boat tied to a dock—Apollo's initial vehicle of pursuit. While it maintains the previously established rhythmic persistence, it contrasts tonally with the first motive in its clear arpeggiation of otonalities and utonalities and in its rapid rate of harmonic change.

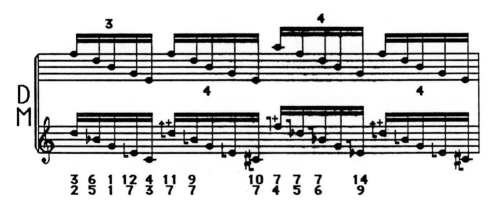

Example 2

In measure 34 Apollo is introduced into the action by the Bass Marimba. This first character motive (A1) provides an abrupt contrast to the previous rhythmic texture and is quite clear in its tonal implications; alternating between elements of a 1/1 utonality and a 4/3 otonality or in conventional terms: C major and C minor. While this theme is initially quite significant from a dramatic perspective, it ultimately proves to be of minor consequence; dissolving back into the "river music" never to reappear.

Example 3

Apollo's principal motive (A2) is later introduced in measure 55 by the Blue Rainbow and the Bamboo Marimba. It retains the energetic tempo and rhythmic aggressiveness of the beginning but with the eighth-note as the primary subdivision of the beat.

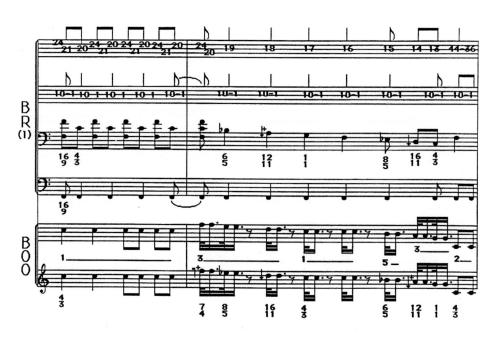

Example 4

The constant 16/9 drone in the Blue Rainbow together with a frequent use of 4/3 render this section quite stable tonally, projecting the 1 and 3 identities of a 16/9 otonality. However the remaining material is drawn from a scale constructed of two identical tetrachords which descend from the primary pitches of the drone. The combination of this scale with the strong pedals in the drone creates a subtle conflict when viewed in light of Partch's theoretical system. Considering the presence of 16/9 and 4/3 as the tonal foundation of this passage, the most logical ratios to include in the scale would have been either 10/9 (completing the 1–3–5 identities of a 16/9 otonality) or 16/15 (completing the 1–3–5 identities of a 4/3 utonality). However, this particular scale formation provides only 12/11 as the possible "third" of the triad; a ratio which falls roughly in between the expected pitches and creates ambiguity regarding the precise tonality.

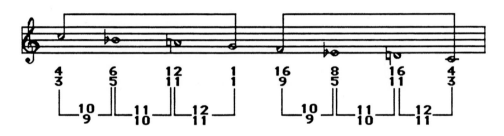

Example 5

Both A1 and A2 are constructed to offer some insight into Apollo's dramatic role. Their brisk tempos, rhythmic aggressiveness, and percussive nature success fully project his athletic prowess and sexual aggressiveness while their tonal clarity, the stability and consistency of his character. Even Partch's use of the synthetic scale in Apollo's second motive could be interpreted as having programmatic implications. While this scale is in a sense diatonic, it is not the diatonicism of a simple 5-limit scale but rather one of greater complexity and sophistication—attributes which suggest additional facets of Apollo's personality as well.

Daphne is represented musically by two different character motives. Both offer a radical contrast to those of Apollo and most of the composition's remaining material. The tempos are always set at a slower pace and the primary pulse mixes quarter-note and eighth-note values resulting in a much less active texture. Whereas much of Apollo's material relies heavily on percussion, Daphne's music is scored almost exclusively for strings. With both of her motives the accompanying visual action of *Windsong* is primarily symbolic, relying on trees, grass, poplar leaves, and driftwood as representations of Daphne with only occasional glimpses of the actual character. In *Daphne of the Dunes* these sections generally trigger her entrance onto the stage.

The first character motive (D1) appears in measure 68 scored for the Adapted Viola with the Blue Rainbow and the Kithara II in accompanying roles. The primary pitch center is secured by a 5/4 pedal throughout most of this section in the supporting instruments and in key pitches of the Adapted Viola. At the same time, strategically placed occurrences of 16/9, 10/9, 4/3, and 14/9 provide brief references to the primary 16/9 otonality (the 1–5–3–7 identities) which will prove to be significant in the motive's future appearances.

Example 6

With a few exceptions, the pitch material is relatively simple in its ratio components, the majority belonging to the 13-tone, 5-limit scale. The frequent use of 5/4, 3/2, and 15/8 (the 1–3–5 identities of a 15/8 utonality) generate a "minor" quality that, together with the dark sound of the viola, contributes to the lamenting character of this motive.

Daphne's second motive (D2) is first introduced by the Kithara II in measure 149. This passage initially centers around 3/2 with 6/5 and 1/1 (the 3–5–1 identities of a 1/1 utonality) generating an overall "minor" quality. However, during the course of the entire section (measures 148 to 159), Partch progresses through a wide variety of tonalities and since this passage is missing the secure foundation of a continual pedal, it projects a somewhat transient quality. (This characteristic is absent, however, in both later appearances of D2 in which the Kithara II appears over a 16/9 drone in the Castor and Pollux).

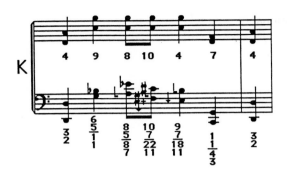

Example 7

Similar to Daphne's first motive, the lament-like character of this theme is established through its tempo, the "minor" feel of its pitch material, and the expressive character of the Kithara II. As in the Adapted Viola, the lower strings of the Kithara II project a dark, rich resonance and the characteristic portamento of the viola is available on the kithara in a more exaggerated form due to the fitting of four of its string banks with sliding pyrex rods which enable the performer to gliss from one tonality to another.

The pursuit of Daphne is primarily represented by a motive (P1) that is closely related to the material which characterized the river setting. First introduced in measure 79, it employs only percussion instruments, relying principally on the Diamond Marimba, the Bamboo Marimba, and the Bass Marimba with occasional appearances of the Cloud-Chamber Bowls and the Gourd Tree. This particular instrumental selection is especially appropriate from a symbolic perspective as it is Apollo who initiates and dominates the action during these sections of the composition. Constant sixteenths at the original tempo again regulate the rhythmic texture, reestablishing the aggressiveness of the work's opening. Their grouping, however, has been sequentially expanded from constant units of five, to an asymmetrical division of the 31/16 measure into beats containing 5, 5, 7, 9, and 5 sixteenths.

Example 8

An additional motive relating to the pursuit (P2) appears once during the work in measures 113 to 125. While the main motive (P1) is most closely related in its rhythm and instrumentation to Apollo, this section draws heavily on Daphne's first motive (D1) for its content. With the exception of two pitches in the Cloud-Chamber Bowls, the instrumentation is confined to string instruments: the Castor and Pollux and the Blue Rainbow. This scoring together with an extremely simplistic rhythmic texture creates a playful, naive character, in contrast with Daphne's other, more somber, musical representations.

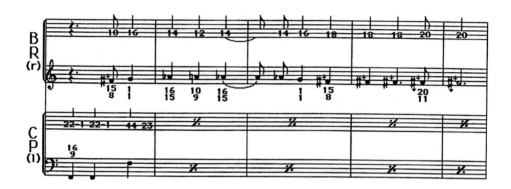

Example 9

The Castor and Pollux provides 16/9 as the underlying foundation for this section while the Blue Rainbow presents melodic fragments originally found as accompanying material to Daphne's first motive (D1). This material, however, has been significantly altered to project a different tonal emphasis. In D1 the motive chromatically spanned 5/4 to 16/9; appropriately so since these boundaries constitute the primary and secondary pitch centers of this section. In P2 the main emphasis has been shifted entirely to 16/9. Consequently the scale material extends only from 20/11 which is now heard as a chromatic upper neighbor to 16/9 to 10/9, the 5 identity of a 16/9 otonality. The presence of 16/15 as a lower neighbor to 10/9 produces a constant fluctuation between the "major" and "minor" third above the 16/9 drone.

The symbolic implications of this small section are quite significant. Daphne has reacted to Apollo's advances but in a naive manner consistent with her character. Her attempt to relate to Apollo is further suggested by the alteration of one of her previous motives to conform to the 16/9 center—a domain which clearly belongs to Apollo.

Apollo's attempted seduction of Daphne is portrayed musically by a single theme (S) which appears twice in the composition. First presented in measure 169, its melodic emphasis on the Bamboo Marimba and Bass Marimba maintains the percussive quality which is characteristic of both the river music and the pursuit and is symbolically representative of Apollo's continued dominance of the dramatic action.

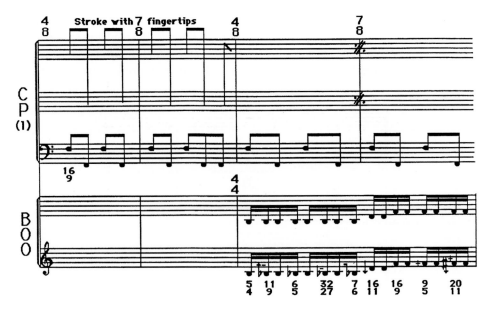

Example 10

Carrying the aggressiveness of the pursuit to an even higher level, the seduction continues the basic sixteenth-note pulse but at a faster tempo of ♩ = 112. This underlying rhythm is cast into a polymetric scheme in which the Castor and Pollux fluctuates between 4/8 and 7/8 while the Bamboo and Bass Marimbas present an alternation of 4/4 and 7/4; the two fields intersecting every four measures of the Castor and Pollux's ostinato.

As in the river music and the pursuit, the melodic statements of the Bass Marimba project elements of the 4/3 otonality and the 1/1 utonality, and the Bamboo Marimba is cast into a chromatic role whose intensity extends beyond that of any of the earlier sections. However, unlike the principal motive of the pursuit (P1), this section features a continual 16/9 pedal in the Castor and Pollux which provides a strong pitch center, keeping the chromatic excursions of the Bamboo Marimba in check. Its emphasis on a heightened sense of rhythmic activity, polymetrical structuring, extensive chromaticism, and polytonal features underscore the increased tensions emerging between Daphne and Apollo during this portion of the drama.

The climax of the dramatic action occurs in the transformation scene, a large section of the composition which is internally divided, both musically and dramatically into three distinct parts: an introduction (measures 286 to 305), the transformation (measures 306 to 326), and Apollo's reaction to its completion (measures 327 to 341).

The first section (T1) is scored only for members of the percussion family: the Bass Marimba, Cloud-Chamber Bowls, Spoils of War, and the Gourd Tree. Rhythmically this passage is set in a 3/4 meter but the internal division of the measure at its mid-point by the Spoils of War generates an actual feeling of 3/8. Its tempo of ♩ = 116 is the fastest of the work with the eighth-note rendered as the basic pulse.

Example 11

The pitch content of this section is stabilized throughout by a 9/8 pedal in the Spoils of War. The Bass Marimba again articulates passages which generate linearly the 4/3 otonality/1/1 utonality combination, and the incompatibility of 9/8 with either of these tonalities creates a continuous polytonal character. The Gourd Tree, Cloud-Chamber Bowls, and shells of the Spoils of War contribute long, chromatic lines which at times support the tonal implications of the Bass Marimba or the 9/8 pedal, and occasionally project contrasting tonalities.

The transformation (T2) follows without interruption and continues to rely on the instrumentation of the introduction, adding only the Castor and Pollux near its mid-point. In the film this section is characterized by dramatically alternating images of the tree to which Daphne is eventually transformed and total darkness. Although the tempo of ♩ = 116 remains intact, the basic pulse centers on the sixteenth-note creating even more linear activity than was present in the previous section.

Example 12

The tonal implications are again oriented around the melodic use of the Bass Marimba and the 9/8 pedal in the Spoils of War. In the first few measures the ostinato figure in the Bass Marimba provides the 1 and 3 identities of a 1/1 utonality. The 8/5 of the Cloud-Chamber Bowls in measure 306 adds its 5 identity while the shells of the Spoils of War articulate a chromatic movement to 16/11: the 11 identity. In measure 307 the large cone gong of the Gourd Tree provides the 9 identity and the Cloud-Chamber Bowls a chromatic inflection (10/7) on 16/11. This entire movement is suspended over the 9/8 pedal articulated by the pernambuco block of the Spoils of War.

62   *Glenn Hackbarth*

    The final section (T3) depicts Apollo's reaction of shock to Daphne's transformation. Its instrumentation relies primarily on the Kithara II and taped material[10] in the Diamond and Bamboo Marimbas with the Chromelodeon I providing chromatic clusters of sound. Although the tempo slows to $\downarrow$ = 76, the constant pulse of sixteenth-note sextuplets produces a linear density which nearly equals that of the transformation (T2).

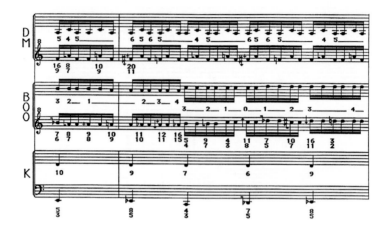

Example 13

    Ostinato patterns are articulated in both the Diamond Marimba and the Kithara II. The former returns to a 16/9–10/9 pattern similar to that of the work's opening with 8/7 and 20/11 providing upper neighbors to each of these pitches. The latter oscillates between elements of a 4/3 otonality (4/3 and 5/3) and a 1/1 utonality (4/3 and 8/5) with 7/5 used "non-harmonically".

    Above these ostinato patterns, the Bamboo Marimba presents chromatic scale segments whose outer boundaries usually support the implied tonalities of the Diamond Marimba and the Kithara II, and eventually comes to rest on a repeated 7/6: the 7 identity of the 4/3 otonality.

    The polytonal complexity of the actual transformation together with its increased tempo carry the growing intensity of the pursuit and seduction to a climax which corresponds precisely to the dramatic action. In T3, Apollo's confusion and momentary shock are appropriately depicted by the continued—although less

---

[10] With most of Partch's instruments, the particular tuning arrangement prohibits octave transposition of even relatively simple material. In *Windsong* Partch initially recorded several sections at half tempo and then played them back at twice the speed resulting in a transposition up an octave. These sections remained as a tape part in *Daphne of the Dunes*.

intense—polytonal structures, the chromatic lines in the Bamboo Marimba which phase in and out of tonal focus, and the large chromatic clusters in the Chromelodeon I during measures 334 to 337. All of these factors contribute significantly to an analogous sense of aural confusion within this section.

Following the transformation scene Partch returns to the opening river music and with this addition the basic framework of the form has been completed. But while this preliminary overview of the drama presents a straightforward realization of the action, the final form of DD and WS has been made much more complex through a web of interruptive excursions and regressions in the dramatic action.

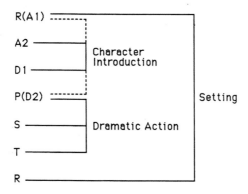

Example 14

First of all, primary material related to the pursuit (P1) appears in three different locations of the composition. Its first and second occurrences are separated by the secondary motive (P2) whose character constitutes a regression from the rhythmic aggressiveness of the main body of the pursuit (P1). The third appearance of P1 occurs between two statements of the seduction (S) where it now functions dramatically and musically to interrupt the action's progress.

At the same time Partch has structured the interlacing of the pursuit and seduction on this level in a telescoping fashion which enhances the momentum toward the transformation. Although roughly the same amount of total time is spent in P1 and S, successive appearances of P1 diminish in size by about the same durational interval while the second appearance of S has increased.

Second, the main thematic material related to Apollo (A2) and Daphne (D1 and D2) is not restricted to any single section of the form but appears continually throughout most of the composition. Daphne's motives function consistently to interrupt the flow of the drama. Their slow tempos ($\quarternote = 60$ and $\quarternote = 66$) and characteristic mixture of quarter and eighth-note rhythms result in sections of sharp contrast which resist the growing rhythmic energy of the principal action. Thus they provide constant musical allusions to Daphne's contrasting character and her reluctance to submit to Apollo's desires.

Motive	Measures	Appx Pulse/Min.	Appx Timing
P1	79-92	430	61 sec.
P2	113-125	160	29 sec.
P1	138-147	430	43 sec.
S	169-202	448	50 sec.
P1	224-232	430	26 sec.
S	235-280	448	66 sec.
T1	286-305	464	31 sec.
T2	306-326	464	44 sec.
T3	327-341	456	48 sec.

Example 15

Successive statements of Apollo's main motive (A2) are strategically placed to introduce portions of the pursuit and the seduction. Being highly aggressive in their character, they function to reinitiate the dramatic flow.

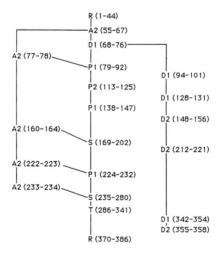

Example 16

Although the pitch substance of Apollo's primary motive and those of the river, the pursuit, and the seduction recurs in subsequent statements without major change, Daphne's motives undergo significant transformations. The final two appearances of both her first (D1) and second (D2) themes are positioned over a 16/9 drone in the Castor and Pollux; a pitch center reserved for Apollo and his actions. Symbolically, Daphne has become increasingly involved with both while the resulting polytonal nature of these sections serves to underline the fact that the basic dramatic conflict remains unresolved.

And finally, four additional motives originally employed to accompany the symbolic actions on the film are encountered with some regularity throughout the composition. The first of these (W) is used in three different locations to represent gulls in flight, an illusion depicted by sweeping glissandi over the entire range of the Surrogate Kithara.[11]

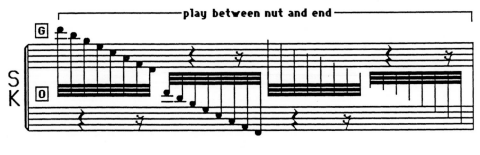

Example 17

A second motive (X) appears twice to accompany the filmed images of snakes in the sand; symbolic representations of Apollo's pursuit. First introduced in measure 103, these passages are scored exclusively for the Castor and Pollux, utilizing both canons with the right canon primarily on tape. The left canon provides a firm foundation for the motive by presenting a drone on 16/9. The right canon has been tuned so that it will produce coloristic glissandi of a highly chromatic nature—an apt choice for a motive which functions to depict slithering snakes. (See example 18.)

Partch occasionally employs a variant (Y) of the snake motive in which full glisses of the Castor and Pollux right canon, instead of small segments, are presented over the constant drone in the left canon. However, unlike either of the earlier motives, its appearance is not consistently related to the same dramatic action. In measure 109 it depicts a gull in flight; in measure 133, sand; in measure 165, a fish in water; and in measure 281, a snake struggling in the sand. (See example 19.)

---

[11] Since Partch indicates that the Surrogate Kithara not be played in the normal manner but be played alternately between the "nut and end" and the "bridge and nut" (similar to playing behind the bridge of a violin), this section is left untranscribed.

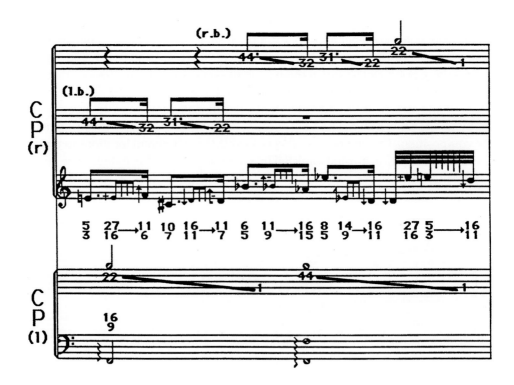

Example 18

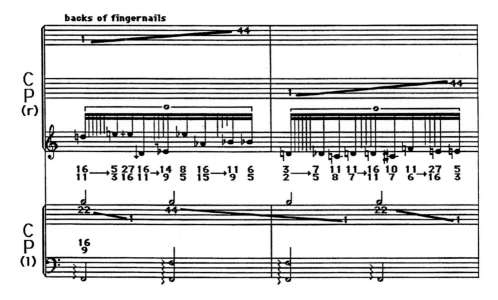

Example 19

A similar observation concerning the relationship between music and drama can be made about the last symbolic motive (Z). Its initial appearance (measure 135) accompanies shots of a tumbleweed rolling; its second (measure 210), a branch falling on the sand and Daphne's hand; and the third (measure 282), a snake struggling and Daphne staggering. Scored for the right canon of the Blue Rainbow and the left canon of the Castor and Pollux, its pitch content centers around a 16/9 pedal in the latter. The Blue Rainbow projects a 5/4–16/9 conflict with 16/9, 10/9, and 14/9 providing the 1–5–7 identities of a 16/9 otonality, and 5/4 with 10/9 the 1 and 9 identities of a 5/4 utonality.

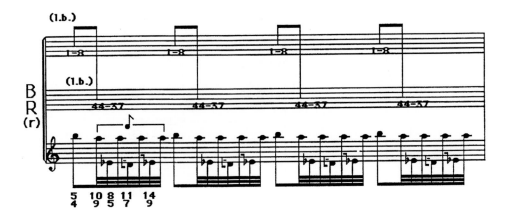

Example 20

The inclusion of these four motives completes the formal layout of the composition. Both the initial and final appearances of W are closely linked to the river music. The first functions to extend and conclude the opening section of the work while the last initiates its return. The remaining statement in mm. 157–159 retains the tempo and supporting instruments from the previous section (D2). Here it functions in a dual capacity to close Daphne's theme and at the same time introduce Apollo; a role that it also had in its initial appearance (mm. 45–54).

Although the tempos of the remaining three motives vary considerably in their individual statements, all lack the feature of a strong underlying pulse. Consequently they function to suspend the musical and dramatic flow. In measures 102 to 112, X and Y continue Daphne's interruption of the action, as does the appearance of Y and Z in measures 132 to 137. The interjection of X and Z in measures 203 to 211 halts the progress of the seduction and introduces a statement of Daphne's second motive. Similarly, the appearance of Y in measures 165 to 168 and the combined statement of Y and Z in measures 281 to 285 provide independent interruptions of the musical flow without a reliance on either of Daphne's themes. (See example 21.)

In its final stage, the form of *Windsong* and *Daphne of the Dunes* reveals a complex struggle between Apollo and Daphne, musically depicted in the continual interruption of sections whose character is rhythmically aggressive and persistent by passages whose contrasting nature delays and resists this momentum. Although the dramatic action moves constantly toward its ultimate goal, the overall implications, planted by the return of the river music at the work's conclusion, are in part circular. It is Daphne who has been transformed and her transformation clearly provides a solution but not a resolution to the basic dramatic conflict. While Apollo experiences momentary shock, he reflects on Daphne's original character

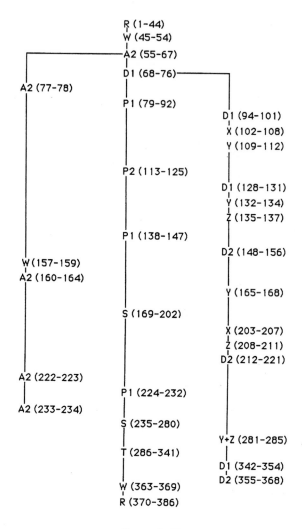

Example 21

(in measures 342 to 358) and returns to the river, whose unchanged music affirms the ongoing nature of the drama's underlying theme.

Thus Partch's perception and musical representation of the drama proves to be remarkably thorough. In view of the extent to which he went in integrating the dramatic element into all of his compositions, it is of little wonder that he came to categorize his work as total theater. Its creation was the result of an ongoing search for an alternative to abstract music. Its roots lie in the integrity of its corporeal substance, in an attempt to create a music of a highly dramatic and communicative nature.

5

A TEXT ON THE MUSIC OF HARRY PARTCH TAKEN FROM NOTES AND COMMENTARIES ON NOTES MADE DURING AND AFTER AUDITIONS OF THE MUSIC OF HARRY PARTCH

Elaine Barkin

obsessive recurrent patchblends defiantly resisting

interior aphony

Mix of the yokel and the sophisticate, the
naive and the systematic, from the ministerial
to the banal, distorting the already distorted;
splintered voices of the speakingeasy; Pierrot's
native American twice-removed stepcousin warbles
from the East; a bunch of guys unkempt with
baggy pants, holes at the knees, woolen caps
with brims, sittin' 'n gabbin', shootin' the
breeze; pulsations, fits and slides of riding
the rails wheeling and pumping for a lifetime
in his head, we get drawn along within the cracks,
drawls and tunes schizophrenically alternating.

Songs, Barstow, CloudChamber Music
U.S.HIGHBALL & Delusion of the Fury

A MUSIC OF ENERGIZED EOCENTRICITY
WHOSE INCESSANCIES GRABS ITS FLEDGLING LISTENER!

Drama of the travelling vaudeville/medicine/carnival show,
dance of the bluesyfloozies, round up the usual shrieky
delirious suspects; pounding lugubrious superwhine,
jittery trills, quavery glides and strums;
voices text&number-tied, all making and
crying with the tumult;
evoking the never-
ending as the
end strokes
on and...   More than
peters..   not IT seems
.out.   always to be THERE,
  ..   over and over, locked
            in to ITself; continually
         filling in/up a temporal expanse/
       surface, as if slowing up or leaving
        tacit was to admit failure; a hands
          on music holding on fast to its
           reality, the madness going by quickly.

Oedipus

Castor and Pollux

I strain to put **IT** in a place and can not.
I strain to hear as tuned those dis/dys/mis tunes.
I hear them as harmonious with each other
I hear my viscera queasing.   but not with me.

...it anoints the hair, it titillates the brow, it mizzles on
the temples, and this wretchedest of intellectual infamies in
the name of music—mark the term!—is called "musical tone." °

Hyperkinetic soundbands and scratches and cries
and stretches jump out at you, layered multi-
discotempoed clumps, longpassing parade in and
out of sync with itself, more densely layered
and peculiarly differentiated as it passes;
interior ghosts exteriorized, sounding in
order to exorcise and control demons, he is
his own shaman searching for ways to rid his
self of those throbbing inner voices; for ways
to restrain yet express rage and prevent silence; for ways
to adapt, negotiate, and maneuver around and about the
psychological, the physiological, and the creative; to
acceptably dispense violent libidinal energy by permissible **pounding
and striking and vellicating and banging with fingers, sticks, gloved
hands and fists.**

Yet here and there lush sensual resonances emanate.

*Windsong
The Dreamer That Remains*

*Daphne of
the Dunes*

| Music for the masses. | Music not for the masses. | Some are already too far gone. | Some not gone far enough. |

Much like the Great American Desert, where things live in
clusters, where suddenly a coalescence of forces produces
an environment hospitable for the habitation of some spec
ies and there, and often only there, some flora (or fauna
) roots or outcrops, and just as suddenly, or so it seems
as one passes on through or makes a sharp turn, another e
nvironment, another habitat, another something erupts and
has its place, its space, its time, its presence.

A mundane music of sensations--of touch, sight,
hearing; a sensationalist's music wanting so to
"influence",[+] shock, incite, and soulstir;
sounds of the new overtaking, surging over what
was, territory invaded, abrupted moments abruptly
changing, an irrepressible music of possession
and possessiveness, unsoberly shaking and rocking
and twisting...

Plectra & Percussion Dances

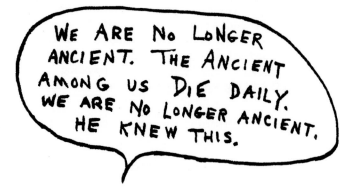

All those entanglements and aggregations, each obscuring
the other, each allowing the other to resonate; ribaldry
animated, libidinal agitation barely but nonetheless tamed
and clothed; disordered canons never quite making it (nor
wanting to), all moving inexorably on and on; steely
fingers, marionettelike feet clacking, NewMusic mewls and
tortures, pulling out all stops, bombarding themselves and
us, force projected at every moment of its own intensity,
EEEE OOOH   EEEE OOOH out of someone's inner depths;
and I take it all in, taking it all seriously and unseriously,
wondering if all the silliness and banality are intentional
parody or just plain sophomoric & freshmanically silly and
weirdly banal with that sleazy "obnoxity" # and those truly
stunning instruments being vibrated by thumping limbs and
twitching bodies, high on their own power and intensity.

The Bewitched

That Partch (& <u>The Bewitched</u>) and Elvis (& <u>The
Sun Sessions</u>) made the scene synchronistically
is no accident. High time for white man to cast
off millenia of donts and postures and blinders
and respectabilities, to color himself **anything**
but 'white', to try on some of those earthtones.
Although both were interested in "shared culture"[@]
and engaged in a miscegenated bodymusic, further
comparison pales. Unlike Elvis's unmitigated
corporeal, textual, and vocal eroticisms--coming
out of his lowdownhome macho guts--Partch's
sexuality is manifest as raw aggression, the
eroticism sublimated; his mythic, androgynous
women sleep with or eat their sons; trickery and
deception rule the roost. There isn't much Romance.

Fanfares and never-quite-right
licks of park band music behaving
rowdily and smelling of popcorn,
accompanied by intoxicated swooning
females--both divine and profane--,
their heaving and aroused voices
complementing instrumental textures,
their phonemic exclamations matching
tunescrap 'motifs'; the entirety
analogous to a C.B.DeMille spectacular
synesthetically turned into its own
soundtrack, albeit a far cry from
music for the millions.

Revelation in the
Court House Park

NO WAY REALLY TO HAVE A SOUND WITH NO TIME, YET

SO OFTEN SO MUCH SEEMS PREOCCUPIED WITH JUST HOW

TO GET THE MOST OUT OF THOSE INSTRUMENTS, HOW TO

MIX AND MATCH AND UNMATCH, SYNC AND NONSYNC, OR

MAYBE IT'S THAT THE TIMES THEMSELVES ARE UNFULFILLED

BUT THERE--FORTUITOUSLY GLUEDSOLID LIKE EXPOSED

LAYERS OF UPTHRUSTED, EARTH(IN PAIN)QUAKED, OR

VOLCANICALLY SPEWNCOOLED&HARDENED MATTER-MULTI-

HUED&PATTERNED, MONOCELLULAR, MONO-LITHIC.

At the start, a long slow expectantly
undulating luxuriant wave, taking its
time, ascending up and on up, dipping
then into those dancing bones-evoking-
bodysource hollowsounds, pulsating
sonic labyrinths, congregations of
whoops, unheard sighs and cackles,
crying out to be seen and felt, not
in a time but a space, a place; not
enough to just hear hearing; always
wanting to be heard felt&seen.

Delusion of the Fury

HP retrieves all those sounds we throw down the tubes,
in the trashbins, out the window; of beginners' practice,
of tuners' rejects; tunes of the shower and the monotones;
spidery X-rated cries of the interstices; outcasts and
runaways of a sonic society rehabilitated--each one now
having acquired a particular identity and place in a world
--even if they do sound a bit rubbishy and unfit; capturing,
reproducing, making effable--by rationally and digitally
enabling--those now-discrete (yet still somewhat indiscreet)
tones, whose intimacy with each successive other borders on
the unchaste, the incestuous, as each almost occupies its
neighbor's turf; parcelling out this sonic riffraff in
checkered uneven wayward beats, fine for any Walpurgisnacht
but hardly suitable for the ballroom or for those in 'gowns
and tails' "afraid [to] loosen their full-dress G-string"*

> ...most cellists would rather commit
> an indecent act than allow another cellist
> to catch them with a colored fingerboard...¢

So what he was doing was
attempting to invoke music theater as if
in its early, albeit highly sophisticated
stages of social evolution;
acting out the dispensability of acquired
Culture yet addressing 'cultured' persons;
rejecting conditioning and
inventing possible ways of inhabiting a world
in which he felt uncomfortable,
from which he felt estranged.

Let us loiter together and know one another. %

NOTES

°   Harry Partch, <u>Genesis of a Music</u>, Second Edition,
      Enlarged, Da Capo Press, New York, 1974, p. 53

+   HP, p. xviii

HP, p. 205

@   Greil Marcus, <u>Mystery Train</u>, E.P.Dutton & Co.,
      New York, 1975

*   HP, p. 215

¢   HP, p. 201

%   HP, from <u>The Dreamer That Remains--A Study in
            Loving</u> (1972)

Elaine Barkin
August 1987

The text was written during a residency at the
Djerassi Foundation's SMIP Ranch in Woodside, CA.

6

HARRY PARTCH: VERSES IN PREPARATION FOR *DELUSION OF THE FURY*

Paul Earls

[*Editor's Note : This paper was written in 1967. Due to the intervening years, a few of it references are no longer valid. Because of its historical significance, the paper is herein reprinted without alteration.*]

For the past forty years an amazing creative personality has been quietly at work in the United States completely out of the mainstream of recognized musical fashions. The accomplishments of Harry Partch are manifold, encompassing profound challenges to the fundamental assumptions of music as it is now practiced in the West, technical innovations of instrumental construction and performance, thorough research resulting in a new concept of tuning and scale formation, and, most importantly, a body of compositions which transforms these theoretical abstractions into highly original works of art.

Partch's work has received peripheral attention from the musical world. He is a member of BMI, and he has received aid from the Carnegie Corporation of New York (1934), the Guggenheim Foundation (1943–45 and 1950), and the Fromm Foundation (1956). He has also been associated briefly with two educational institutions, the University of Wisconsin (1944–47) and the University of Illinois (1956–57; 1959–62), but without normal faculty status. He has a small but highly partisan following, mostly on the West Coast.

Yet little serious attention has been given to his position as a composer. The standard reference source for musicians, *Baker's Biographical Dictionary of Musicians*, in its fifth edition (1958) had no mention of Partch, although Albert Ross Parson and Odön Partos do have entries at the point one should find a Partch listing (that oversight is corrected in the 1965 Supplement).

Discussions of Partch usually are devoted to factors other than his music, and even those are rare.[1] The best source of information remains his own book.

---

[1] His music, however, receives laudatory recognition in America's Music (1955; 2nd. rev. ed., 1966) by Gilbert Chase.

Genesis of a Music, largely written before 1930 and which took close to twenty years
to publish.[2] It contains a detailed treatment of his basic theories about music and
the results of his intensive scale research. He convincingly arrives at a number of
conclusions, the most basic of which is his concept of a visceral/corporeal music,
essentially monophonic, employing an "acoustically perfect" scale of forty-three
unequal pitches per octave.

Partch was also an early advocate of "total theater." To Partch this meant,
among other things, that the concept of a pit orchestra is artificial. He insists that his
instrumentalists and their instruments be on stage and part of set design. Performers and their equipment must be dramatic and pleasing to the eye. He says, referring to his own instruments,

> *There is surely some special hell reserved for the player of one of the more dramatic instru-*
> *ments who insists on deporting himself as though he were in tie-and-tails on a symphony*
> *orchestra's platform (such as experimental hanging by the gonads on a treble Kithara string*
> *until he relents).*[3]

It is beyond the scope of this article to deal with Partch's dramatic and theatrical
concepts except in passing. The intention is rather to focus attention upon his musical
thought, which has not received proper examination by others;[4] para-musical
issues are eloquently put by Partch himself.

Partch does not write absolute music, so a discussion of the purely musical
aspects of any work of his yields only partial insight. Much of what may appear relatively routine on paper may become truly gripping when effectively staged. This
is true of other composers and their music and has not inhibited analytical studies
of Wagner, Verdi, Weber, Berlioz, and other theatrical composers. Unfortunately,
no satisfactory film record of any of his staged works exists.

Partch's earlier works are known primarily through his own release and
sale of recordings under the Gate 5 label. Until recently these could be obtained
only from Partch himself, but they are now available through SOURCE records
(Davis, California.)[5] Partch's primary source of income for many years were these

---

[2] University of Wisconsin Press, Madison, 1949.

[3] *New (revised) Manual on the Maintenance and Repair of—and the Musical and Attitudinal Techniques for—Some Putative Musical Instruments*, unpublished manuscript, dated 1963, p. 2.
(Hereinafter referred to as *Manual*).

[4] Such a study is made possible through Partch's generosity in allowing the author to use the
master sheets of many of his scores in order to have personal copies made. All were unpublished until *SOURCE* (Vol. I, No. 2, 1967) printed his latest score, the topic of this paper.

[5] Composers Recordings Inc. used the same master tapes for their release of selections from
the music of Harry Partch (CRI, 193), issued in 1966 with the assistance of the Alice M. Ditson
Fund of Columbia University.

recordings (supplemented by an annual grant from BMI and scattered gifts from individuals), and although it would be considered completely inadequate by twentieth-century standards, he has been able to support himself by his music.

His latest work is another large-scale piece containing all the characteristic Partch elements as well as some newer innovations. The score of the work bears the title *And On The Seventh Day Petals Fell In Petaluma*, a possible reference to his forced move from a studio he had set up in a former chicken hatchery in Petaluma, California, in 1965.[6] The music was conceived as a study for, and to be used with, a major theatrical production, *Delusion of the Fury*, which has not been staged to date. A detailed scenario (unpublished) has been prepared by the composer, which contains references to specific sections of the musical score.

Portions of the work (selected Duets) were performed under the collective title *Verses* in the Los Angeles vicinity, beginning in 1965. Additional titles have been used by Partch, such as *Seventh Day, Petals, Delusion*; they all refer to the same work. I shall refer to the music itself as the *Verses*.

The original score consisted of thirty-two minutes of instrumental music, arranged as "23 one-minute Duets, which later become five Quartets, three Sextets, and one Octet" through a process of overlay and electronic synthesis. A similar overlay process was used in earlier works, such as *Castor and Pollux* (1952) and *Windsong* (1957). The procedure is to design a large ensemble so that separate parts, normally two at a time, are musically complete. In *Castor and Pollux* three duets—each of a different textural character—are later combined into a large ensemble with all parts played simultaneously. Theoretically, any two lines could work together, although certain combinations as indicated in the score of both *Castor and Pollux* and the *Verses* are most effective for structural reasons.

To return to the *Verses*, the original structure was tentative. In August, 1966, after a recording session which took place in his Venice (Calif.) studio the previous month, Partch made a new arrangement of the *Verses* scheduled for release late in 1967 by Composers Recordings Inc. Since these changes—made within a week's time—are interesting themselves, both versions of the *Verses* will be discussed in this article. The 1966 version retains the basic twenty-three Duets, but the larger ensembles now consist of ten Quartets and one Septet. As will be seen, this recorded version is less complex than the original design.

A complete list of the original order and recombination of ensembles in the *Verses* appears in the preface to the score (Figure 1). The new order is given in Figure 1A. The nature of each instrument has been indicated by a letter after its

---

[6] The author's copy bears the following annotation on the last page, in the composer's hand: "Petaluma, California, March–April, 1964 (48th anniversary music—*Death on the Desert* written March–April, 1916."

name, with I representing idiophone, C chordophone, and A aereophone. The
vibrating materials have been indicated for the idiophones and the method of
sound production for chordophones and aereophones. The re-numbered *Verses* are
shown in Figure 1A by citing their original number.

The 1964 version used twenty-one instruments; the revision uses twenty-
four. There is a balance between idiophones (nine in the first, ten in the second) and
chordophones (eight in the first, ten in the second) in both versions. All combinations in the Duets and larger ensembles are unique. The earlier version was dominated by four instruments, Zymo-Xyl, Harmonic Canon I, Koto, and Castor &
Pollux, each of which was used four times. The later version uses only Harmonic
Canon I and the Koto four times.

There are a few instrumental changes in the later version. The Adapted
Viola is dropped from the ensemble, replaced by the Blue Rainbow in Verses 3 (old
Verse 5), by Chromelodeon I in Verse 15 (old Verse 17), and by Chromelodeon II in
Verse 4 (old Verse 6). The Drone Devils in Verse 19 (old Verse 18) have been joined
by the Gubagubi; the Blue Rainbow, the Gourd Tree and Cone Gongs have
replaced Castor & Pollux in Verse 23 (old Verse 18). The Zymo-Xyl has been dropped
from Verse 12 (old Verse 21).

The work includes the entire gamut of Partchian instruments, although
many (Adapted Guitar II, Gubagubi, Gourd Tree, Cone Gongs, Bloboy, Drone

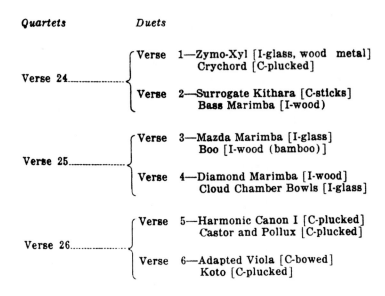

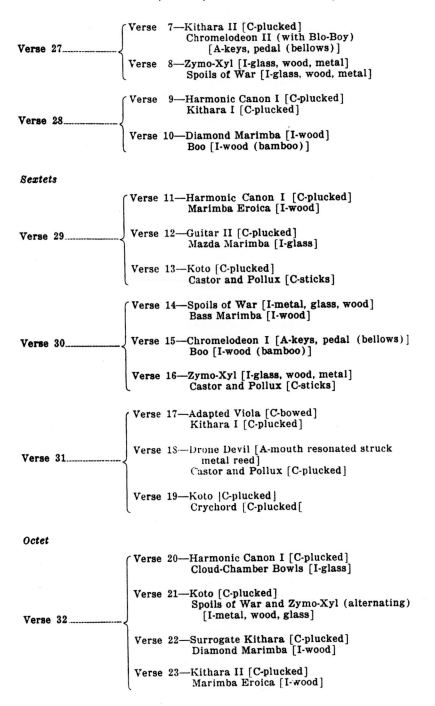

Verse 27
- Verse 7—Kithara II [C-plucked]
  - Chromelodeon II (with Blo-Boy)
    [A-keys, pedal (bellows)]
- Verse 8—Zymo-Xyl [I-glass, wood, metal]
  - Spoils of War [I-glass, wood, metal]

Verse 28
- Verse 9—Harmonic Canon I [C-plucked]
  - Kithara I [C-plucked]
- Verse 10—Diamond Marimba [I-wood]
  - Boo [I-wood (bamboo)]

Sextets

Verse 29
- Verse 11—Harmonic Canon I [C-plucked]
  - Marimba Eroica [I-wood]
- Verse 12—Guitar II [C-plucked]
  - Mazda Marimba [I-glass]
- Verse 13—Koto [C-plucked]
  - Castor and Pollux [C-sticks]

Verse 30
- Verse 14—Spoils of War [I-metal, glass, wood]
  - Bass Marimba [I-wood]
- Verse 15—Chromelodeon I [A-keys, pedal (bellows)]
  - Boo [I-wood (bamboo)]
- Verse 16—Zymo-Xyl [I-glass, wood, metal]
  - Castor and Pollux [C-sticks]

Verse 31
- Verse 17—Adapted Viola [C-bowed]
  - Kithara I [C-plucked]
- Verse 18—Drone Devil [A-mouth resonated struck metal reed]
  - Castor and Pollux [C-plucked]
- Verse 19—Koto [C-plucked]
  - Crychord [C-plucked[

Octet

Verse 32
- Verse 20—Harmonic Canon I [C-plucked]
  - Cloud-Chamber Bowls [I-glass]
- Verse 21—Koto [C-plucked]
  - Spoils of War and Zymo-Xyl (alternating)
    [I-metal, wood, glass]
- Verse 22—Surrogate Kithara [C-plucked]
  - Diamond Marimba [I-wood]
- Verse 23—Kithara II [C-plucked]
  - Marimba Eroica [I-wood]

Figure 1   Ensemble Movements in the Verses—1964 version

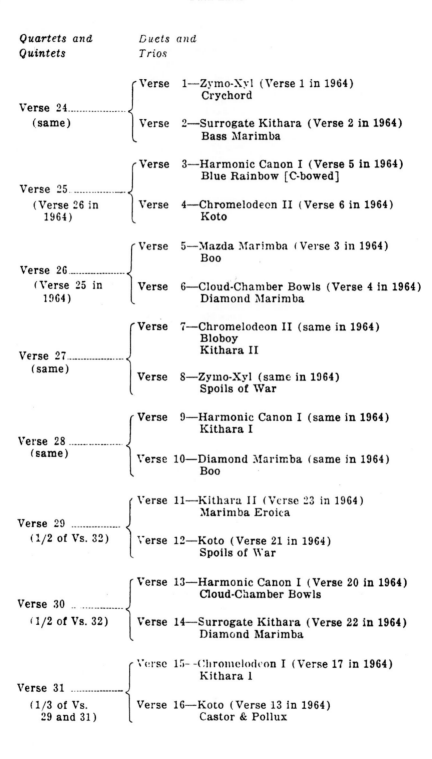

Quartets and   *Duets and*
Quintets   *Trios*

Verse 24............
    (same)

Verse 1—Zymo-Xyl (Verse 1 in 1964)
    Crychord

Verse 2—Surrogate Kithara (Verse 2 in 1964)
    Bass Marimba

Verse 25............
   (Verse 26 in
    1964)

Verse 3—Harmonic Canon I (Verse 5 in 1964)
    Blue Rainbow [C-bowed]

Verse 4—Chromelodeon II (Verse 6 in 1964)
    Koto

Verse 26............
  (Verse 25 in
    1964)

Verse 5—Mazda Marimba (Verse 3 in 1964)
    Boo

Verse 6—Cloud-Chamber Bowls (Verse 4 in 1964)
    Diamond Marimba

Verse 27............
    (same)

Verse 7—Chromelodeon II (same in 1964)
    Bloboy
    Kithara II

Verse 8—Zymo-Xyl (same in 1964)
    Spoils of War

Verse 28 ....
    (same)

Verse 9—Harmonic Canon I (same in 1964)
    Kithara I

Verse 10—Diamond Marimba (same in 1964)
    Boo

Verse 29 ....
  (1/2 of Vs. 32)

Verse 11—Kithara II (Verse 23 in 1964)
    Marimba Eroica

Verse 12—Koto (Verse 21 in 1964)
    Spoils of War

Verse 30 ....
  (1/2 of Vs. 32)

Verse 13—Harmonic Canon I (Verse 20 in 1964)
    Cloud-Chamber Bowls

Verse 14—Surrogate Kithara (Verse 22 in 1964)
    Diamond Marimba

Verse 31 ....
  (1/3 of Vs.
   29 and 31)

Verse 15—Chromelodeon I (Verse 17 in 1964)
    Kithara I

Verse 16—Koto (Verse 13 in 1964)
    Castor & Pollux

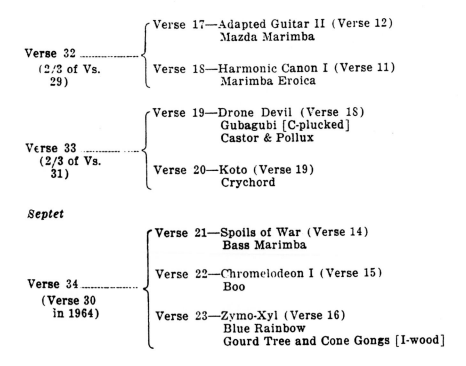

Figure 1A   Ensemble Movements in the Verses—1964 version

Devils) are only used once in the Duets. Additional instruments will be used in a stage presentation (see the section below on instruments), so this work represents a complete exploitation of all of Partch's contributions to original instrument construction. The only quality lacking is the human voice, which also is planned for the theatrical applicatins. The only conventional instruments are the Koto and Drone Devil (jew's harp; or, more properly, jaw's harp); unlike other large stage-works (such as *Oedipus, The Bewitched,* and *Revelation in the Courthouse Park*) no instruments are borrowed from the Western orchestra.

     A closer look at the classification of instrument types reveals a careful plan of sonority combinations which become most evident in the larger ensembles.[7] Originally, the first Quartet combined equal portions of idiophones and chordophones, the second and third Quartets were exclusively idiophonic and chordophonic respectively, while the fourth Quartet added a new texture, the aereophonic,

---

[7] "The strings in general represent the soul of my work...Percussion represents the bodily structure..." (*Manual,* p. 4).

to one idiophone and two chordophones. The last Quartet was like the first, i.e., an equal portion of idiophones and chordophones, achieved in this case by combining like categories, whereas the first combined unlike textures.

Chordophones dominated the first Sextet, although the use of felted sticks on Castor and Pollux in Verse 13 moved it closer to the idiophonic group. Still, the idiophones were out-numbered two to four. The second Sextet (Verse 30) reversed this relationship by using four idiophones, one chordophone (played with sticks) and an aereophone. Verse 31, the last Sextet, was all chordophonic in texture. The "jaw's harp" used in Verse 18 actually sounds more like a stringed instrument than the previously used Chromelodeon (an adapted reed organ).

The largest ensemble, the Octet of Verse 32, was a return to the textural construction of the first Quartet by evenly balancing idiophones and chordo-phones. All of the chordophones were in their most 'primitive' state—plucked—and all varieties of vibrating materials—metal, wood, glass—were present in the idiophones.

The revised version deletes the larger ensembles, resulting in ten Quartets and only one Sextet. The most common texture in the Quartets is a balance between chordophones and idiophones; Verses 24, 28, 29, 30, and 32 are of that nature. Verse 25 is actually entirely chordophonic; the Chromelodeon part replaces the Adapted Viola.[8] Verse 26 is all idiophonic, Verse 27 has a balance between two aerophones and two idiophones (along with one chordophone), Verse 31 is again chordophonic with the Chromelodeon again substituting for the Adapted Viola, and Verse 33, the last Quartet, is again chordophonic. The Sextet, Verse 34, has four idiophones with one aerophone and one chordophone. Only two of the large ensembles (Verses 26 and 34) are predominantly percussive in texture; thus Partch's feeling about the respective rôles of strings and percussion operated in his reorganization of this work.

This modular construction could continue indefinitely through the addition of further duets, sextets, octets, nonets, etc., and the various combinations possible which could be drawn from Partch's basic matrix. It is the most complex construct of its type Partch has ever used. The implication of his statement that this work was " originally conceived as experimental studies in preparation for *Delusion of the Fury*" is now apparent.[9] He has arrayed a wide palette of textures (and rhythmic orders—see below) from which he can choose those segments appropri-

---

[8] Although an aereophone, the Chromelodeon (a reed-organ) is meant to be used like a bowed string instrument. Partch tells Chromelodeon players in his *Manual* to emulate the sensitivity of the violinist's bow in their use of the pedal-operated bellows. He tried and discarded motors for the bellows, preferring the control available with the original system.

[9] *Delusion of the Fury* (unpublished manuscript dated Jan. 17, 1965), p. 4.

ate for use in the larger dramatic work, and which could be expanded without destroying the architecture of the whole.

Since Partch usually trains his performers to double on various instruments within a basic category it is difficult to calculate the total number of performers needed for the *Verses* in the sequence he lists. Chordophone specialists can play all of the Canons (Harmonic Canon I, Castor and Pollux), as well as the Kitharas and Koto, and much of the Surrogate Kithara material.[10] The Marimbas are usually played by trained percussionists, with only the Diamond Marimba demanding special virtuoso skills. Thus, conceivably two chordophone and two idiophone performers (with one doubling on the aerophones) could, under great strain, play each of the duets for a *studio* recording session. The larger ensembles would be put together by replaying a recording of a previous smaller ensemble and adding the extra parts "live." Or, all could be combined by careful recording of the separate duets which could then be mixed electronically.

Partch asks for nineteen instrumentalists for a "live" staged performance, which is not excessive (if they could be found). As he states:

> *Where necessary, instrumentalists must memorize parts, or know them so well that faint light is enough. The effect of stand lights on white music paper—on stage—tends to destroy even the most elementary lighting concept. Actors and singers have always memorized parts, and it is irrational to exempt instrumentalists, especially when they are cast in such a way as to be indispensable to the action.*[11]

All lines are carefully written in Partch's own unique notation—to be discussed later—except for Verse 18, where the Drone Devil part is left blank. This part was improvised by one of Partch's most experienced performers, Danlee Mitchell, under Partch's supervision, for a tape made in 1965.

The *Verses* employs four generations of Partch's own instruments, many of which are not represented as completely on previous recordings, and some of which have not been described in print. The older instruments, for which adequate descriptions and pictures can be found elsewhere,[12] include the Kitharas, Marimbas,

---

[10] The instruments are not as difficult to master as might be imagined. The author gained respectable competence on two chordophones (Castor and Pollux and Kithara II) and one idiophone (Boo) in two months of serious study.

[11] *Delusion of the Fury*, p. 6.

[12] *Genesis of a Music*, and, more recently, *Photographs of Instruments Built by Harry Partch and Heard in His Recorded Music*, June, 1962 (the insert to sets of Gate 5 recordings).

Bowls, the Canons,[13] Chromelodeons, Boo, Koto,[14] Spoils of War, and the Adapted Viola and Guitar.

Three instruments built in the last decade, with the help of Industrial Design students at the University of Illinois, are used prominently in the *Verses*: the Zymo-Xyl, Crychord, and Mazda Marimba. These instruments are described in another unpublished manuscript: *New (revised) Manual on the Maintenance and Repair of—and the Musical and Attitudinal Techniques for—Some Putative Musical Instruments*, August, 1963. My comments are drawn from this source and from personal memory.

The Crychord (Cry-Chord) consists of one steel string under tension over a wooden resonator. Tension can be altered on the string by means of pulleys and a hand level; control is maintained by a curved pitch bar that locates the desired pitches. It can be plucked or bowed and comes closest to functioning as a one-stringed string bass, although its primary characteristics are its powerful and smooth glissandi and its prominent vibrato.

The Mazda Marimba is constructed of twenty-four viscerated light globes. The resulting glass spheres vary from six to two inches in diameter. Its range is from the C below middle C to the B two octaves plus a seventh higher. Played with very light mallets that have rubber chair-dowels inserted on the striking edge, it cannot hold its own in an ensemble with the more powerful instruments. As with many other instruments, including most of the strings and Chromelodeons, it must be closely miked for balance to be achieved. A live performance without the proper placement of adequate microphones is a severe handicap in any large work of Partch. The Mazda Marimba has been used prominently in *Bless This House*.[15]

The hyphenated prefixes in Zymo-Xyl refer to its sounding materials: wood (xyl) and glass (zymo).[16] As Partch writes:

> *Alpha impregnated Omega in all seven apertures and the kettle top blew off. Out came Zymo and Xyl in multiple births: seventeen liquor and wine bottles, fourteen blocks of walnut with a single resonator, two Ford hubcaps, and—of course—one kettle top.*[17]

---

[13] This adaptation of the ancient monochord has two varieties: a pair of single canons, treble and bass (Castor and Pollux), and a double canon, Harmonic Canon I, which contains two sets of forty-four intersecting strings with a Pyrex glass rod mounted on an incline for gliding tones. Partch constructs his own bridges for these instruments which often are re-used in different works.

[14] Partch has used this traditional (and basically unmodified) Japanese instrument before in *The Bewitched* (1956).

[15] Available on Gate 5 Records, Issue A.

[16] Zymo is a prefix relating to fermentation, Partch's method of indicating the use of liquor bottles in this instrument.

[17] *Manual*, p. 41.

With a range of a seventh, Zymo's list of bottles ranges from Cheap Heaven Hill through Gordon's Gin (two different bottles having different frequencies) to Calvet Chateauneuf du Pape. Xyl covers a gapped three-octave span. The two hub-caps have different pitches, as well as two different pitches each, depending upon the edge tone and the center boss. The kettle top is notated as omega in the score and all surfaces are played with either wood or hard rubber mallets.

The Drone Devil is Partch's fanciful and descriptive name for the familiar "jaw's harp." He also has mentioned the possibility of using the Korean variety, the Piri, instead of the dimestore metal instrument. The Gubagubi is drawn from East Indian folk sources. Consisting of a drum with a steel string attached to the inside of the drum membrane whose tension is adjusted manually while the string is plucked, its primary characteristic is continuous glides combined with rapid plucking.

Additional instruments have been built in the past few years that Partch lists for use in *Delusion of the Fury*.[18] Three of them are percussion instruments: the Quadrangularis Reversus (another virtuosic marimba), the Gourd Tree, and the Boodongs. He has also constructed an array of hand-instruments to be carried and played by the Chorus. These include Oriental (particularly Far-Eastern) instruments, such as the Formosan drum, East Indian drum, Japanese pancake drums, Chinese gong; his own version of the African musical bow, the Ugumbo (Zulu), which requires a bare stomach to regulate the resonance;[19] along with two American instruments (the afore-mentioned "jaw's harp" and the American sled gong), and bamboo bouncing poles such as are found in Africa and in the Philippines.

Partch lists the application of the various *Verses* for appropriate sections of *Delusion of the Fury*. The *Verses* are not used in their numbered sequence, and the newest instruments, with the exception of the Drone Devil, were not scored in the original version of the *Verses*. The other hand-instruments would be choreographed during the preparation of the staged work, adding dramatic emphasis and color where appropriate. And Partch may very well write some more music in the meantime; he was still building hand-instruments in the summer of 1965.

Metrical Structure

The device of combining duets (as seen in Figures 1 and 1A) is made more complex because, when included in larger ensembles, all parts do not necessarily share the

---

[18] *Delusion of the Fury* (scenario), p. 3.

[19] For a description and illustrations of this gourded musical bow see Kirby, P. R., *The Musical Instruments of the Native Races of South Africa*, Johannesburg, 1965, pp. 197–206, pl. 55; and Balfour, H., *The Natural History of the Musical Bow*, Oxford, 1899. Partch's model is the *regwana/ligubu/ugubu/thomo*. This is the origin of his new instrument, The Blue Rainbow.

same metrical structure. In *Castor and Pollux*,[20] which also uses this overlay technique, all parts do share the same metrical structure, with identical numbers of identical measures. Each measure has the same basic beats, e.g., 3/4–4/4 (repeated), or 4/4–5/4 (repeated). In the Introduction to *The Bewitched*[21] Partch employs another rhythmic technique: variable beat lengths. Although the parts are not subjected to dual overlay, succeeding measures use a slightly different sized beat, e.g., 5/4 alternating with 25/16 (played as five beats, each of which contains five sixteenth-notes); the sixteenth-note is kept constant, but each beat is increased or decreased by one one-fourth.

The *Verses* combine both techniques together, i.e., the overlay process combining differing metrical units, which also, at times, have a differing unit as the beat. The preface to the score refers to this process:[22]

> RHYTHMS   However the patterns below are used, the final tone or chord ends each duet in one minute.
>
> 1. The sequence 5½/4–6½/4–7½/4, repeated. 120.
> 2. 20/16.   96.
> 3. 6/4   180, or 6/4   60.
> 4. 3/4 90, or 18/16   90.
> 5. 5/4   150.
> 6. 10/8   58.
> 7. 4/4   120.

The mixed-meter pattern of No. 1 is used the most in both versions of the Verses, occurring six times in each. The 20/16 pattern is used only twice; No. 3 (6/4) is used only once, although a variant not listed, 3/2, occurs once in the early version which is changed to 3/4 in the 1966 revision. The 3/4 pattern of No. 4 is used five times; its variant of 18/16 is used once. A pattern not listed, 6/8, is used once, paired with a 3/4 meter. Nos. 5 and 6 are each used twice, and No. 7 (4/4) is found three times.

Neither the foregoing tally nor Partch's list tells the complete story. Pattern No. 1 actually consists of five repetitions of the 5½/4–6½/4–7½/4 series followed by five measures of 4½/4 for a total of 120 quarter-note beats. 20/16 is written as four equal beats, each containing five sixteenth-notes. The 6/4 subdivides each measure into two equal units of a dotted-half-note, while 3/4 (3/2) has three equal

---

[20] Gate 5 Records, Issue C.

[21] Gate 5 Records, Issue E.

[22] The numbers at the far right of each line refer to either the proper metronome setting or to the number of beats of that meter in a movement.

pulsations per measure. Pattern No. 4 is conventional; its 18/16 variant is written as three equal dotted-quarter-note (or six sixteenths) beats. Patterns Nos. 5 and 6, although superficially similar, are not the same. In Verse 7 the 10/8 is much like 5/4, except that rhythms of ♩.♩ and ♩ ♩ ♩ are frequently used. Verse 11 (Verse 18 in the revision) is a diminution of one of those rhythms (♪.♪ ♪.♪) dividing each measure into two equal units of five eighth-notes each. The 5/4 is more conventional in Verse 13 (Verse 16 in the revision), with patterns of ♩ ♩ ♩ ♩ often used.

Each verse has at least one introductory measure which serves as an upbeat cue for the larger ensembles. These are not played, with one exception, on the tape copy I have.[23] This introductory measure (with its first beat silent) links up with the last measure of each duet which consists only of a first beat in an open-ended measure, i.e., the final beat of that duet. These framing measures, necessary when performed by large ensembles, will be disregarded in the analysis that follows.

Since the individual lines for each Duet share the same meter, it is only when these duos are combined with others in a differing meter that the rhythmic complexity of this work is realized. This complexity of the larger ensembles can only be appreciated through aural realization; the visual representation that follows deals with the *1964 version*, as it is more ambitious than the 1966 revision. Also, all combinations used in the 1966 revision are found in the earlier version.

The first Quartet (Verse 24 in both versions) combines the 5½/4–6½/4–7½/4–4½/4 sequence with a duet in 20/16. The added half-beats of Pattern No. 1 are either upbeats to the next measure or accents ending the previous rhythmic pattern. In either case they constitute a separate short beat. As the complete cycle of Pattern No. 1 totals 19½ quarter-note units, it follows that the quarter-note unit (which serves as the metric unit for both Duets) undergoes a half-beat displacement on each repeat of the cycle. This becomes intensified in the repeated measures of 4½/4 at the end of the pattern.

This Quartet has all four parts sharing identical note-values, but treating that note-value (the sixteenth-note) differently. The mixed meter Duet (Pattern No. 1) uses the traditional method of considering the sixteenth-note as one-fourth of a quarter-note beat, or half of an eighth-note beat. The 20/16 duo uses this same value as one-fifth of a pulse, which results in constant divergence between both metrical structures (patterns) and individual beats. Except for the beginning and end, there are only two occasions when primary accents coincide in all parts, and then at a different point in each pattern.

Verse 25 presents no such complexities; all four lines are in the same pattern (No. 1), as is the case with *Verse 26*, where all parts are in ½.[24] *Verse 27* again

---

[23] Made in 1965.

[24] These two quartets are reversed in the 1966 version.

Graph of Vs. 24 (First Quartet, combining Vs. 1 and 2)

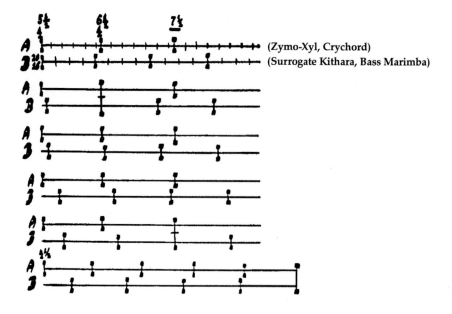

Tempi: A[Vs. 1] ♩ =120 ⎰ 96 beats [24 measures of B=
      B[Vs. 2] ♪♩=96 ⎨ 120 beats [20 irregular measures]
                  ⎩ of A

Figure 2

combines differing meters, this time with no unit common other than coinciding barlines. The Quartet is made up of *Verse 7*, a Duet in 10/8 with a good deal of syncopation across barlines, and *Verse 8*, which is in 18/16. A sample illustration is sufficient for this relationship, which is five against three (Figure 3).

    The last Quartet in the early version, *Verse 28*, again combines beats of a different length, as was done in the first Quartet. Half of the ensemble is in 3/4. The other half is in 20/16 with the same beat construction as in Verse 24, i.e., four equal beats of five sixteenth-notes. Only five of the thirty measures of 3/4 are shown in the illustration (Fig. 4) which cycles exactly with three measures of 20/16. On another level this is an extension of the five-to-three relationship of Verse 27.

Graph of Vs. 27 (Fourth Quartet, combining Vs. 7 and 8), four measure sample.

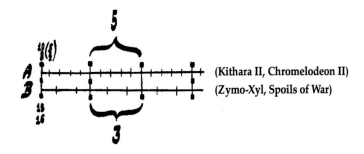

(Kithara II, Chromelodeon II)
(Zymo-Xyl, Spoils of War)

Tempi: A[Vs. 7] ♩ =150 ⎰ 90 beats [30 measures] of B=
       B[Vs. 8] ♩ =90 ⎱ 150 beats [30 measures] of A

Rhythms: (Samples)

Figure 3

Figure 5 is of the Sextet (Verse 29) which, like the first Quartet (Verse 24) is another rhythmic challenge, except that the challenge is of a reverse nature in this case.[25] Now only two of the three Duets share any common unit, but all three share

---

[25] Figures 5—8 show instrumental combinations projected in the 1964 version. Many were not actually used in the CRI recording. However, all rhythmic combinations selected by Partch for that recording are to be found in these graphs. The newer verse numbers are given in parentheses.

common barlines and primary accents. Also, the internal rhythmic patterns become more varied and give further cross-accents.

Graph of Vs. 28 (Fifth Quartet, combining Vs. 9 and 10), one cycle.

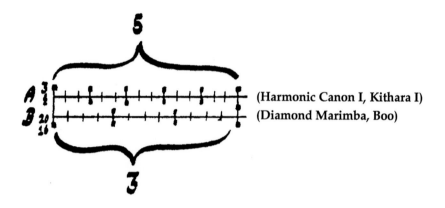

(Harmonic Canon I, Kithara I)
(Diamond Marimba, Boo)

Tempi: A[Vs. 9] ♩ =90 $\Big\{$ 96 beats [24 measures] of B=
B[Vs. 10] ♪♩=96   90 beats [30 measures] of A

Figure 4

The 10/8 Duet (Verse 11) divides each measure into two equal groups of five eighth-notes each, then further subdivides that unit unequally into dotted-quarter, quarter. The 5/4 Duet (Verse 12) has many levels of micro-rhythm with note-values ranging from sixteenths to double-dotted halves. The glue here is the 4/4 Duet (Verse 12) which adheres closely to constant pulsing values in half notes and to a perpetual-motion sixteenth-note figure in the Mazda Marimba.

Verse 30 (Fig. 6) is midway between the two extremes of non-coincidental barlines (where note-values are shared), and non-coincidental beats.[26] Four of

---

[26] This is Verse 34 in the 1966 version, and is the largest ensemble contained on the CRI recording.

Graph of Verse 29 (First Sextet combining Vs. 11, 12, 13), four measure sample.

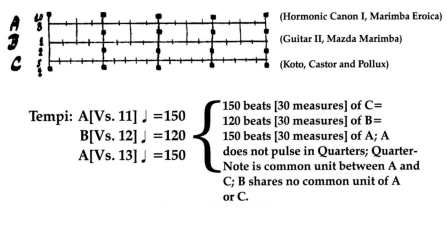

(Hormonic Canon I, Marimba Eroica)

(Guitar II, Mazda Marimba)

(Koto, Castor and Pollux)

Tempi: A[Vs. 11] ♩ =150
 B[Vs. 12] ♩ =120
 A[Vs. 13] ♩ =150

{ 150 beats [30 measures] of C=
 120 beats [30 measures] of B=
 150 beats [30 measures] of A; A
 does not pulse in Quarters; Quarter-
 Note is common unit between A and
 C; B shares no common unit of A
 or C.

Rhythms:

Figure 5

the six lines are in the same meter (4/4), and, although they have a good deal of syncopation in small note-values, the primary accents and the basic metrical pattern is not obscure. The other one-third of the Sextet is in the by now familiar 5½/4–6½/4–7½/4 pattern.

All lines give the same value to the quarter-note. This verse makes an interesting comparison with Verse 24, where the irregular pattern was used with another four-beat pattern, but in this case (Verse 30) the size of each of the four beats per measure has been truncated by one-sixteenth-note. Again, as in Verse 24, only two occasions other than the beginning and end have primary coincidental accents.

The last Sextet, Verse 31, has all parts sharing primary accents, although the internal subdivisions are not common between any of the duos (Fig. 7).

The Duets in 3/4 (Verse 17) and 6/8 (Verse 18) share common note values, but this is only academic, as their micro-rhythms make no use of this coincidence. The 5/4 Duet (Verse 19) is odd-man-out, sharing values with neither duo. At times Partch has a measure of the ensemble subdividing into equal portions of five, six, and three—all at once.

Graph of Vs. 30 (Second Sextet, combining Vs. 14, 15, 16).

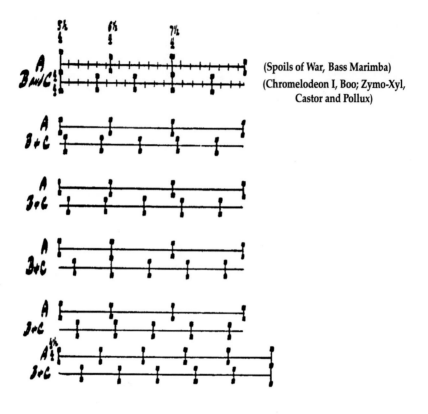

(Spoils of War, Bass Marimba)
(Chromelodeon I, Boo; Zymo-Xyl,
Castor and Pollux)

Tempi: A(Vs. 14)[Vs. 21] ♩ =120

B+C (Vs. 15+16)[Vs. 22=23] ♩ =120

⎰ 120 beats [30 measures] of
⎱ B and C=120 beats [20 irregular
  measures] of A. All parts share
  quarter-note.

Figure 6

    The last ensemble, Verse 32—and the only Octet—recalls procedures used
in Verses 24 and 30. Half of the ensemble is in the mixed irregular meter (pattern
No. 1) that forms the core of this work. The other half (four lines) is in a hemiola (6/4
and 3/2) relationship (Fig. 8).

    The new element here shows the inadequacy of our notational system, and
appears like one of the illustrations Henry Cowell used in advocating a more

Graph of Vs. 31 (Third Sextet, combining Vs. 17, 18, 19). Three measure Sample.

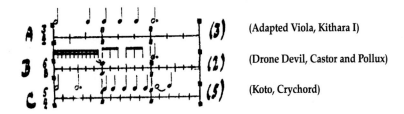

(Adapted Viola, Kithara I)

(Drone Devil, Castor and Pollux)

(Koto, Crychord)

Tempi:

A (Vs. 17)[Vs. 15, with Chromelodeon I substituted for viola] ♩ =90

B(Vs. 18)[Vs. 19 with Gubagbi added] ♩ =180

C(Vs. 19)[Vs. 20] ♩ =150

{ 150 beats [30 measures] of C= 180 beats [30 measures] of B= 90 beats [30 measures] of A; A and B share makes (beseiol A); C has no common unit except measure length with either A or B.

Figure 7

graphic rhythmic notation. In order to make this combination work, Partch has had to make four beats of Pattern No. 1 equal six beats of Pattern No. 3 (6/4). The relationships vary in this movement, with six (basically in two) against three all against the changing pattern of 5½/4–6½/4–7½/4. Although each half of the ensemble shares primary accents, all four duos (eight lines) share primary accents only twice in the movement, and then at a different segment of their macro-structure.

An aural realization of these graphs in fascinating. These are not paper rhythms; Partch's rhythms have definite primary and secondary accents along with much real syncopation. It is evident from the above that Partch's music demands skilled professional performers. He has stated that he will not write easy music which amateurs can mutilate. Certainly no amateur would attempt these problems; for it is apparent from the preceeding that Partch's music—and particularly this work—relies to a high degree upon sophisticated and complex textural and rhythmic structures.

Graph of Vs. 32 (Octet, combining Vs. 20, 21, 22, 23).

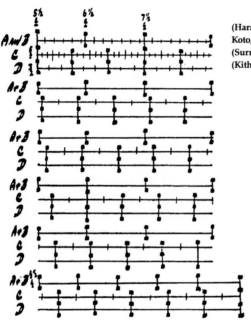

(Harmonic Canon I, Bowls,
Koto, Zymo-Xyl-Spoils of War)
(Surrogate Kithara, Diamond Marimba)
(Kithara II, Marimba Eroica)

Tempi: A and B(Vs. 20, 23)[Vs. 13, 12] ♩ =120
C(Vs. 22)[Vs. 14] ♩ =180
D(Vs. 23)[Vs. 11] ♩ =90

{ 90 beats [30 measures] of D=
180 beats [30 measures] of C=
120 beats [20 irregular measures]
of A and B.

Figure 8

Although Partch could have strictly adhered to his original plan of duet combinations, as these were accomplished by electronic mixing of previously recorded smaller units, he chose to present no more than two levels of metric units at any one time. The original scheme has been given in detail here for the benefit of those who may themselves wish to experience these fascinating combinations; one can simply make further mixtures using the CRI recording.

Pitches

Partch's notoriety, such as it is, stems from his highly chromatic tuning system of forty-three unequal pitches per octave, although the foregoing demonstrates that his musical inventiveness in other areas is worthy of serious attention. His division of the octave is not purely theoretical.[27] Association with Partch, his music, and his instruments will convince the non-prejudiced musician that he makes no impossible demands upon human aural capabilities.

Initially a musician with fine pitch discrimination[28] (such as the author) recognizes pitches in the only way he knows, i.e., a group of C-sharps, D-flats, etc. Rather quickly, however, clearer distinctions are sensed between the different kinds of 'fifths' and 'fourths'; later, more precise delineations are recognized in his wide vocabulary of 'seconds' and 'thirds.' It is these latter intervals that are the most crucial in Partch's system. They are responsible for many of his most expressive musical moments.

The greatest obstacle in this process comes from Partch's pitch nomenclature. He uses ratio names for pitches, all calculated from his starting point, G. Thus, in a real sense, one is faced with learning a new language, a process extremely difficult as there are no terms in one's old language equivalent to those in the new language. A good ear can be a handicap, as it leads one into a blind alley through attempts to effect translations, e.g., 4/3 is close to a C, 3/2 approximates a tempered D, etc. This unconscious search for equivalents makes super-particular ratios (16/15, 12/11, 11/10) relatively inaccessible, and more complex ratios such as 16/9, 15/8, 64/33, 40/21 and 160/81, impossible.

A discussion of pitch elements in the Verses would be meaningless without a preliminary conversion of these pitches into a form more meaningful to traditionally-trained musicians. Rather than attempt to do justice to both projects, the author has chosen to discuss Partch's scale formation itself, as this can be useful for all of his music, and allows interested individuals who find this discussion helpful to pursue their own investigations.

Figure 9 gives the complete list of forty-three pitches Partch uses, in ascending sequence by their ratio names.[29] I have added the alphabetic pitch equiv-

---

[27] It is soundly based upon careful research and study. About two-thirds of *Genesis of a Music* is devoted to the results of that research.

[28] The substitute term "perfect-pitch" is misleading in this context—and probably in all others.

[29] After *Manual*, p. 10, where bridge measurements that will produce this complete scale are given for the Harmonic Canon.

1/1 — G	32/27	10/7	12/7
81/80	6/5	16/11	7/4
33/32	11/9	40/27	16/9
21/20	5/4 — B	3/2 — D	9/5
16/15 — G#, A♭	14/11	32/21	20/11
12/11	9/7	14/9	11/6
11/10	21/16	11/7	15/8 — F#
10/9	4/3 — C	8/5	40/21
9/8 — A	27/20	18/11	64/33
8/7	11/8	5/3 — E	160/81
7/6	7/5	27/16	2/1 — G

Figure 9   List of ratios

alents as they would be placed according to just intonation calculations,[30] with G as the base.[31]

This looks very close to an equally tempered system, as there are often six pitches between successive whole steps; but such is not the case. The gamut does divide itself, however, into two equal units, at pitches No. 22 (7/5) and No. 23 (10/7). These two ratios are the inverse (divided by an octave) of each other.[32] In like manner, 11/8 is so related to 16/11, 27/20 to 40/27, etc. Thus, the *intervals* formed by pitches 1–2 and 42–43 are the same, as are the intervals between pitches 2–3 and 41–42, etc. For the remainder of this discussion only the first half of the scale will be considered, as the last half is its retrograde.

Partch converts 340 intervals narrower than an octave into Cents in Appendix I of *Genesis of a Music*, which includes his chosen forty-three. The distances between adjacent pitches in his system varies greatly, from 14.4 Cents to 38.9 Cents.[33] Had Partch used an equally tempered system of forty-three

---

[30] Partch: "acoustically perfect intonation'"; see earlier comments in this article.

[31] Partch, like Guido, prefers this point of origin. He uses the G a fourth below 'middle' C, or 'small g'.

[32] 7/5 1/2 = 7/10, the inverse of 10/7.

[33] Only one decimal point is retained in these calculations, which invites round-off error. However, since 100 Cents is the distance of a tempered duodecaphonic semitone, one extra Cent may not be too significant.

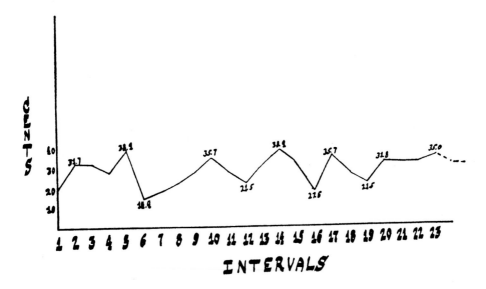

Figure 10

intervals each interval would be 27.9 Cents. Partch has thirteen different intervals in his fabric whose average is, for all practical purposes, the same: 27.8 Cents.

Figure 10 illustrates the size of the first twenty-three intervals in successive scale order. The successive intervals are quite irregular. The only smooth relationship among adjacent intervals occurs between the smallest (No. 6) up to the second largest (No. 10). His largest interval is immediately followed by his smallest (Nos. 5–6) on its first appearance; the second time this peak is reached (No. 14) it is quickly followed by an intermediate interval, then by the second smallest (No. 16). The large intervals are roughly spread out in the fabric (Nos. 5, 10, 14, 17, 22), as are the smaller intervals (Nos. 6, 12, 16, 19).

A different method of illustration is used in the next graph (Figure 11). Here the intervals are seen linearly, with Partch's ratio nomenclature and the addition of the just intonation pitch zones underneath.[34]

Partch's division point (7/5—10/7) exactly splits the 600 Cent mid-point of an octave; i.e., he has no pitch that is exactly half of an octave: 7/5 is 17.5 Cents lower than this mythical mid-point tritone while 10/7 is the same distance higher.

Partch has arrived at a system that gives him both precision and variety. An equally tempered system might achieve the former, but it would be at the expense of the latter. This is exactly what has happened to us by our blind

---

[34] Partch uses a stair-step representation for the complete octave in *Genesis of a Music*, p. 134, without Cents measurements.

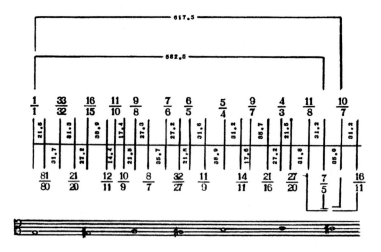

Figure 11

allegiance to equal temperament. There are many (including the author) who are convinced that the human ear can make distinctions in the zone of one-fifth to two-fifths of a tempered semitone—more or less, depending upon the frequency and amplitude—and this contention is supported by the pitifully small amount of psycho-acoustical research that has taken place.

Electronic music composers testify to the remarkable (to them) precision their ears develop while working with their medium, in all parameters, including pitch. It is self-evident that one can only hear what one is accustomed—or wishes—to hear. The limits of our aural sense have not been defined, as ethnomusicologists would be the first to state.

There is an effect of a continuous glissando when all forty-three pitches are closely stacked in a rapid complete scale passage. No differences in interval sizes are apparent. This effect is rarely used by Partch, although chromatic scale segments do appear in Chromelodeon passages. The standard keyboard of that instrument lends itself easily to that finger technique. Also, Partch insists that Chromelodeon performers use a flat hand so as to connect pitches.

The melodic interest of the *Verses*, as with earlier works, is derived from the wide range of choices available in varying intervals of the same general class, i.e., three kinds of 'fifths', three kinds of 'tritones', and most prominently, a large selection of 'seconds' and 'thirds' that show our 'major' and 'minor' varieties to be what they are: pallid compromises.[35] This is one of the main reasons why the tex-

---

[35] Although it may seem reactionary to equate these intervals to our system of equal temperament, Partch also does so, and conditioning cannot be dismissed.

ture is primarily monophonic and contrapuntal. Chordal passages do occur, partic- .
ularly on the Kitharas; these are fixed in Partch's own system of consonance and
dissonance which he calls U and O Tonalities.[36] These arpeggios are the one most
familiar pitch element to conventional ears, as they frequently are simple ninth,
eleventh, and thirteenth tertian sonorities.

Notation

Any Partch score which primarily employs instruments of his own construction
presents substantial notational problems.[37] His notational system is almost meaningless to anyone not willing to study his scale construction and the construction of
the various instruments. The uninitiated can only follow rhythmic patterns without reference to pitch, and even that parameter looks puzzling through Partch's
frequent use of repeat abbreviations and parentheses for the end of gliding tones.
The addition of unique symbols to designate a particular segment of an instrument
contributes to the confusion.

    This is the one element in Partch's pioneer work which seems to be at vari-
ance with his effort to eliminate the barrier that exists in traditional practice
between the performer, his instrument, and the music. Partch's performers are
expected to understand their instruments thoroughly, and be prepared to both
tune and repair them:

> *Musicians, who are generally so awkward with common tools that they would not hesitate
> to use a screwdriver for a chisel, expect faultless perfection in their instruments. And the
> conclusion one must draw, inevitably, is that music education has failed, and tragically, to
> convey the nature of music: the versatility of the vocal organ, as one outstanding example;
> the fact that musical instruments are mechanical contrivances, the fact that common tools
> and elementary skills can be developed to maintain them, the fact that developing the ele-
> mentary skill of tuning them is of supreme importance to musicianship, and the fact that—
> as a consequence of all this—a deeper understanding ensues.*[38]

---

[36] The Diamond Marimba and the Quadrangularis Reversus are constructed so that a single
mallet stroke produces consonant arpeggios.

[37] Mixtures of conventional and original instruments are found in *Oedipus, The Bewitched,
Ulysses,* and *Revelation in the Courthouse Park.* He uses a color-modified conventional pitch
notation for these instruments, explained in the preface to *Oedipus.*

[38] *Manual,* p. 2. Documentation of his complaint is easy to assemble. Consider, for example,
the inability of a professional violinist to cope with a sound post, a pianist to regulate action
(let alone tune his instrument), and the reluctance a wood-wind player has in replacing pads
and springs—preferring celophane and stale popcorn as 'temporary' substitutes. The best
double-reed performers must make their own reeds, but not without complaint. One of the
most flagrant examples of this indifference and ignorance is demonstrated when performers
(or composers) are asked precise questions about electronic sound-recording mike-place-
ments, the difference between low and high impedence, etc.

Partch's notation is a mixture of ratio tags (discussed earlier) and positional graphs (which use the conventional five-line staff), in the tablature lineage. Its primary purpose is to clearly tell the performer which string, bar, bottle, block, etc., to strike. It does succeed, with few exceptions: little oral explanation is needed to realize a Partch score.

Yet, the reader of such a score, with few exceptions, is told nothing about actual pitches. Experienced students of Partch would be puzzled by notational systems for unfamiliar instruments (or new uses of old instruments) and find them impossible to hear mentally. This sharply limits the choice of conductors. As in conventional music, a conductor must minimally be able to correct pitch mistakes by sight and hearing. Any conductor of this material must possess the same skills required in conventional music, but applied in a new dimension. He must have an intensive knowledge of all the instruments, their playing techniques, and their differing notational systems. There is little transfer of practice across these two cultures. Thus, transportation problems are not the only enemy of performances of this music, and this fact alone may be responsible for the oblivion many see as the fate of Partch's music.

Partch, now in his mid-sixties, can no longer stand the strain of conducting and performance, and there is only a handful of qualified persons capable of presenting his music (Danlee Mitchell is an outstanding example)—and they are geographically scattered.[39] A good deal of foundation money has been spent to preserve foreign cultures (human and animal) threatened with extinction. Here is an instance of a similar danger that will most probably be ignored, as it occurs in our own backyard and is native.

Returning to notational problems, these are compounded by various stop and coupling combinations on the Chromelodeons, different bridge settings on the Harmonic Canons,[40] various methods of tuning the Kitharas, and a choice of striking areas on glass and metal instruments—all affecting the pitches. The composer must laboriously spell out these variables in the preface to each score, somewhat reminiscent of individual tables of ornaments in the eighteenth century. It would be helpful to the reader if a standard reference sheet could be inserted into every score dealing with fixed-pitch instruments, such as the Boo, Bowls, etc., which converts ratios into more accessible figures such as frequencies and Cents; it would be pointless for these scores to be published otherwise.

Since 1/1 and 2/1 are always fixed at G, this is highly possible, involving only a certain amount of tedious work. It is unreasonable to expect the composer to do this mechanical chore.

---

[39] The decision to replace the Adapted Viola with other instruments stems from the fact that only Partch plays that instrument—his first—and only with great strain.

[40] Reused in other works.

This forced obscurity is only one of the prices Partch pays for being unique. No 'theory' courses are given for his idiom except his own pungent treatment in *Genesis of a Music*—now out of print—and that treatise does not contain information about developments of the past twenty years.

Delusion of the Fury

The projected stage work for which the *Verses* were composed has not been produced to date. Partch has prepared a detailed scenario of the work which serves as the basis for these comments.[41] Since many changes will occur during the preparation of a first performance, these brief remarks can only reflect upon the work as Partch originally conceived it. Nothing can take the place of an actual performance, particularly with Harry Partch.

The outline of *Delusion of the Fury* displays some of the myriad sources from which Partch draws inspiration. Act I, titled "Pray for Me", is based on the *Atsumori* legend as used in Japanese Noh plays. Act II, titled "In the Advent of Justice," is a Partchian mixture of an Ethiopian folk tale (drawn from *African Voices*) and American hobo lore. Partch describes his dramatic themes as follows:

> *Act I treats with death, and with life despite death.*
> *Act II treats with life, and with life despite life.*
> *They have this in common: both convey the mood that reality is in no way real, despite the very different locales, subject matter, and the very different paths toward the awareness of unreality.*
> *Both, essentially, are happy in their focus; the reconciliation with some kind of unreal death makes the one with some kind of unreal life possible.*[42]

Act I contains Partch's first use of Japanese subject material.[43] The second Act marks his first deliberate venture into African folklore leavened with his often-used vagabond American material. An entire study could be done on his preoccupation with 'bums;' they form the core of *The Wayward* series and touches of this source are apt to crop up in any of Partch's works. *Delusion of the Fury* continues his interest in the confrontation of the unorthodox personality—anyone who doesn't fit—with more "respectable" society.

It is an impossible but fascinating exercise to disentangle the maze of cultural elements in this or any other Partch work. Into his bag he throws unsung

---

[41] *Delusion of the Fury* (unpublished manuscript), 1965.

[42] *Delusion of the Fury*, p. 1.

[43] His earlier works drew heavily upon Chinese sources. *Oedipus* and *Revelation in the Courthouse Park* are based on ancient Greek plays, the latter on the *Bacchai* (Euripides).

heroes, American folklore (particularly society's outcasts—such as himself), African and Oriental elements, mystical (particularly pre-Christian) thought, and magic, together with strong dashes of parody, satire, studied naiveté, and irony. The result is literally unique.

Partch's life offers a partial explanation or clarification. He spent many years during the Depression (and after) riding the rails as a hobo "carrying socks in a viola." He is also an extraordinarily well-read and informed man. Attempts have been made to categorize him and/or his music as Romantic, Visionary, Reactionary, Folk-Art(ist), Quixotic. Each term has an element of truth as applied to him and his work; but, like all significant figures, he will not fit neatly into a pre-designed slot.

He acknowledges no current influences. In a recent letter he says:

> *I've never seen a survey of contemporary music in which I did not feel a total alien . . . Not a single composer of this century has been the slightest influence on me; a few from the nineteenth century, yes,[44] but aside from this the profound impacts have come from far afield geographically or 2500 years back in time.*

Partch has achieved what normally would take many life-times: the formulation of precise dissatisfactions with current practices, alternatives which are practically realized in metal, glass, and wood; and—most important and most difficult—he has produced convincing results which enter the human consciousness via one of the few senses wherein man cannot restrict and control input—the ear.

---

[44] Berlioz is mentioned in *Genesis of a Music*.

Part II

VISUAL BEAUTY

Harry Partch's parents: Virgil and Jennie Partch.

Harry Partch as a hobo during the depression.

Partch playing the Adapted Viola. The photo appeared in the *Pasadena Star-News*, February 16, 1933.

Partch playing an early version of Adapted Guitar I (with the original frets) sometime in the early 1940s.

Mills College, 1952.

Partch playing Kithara I (with original base), Sausalito, early 1950s.

Partch playing the original Boo. Champaign, Illinois, late 1950s.

Petaluma recording session, 1964. Photo: Bruce Marlow.

Petaluma, Calif., 1964. Photo: Danlee Mitchell.

Partch playing Harmonic Canon I, Van Nuys, Calif., 1966. Photo: Ted Tourtelot.

Harry Partch in the late 1960s.

HP in the early 1970s. Photo: Mark Stevens.

HP playing Kithara, Encinitas, 1972. Photo: Betty Freeman.

HP outside his Encinitas, Calif. home, 1972. Photo: Betty Freeman.
Sign reads: "Jehovah Witnesses—Important notice! Here, everyone needs saving.
But not by Jehovah Witnesses"

HP on the film set for *The Dreamer That Remains*, San Diego, 1972
Photo: Betty Freeman.

Part III

EXPERIENCE–RITUAL

Part III

EXPERIENCE-RITUAL

7

FURTHER MEMORIES AND REFLECTIONS

A Conversation between Henry Brant and Danlee Mitchell

DM: Where did you first meet Harry?

HB: In New York. I believe that Otto Luening brought him to the attention of Douglas Moore at the Columbia University Music Department. Douglas was very intuitively impressed but when Harry started to talk about his theories, he said, "well, this is over my head but there's somebody I know who will be very interested." He called me and said to come over. Harry began to talk about his theories of tuning and how he made chords going up to the ninth harmonic. I asked him why he stopped there. Douglas said, "that's fine, this is all I wanted to hear, somebody who knew what this meant. I know he is a great artist but I want him to be understood also." This is when I first heard about Harry' work and how he made instruments during his travels and had to leave them in place where he could.

Shortly afterwards, a concert was arranged by the League of Composers. The principal work was to be **U.S. Highball**. He had to find somebody who could play the Chromelodeon and I undertook to do that. In the 1940s there wasn't much business for composers and I had a little time. I thought I'd get educated and learn something that I didn't know before. We worked on this for about two months. This was the first performance of **U.S. Highball** although Harry had given abridged extracts of it by himself with his guitar. I also played for him the instruments I had, this double flageoleot made in England about 1810, and my tin whistle which I played with a lot of facility. He wrote **Yankee Doodle Fantasy** for Ethel Luening, me playing the flutes and himself on the Chromelodeon. He checked the pitches carefully that I was able to play on both instruments and wrote down the closest equivalents he had in his tuning and used them. So the program consisted of that big work, the new one, and three other ones also dealing with Americana. I can't remember now what they were. That was the entire concert. Harry came on the stage carrying a hammer, a screw driver and a pot of glue that he had to use during the show to keep these instruments in shape, especially the Chromelodeon.

DM: Wasn't the New York concert his first on the east coast?

HB: I think so. His first formal one man show.

DM: What was the League of Composers?

HB: I think it's still in existence. It's affiliated with the International Society for Contemporary Music. It had a board of directors all of whom were composers. The idea was to present concerts of contemporary music, either important European works that hadn't been heard in New York or new works by Americans which it considered important and which otherwise wouldn't be heard. It had a certain small following. Now, in New York City, there may be thirty such groups. At that time there were only two: the League of Composers and the International Society for Contemporary Music. They were joined in about 1930 by a third one, the Copland/Sessions Concerts. A League of Composers presentation was looked upon as an important event in contemporary music in New York. I don't know how this was managed but it was certainly a big thing for any composer to get a one man show at the League in 1944.

DM: How many people were at that concert?

HB: It was Carnegie Recital Hall and it was full. There were a lot of people who I would call stuffy, self-satisfied hacks as composers. One of them said to me, "what is this, how could you spend your time learning this kind of stuff?" All I could say was when you spend two months on it you'll be in a better position to say that than you are now.

DM: Was the reaction of the audience one of being positive, negative, or apathetic?

HB: Not apathy. I believe that everyone felt themselves in the presence of a formidable new contender. They reacted in various ways. Some were annoyed, irritated, perhaps envious, a little hostile, and on the whole weren't very sympathetic. But I had the impression that they felt, here's a new competitor on the scene and he's going to make a lot of trouble.

DM: What were you doing in New York City during this time?

HB: I was a freelance commercial orchestrator and on the side a composer of concert music that didn't sound like my commercial work. It was an extremely conservative time and anything as experimental and original as Harry's work was a distinct oddity. Something like that would have seldom been heard even under the auspices of an institution like the League of Composers. I had something played by the League of Composers a few years before that. I was afraid to play anything experimental although I wrote experimental music. I was afraid of getting a black eye in the press and losing the slender market I had for my conservative concert music. All this changed after the Second World War. We were able to write as we wished.

DM: You were a friend of Otto Luening and Douglas Moore at the time?

HB: Yes.

DM: Was Howard Hanson influential during these times?

HB: Yes, but as far as I know he had no connection with this concert.

DM: Who were the influential people in composition?

HB: They were the big Europeans. They were Stravinsky, Schoenberg, Milhaud, Bartok and so forth. But everybody was scared to write music as daring as that because they were having a bad time. Their music wasn't getting played often. When it was getting played, it had a hard time with the press. We figured, if these big heavyweight composers are running into stuff like that, we better not try.

DM: So you were worried about press during those times?

HB: Getting jobs. I was afraid of a black eye which would prevent me from getting commercial jobs. I arranged for bands. I did things for singers with club dates who had a band in the background. I wrote scores for documentary films of all kinds. I orchestrated music by other composers. I was a ghost writer for a couple of wealthy men who wanted to have their symphonies played. In fact, anything that anybody would pay somebody to write music for, I was ready to do. No matter how strange or difficult it was. My reputation was that of someone who would try anything: "If nobody else will try it, try Brant, he can do it."

DM: But you got the reputation for being an iconoclast amongst American composers. You, Harry, and Charles Ives, were thought of in this manner more than most composers during your times. Had you heard about Harry before you met him?

HB: No.

DM: His book was finished by that time. It wasn't published, of course, but I think his ideas were fairly organized by the 1930's. He had done most of his theoretical study and back-

ground work during the 1920's and early 1930's, going to the British museum. So, Harry Partch in the 1940s was not well known?

HB: Certainly not by me. The New York composers who came to the concert were very much astonished by what they heard. He was as new a phenomenon to them as he was to me.

DM: Was he considered a folk artist rather than a serious composer?

HB: Many of them took that view: an eccentric amateur. But in 1944, matters were so stone age that many of those same people would have said the same thing of Ives.

DM: Even though Harry played viola in WPA orchestras, and knew many of the currents of music going on at the time, my impression was that he wasn't the type of trained musician that most of us are. Did you have that opinion of him?

HB: He said that he studied piano and he had certain ideas from his teacher. For instance, how Chopin should be played. He demonstrated a Chopin nocturne and displayed a considerable practice familiarity with keyboard styles.

DM: Harry's principal interests were in tuning and theatre. These interests matured in later years but they were certainly evident in the 1940's. How did you react to his compositional preoccupations?

HB: I immediately had the impression of an important and substantial musical personality. This is what attracted me. Quite aside from the novelty of the sounds and the subject matter, the thing that impressed me most was a point of view of considerable breadth comparable to Ives. It's an opinion that I still hold. I was also impressed by the fact that he followed no trend. It came neither from Europe nor was it a stereotypical use of American pop material superimposed on a commercial background. The thing that struck me as especially vital was that he alone of the American and European composers at the time was writing directly from his own experience. What he wrote was not from hearsay or rumour or because it followed another point of view. He wrote the things that he had seen and done. Very few musicians were in a position to have experienced anything that directly and, secondly, to have found the means to do it. But I still don't know to this day why it was necessary for him to use just intonation in order to do that. I think this was a separate interest. He combined two interests in his work as a composer but the two necessities need not have combined. They could have been pursued separately.

DM: He was in his late thirties when you met him. What was his personality like in those days?

HB: In rehearsing his music he was unfailingly patient. He knew exactly what it was that he wished to attain and no amount of trouble was too great for him to help somebody do it correctly. His manner was gentle and courteous but highly concentrated. He'd zero in on something and he'd keep his mind on that. Nothing would distract him. He was socially at ease in groups of people. He didn't behave as a recluse. He knew what to do when there were a lot of people around. His own interests, by that time, had become very concentrated. He'd listen quietly if you were talking about some branch of music other than his, but the thing that he really used his concentration for was his own ideas and how he was going to project them. He had already instinctively arrived at that point where he had to make the choice between where he was going and what the rest of the world was doing musically.

DM: When I knew him he would easily monopolize a party with his humour and his knowledge of non-musical matters. Was that the same in the 1940s?

HB: I saw him on a few occasions at parties and that's not exactly what he did. He was very much at ease but he didn't make himself the center of the group.

DM: With regard to his tuning theory, you said that he probably could have done what he did compositionally without just intonation. What he did was really quite simple: he chose to take advantage of something that was a natural law.

HB: I'm aware of that. What I'm saying is that his use of the material that he discovered was arbitrary in terms of the materials themselves. It wasn't written in such a way that your attention would be forced on the different kinds of consonance in just or tempered intonation. It sort of ignored that and he worked impressionistically with pitches as other composers have in tempered tuning.

DM: I find it a mystery that composers on the level of Luening or Moore couldn't theoretically understand what he was doing. It seems that, in our teaching of young American musicians and composers, we have lost the idea of investigating the very basis of music which is tuning the notes.

HB: We never had this basis of inquiry in the United States. It was always a method of analysis based on the received European theory.

DM: I think Harry latched onto just intonation as a viable mode of investigation but he didn't use it in his compositions all of the time. I find that half of his compositions are based

on just intonation and half are based simply on timbre and rhythm. I think he used just into-
nation as a mystical basis for his music and to give his music individuality.

HB: I do tend to agree with that because Harry was not interested in an intricately textured music which required a lot of layered organization. He wrote for the drama and he took what he needed. Some of the materials he made for himself were justly tuned intervals, but the idea of having the music organized in such a way that your attention would be compelled by the properties of those intervals would have been quite foreign to the way he thought. In fact, he told me that he disliked all theories of composing.

DM: What happen to Harry after that 1944 concert? When did you last see him?

HB: He left New York and we had some sporadic correspondence up until something like ten years ago when we saw each other at Bert Turetzky's house. Harry learned that I was there. He didn't stay long because he wasn't feeling well. We were glad to see each other and had a brief talk, mostly about the new instruments that Gunnar Schoenbeck was interested in making for him.

DM: In his mature years, Harry went into larger theatrical forms and you became one of the pioneers of spatial music.

HB: I've probably written more of such pieces than anyone.

DM: To me, spatial music implies theatre.

HB: It is a kind of theatre. The space makes it so automatically.

DM: Harry was led into the area of corporeality, the idea of the musicians not simply being there as musicians but being visually important as well as sonically.

HB: I must say I'm less sanguine than Harry about the ability of muscle bound musicians to learn how to move. They really need a year of modern dance and karate before they are fit to be seen in public.

8

"I DO NOT QUITE UNDERSTAND YOU, SOCRATES"

Lou Harrison

In the February 1988 issue of "Harper's" appears an article by I. F. Stone entitled "When Free Speech Was First Condemned—the Trial of Socrates Reconsidered". This is an excerpt from his new book "The Trial of Socrates". "Harper's" also published, in 1981, "Plato's Ideal Bedlam" by the same author. Now Mr. Stone is over eighty, and for many years issued from Washington D.C. a weekly journal "I. F. Stone's Weekly" which was one of the most diligently read journals of political comment. In his "retirement" he taught himself ancient Greek so that he could study and write about Athenian political thought and usage. Stone has thus carried forward the flowing current of classical thought which is clearly, despite modernist opposition, an integral and continuous part of culture in the U.S. since its beginnings.

As Americans we have built enormous numbers of classical buildings—they are everywhere to be seen—and it was the "Greek Revival" style which, in its spread coast to coast, became a true vernacular architecture. Our poets and prose writers, both as original artists and as translators have found roots and drive in classic literature. We have in recent years been given the complete works of Horace translated in the original metres by Charles E. Passage, the complete Theocritus similarly translated by Daryl Hines, to mention only two out of many. Gore Vidal, beside deploying political sense and wit stimulated by his vast classic learning, wrote a splendid biography of Julian the Apostate and a panoramic survey of the ancient world in "Creation". Once read, who can forget John Gardner's "Jason and Medeia"? These are recent works and the vein continues. Only a month ago, in Berkeley, I experienced a wonderful theater work titled "OX", the cooperative work of designer Jill Neff and the musician Richard Zvonar. This was a moving and profound stage work which richly explored the classical Cretan labyrinth and Dedaelian flight themes over many centuries. Delightfully, it included in the sound track a Theseus legend written and read in Pidgin. In a program note Zvonar deplores the present omission of classic curricula in our public schools.

In the 19th century and up to the Second World Calamity a classic curriculum was common in Usonian schools and, for Harvard our first great symphonist,

John Knowles Paine, composed a highly successful score for Sophocles Oedipus Tyrannis, setting the original Greek. Isadora Duncan and Ruth St Denis, especially the former, evoke the very image of Greek revival dance, and too, the late works of Martha Graham and Jean Erdman come from Greek sources.

Harry Partch and I used to joke with one another that, whereas we were both publically considered radical modernists, we were actually dealing with, and much more concerned with, Greek and Hellenistic music. Michael McIntyre of BBC, in his splendid 1987 video study "Frontiers of New Music—the West Coast Story" says, "In Harry Partch's opinion music started going wrong at about the time of Gregorian Chant. Getting back to basics he chose as his inspiration the philosophers of ancient Greece." Indeed this was so. He was strongly attached to Athenian drama, and his intent to relate Sophocles' "Oedipus" and Euripedes' "Bacchae" to mid-20th century Usonian life consumed a great amount of his mature energy and much time. His "Two Studies on Ancient Greek Scales (Olympos' Pentatonic and Archytas' Enharmonic)" were composed in 1946, and were a few years later included in a miscellany titled "Eleven Intrusions". They clarify the idea of actually composing with musical material contemporary with the Parthenon. This cue has been followed up. I myself have written in Doric and Hellenistic modes, as have artists younger than I, especially Larry London and Alexis Alrich. The former has created a number of works in this vein, and to my mind, they are most alluring. The "Woodstock Chimes" by Gary Kvistad are also tuned to correct modalities directly derived from Partch's insight.

But it was the ritual and dramatic in ancient theater that most absorbed Harry, and his fame grew from these works. Oedipus, which he subtitled a "Dance-Drama" was given its first performance at Mills College in 1952. Five years later the American Council of Learned Societies convened a set of meetings titled "The Present-day Vitality of the Classical Tradition" at Indiana University. During these sessions O'Neill's "Mourning Becomes Electra" was mentioned and a work of T. S. Eliot. But only Stravinsky's "Oedipus Rex", along with Milhaud's "Oresteia", Satie's "Socrate", and other European works, were mentioned by Roger Sessions in his address about "The Classical Tradition in Music". Sessions also mentioned his own "Idyll of Theocritos", and a few other Usonian works. But he did indeed speak of scales. He said, "First of all, we owe our scale system to the Greeks; or to put it differently, the Greeks organized tones for us. They laid the basis for the whole system of tones on which the music of Western civilization depends." He meant 18th century diatonics and their equal-temperament distortions. Now the great gap here was that Partch's "Genesis of a Music" had already been published in 1949. This is the "age of communication", so that of course no one knows what anyone else is doing. And besides, all the pertinent information had long been available in Sir John Hawkins' splendid work of the 18th century. Sessions, certainly, never took thought that the 19th century 12-tone equal-temperament had/has nothing to do with Greek music. Partch did. The intervals heard in Partch's "Oedipus" would have been familiar to an Athenian audience, if not, probably, their use. In October of 1987 the American Musical Theater Festival presented in Philadelphia the first "professional" performances of Partch's "Revelation in the Courthouse Park", in which he connected mid-20th century Pop Stars' behavior with the Dionysiac cults of Euripedes' "Bacchae". All performances were sold out and the artistic caliber was excellent. Danlee Mitchell (Partch's heir) trained the musicians, and staging, lighting, sets, and acting were "first-class". Two things may be remarked. Harry compares Pop Stars to Bacchantes—sensual overload, drugs, millionairish popularity, etc. (and one may add that Roman gladiators, too, were Pop Stars and had corporate sponsors)—and, second, that here the musical intervals are "for real", not airy-fairy approximations as in 12-tone equal, but genuine, bodied relationships.

"Corporeal" was a word much used by Partch and he used it as though he meant it to signify "incarnation" of musical and social ideas. Here too Harry "thought Greek"; for, truly, on the basis of some earlier Egyptian beginnings, the Greeks "invented" the human body. No one else thought to do it, the Greeks did, and this has proved a lasting matter for social joy, hate, worry, and work. Harry would have been happy if all of his music were played and sung by naked people playing and singing true ratios with grace and gusto. In his last large stage work, "Delusion of the Fury", he did indeed strip his male musicians to the waist.

To embody the ratios which he had found make up the irreducible basis of music, Harry found that he had to build instruments able to play them, and he did that over a long period of time. The received instruments were insufficient to his needs, although Ben Johnston, I, and others have retuned some of them, or caused players to learn how to play the needed notes. Terry Riley, that lovely musician, serenely and fluently devoted to exploring just intonation, moves from concert to concert with a piano technician capable of putting the instrument into what tuning Riley is working on at the time. This is a newer attitude, and one which I've long used, i.e. "just what you need when you need it".

But there was more than a little of the earlier "system-builder" in Harry, and in this he resembled the many renaissance musicians and theorists who hoped to make a usable gamut capable of giving the three Greek genera—Enharmonic, Chromatic, and Diatonic—all on one instrument and within a single tuning; thus Vincentino, Mersenne, and many others. Zarlino, whose 19-toned harpsichord was another such systematic effort, was himself a member of the classicist circle that included the great Palladio. Thomas Jefferson admonished an inquirer to carry Palladio with him as a bible (the Four Books on Architecture) and in his own fine architectural work Jefferson knew and used the ratios of classic orders and design. Discounting the Roman additions of Tuscan and Composite, the original Greek orders were three—Doric, Ionic, and Corinthian, just as they left us the three genera of tetrachords.

So strong was Harry's classical drive that he used classic names for some instruments that little resembled the namesake. His kitharas but vaguely resemble their prototypes. His are very large, and although the generalized shape is indeed there, the stringing, use of glass sliding-bridges, and musical behavior are quite other than in the originals. But this was high poetry in Partch. His "Harmonic Canons" are closer to the root sources. Kanon is Greek for "law". Islamic music still makes use of the "kanun", a many-stringed psaltery not at all unlike the ones that Harry made. He said of himself "I am not an instrument-builder, but a philosophic music-man seduced into carpentry".

Immense care and research went into his "carpentry", both as to his choice of tuning—a forty-three tone gamut entirely within the limit of the 11th overtone—and as to the frequent elegance of his design and cabinetry. For the fully developed ensemble, or for smaller sections of it, he composed his entire extant works. He did borrow from "Northwest Asian" instruments once in a while, and so we hear, without physical alterations, clarinet, bass clarinet, oboe, 'cello, and, in "Revelation in the Courthouse Park" a whole small wind band.

Harry used "high-tech" only in concert amplifiers and in his self- issued "Gate Five Records". So far as I know he had no impulse to attempt synthesized sound, nor to deploy computers, although he was surrounded with these things in his later years. He did, however, use multi-track recording in two works, himself the performer.

In "Castor and Pollux" he celebrated the offspring of Zeus' peccadillo with Leda and wrote the work in a spirit of high relief and joy after the intensities of Oedipus. "Ulysses at the Edge" was composed in 1955, and in "Windsong", on the subject of Daphne and Apollo (and in its version for film), he recorded the music multi-track by himself. Partch had many facets, incorporated elements of Amerindian and Asian thought and music too, and he filled everything that he did with gusto and every kind of enthusiasm. He also, and classically, took time to make things right. He composed deliberately and with Reason.

Like his renaissance forebears he wrote a book, and such a book as theirs were, too. "Genesis of a Music" will remain a major intellectual achievement of Usonian culture. Its high-spirited elegance is inimitable and its contents include all of the fundamentals plus such history as was known when he wrote it. The book is a 20th century masterpiece. It is a classic, like the Morgan Library, the Lincoln Memorial, Henry Cowell's "New Musical Resources", the San Francisco civic center, the Departmental Auditorium and the Philadelphia Museum of Art. I do not think that New York can demolish it as it did Penn Station.

Harry also had a kind of playfulness. He would carefully tune a great number of strings on one of his psalteries and then play on the other side of the bridges. His demonic or "dark" side was also noted by friends, sometimes terrifying those who did not know of it or who might encounter it for the first time. His deeply admired ancient Greeks, too, had an irrational side, and several of them descended into Hell just as Harry, who indeed composed to Rimbaud's "Season in Hell". The Dionysiac was strong in him too, and his mint juleps were made of strong whiskey poured over a mound of mashed mint leaves—nothing more.

He relates: "When I was reading the dialogues of Plato and came across the line 'I do not understand you, Socrates' I laughed and threw the book down. 'That ought to be the title', I mused. 'Very frequently I do not quite understand you either, Socrates!'" Partch greatly disliked academic teaching—after all, his whole teaching is in the book and the music.

He was an affectionate man who warmly gave and received love, and who attained an intellectual majesty that yet included hobos around a campfire—Satyrs perhaps?

6 Feb. 1988

9

BEYOND HARRY PARTCH

Ben Johnston

Most of American culture sees art as a variety of entertainment, and "serious" art as a not very successful variety of high-class amusement. Note the adjective: an interest in serious art is seen as a credential for identification with a higher social class. The government, and the majority of the people, thinks that art should support itself like any other commercial enterprise, and that if a minority wants to indulge in aristocratic pretensions it should pay for these without subsidy.

A minority, mostly wealthy, has never given up an aristocratic stratification of society, and supports an art which imitates European culture in competition with it. With the decline in Europe of political institutions directly based on aristocratic models, the artist, freed somewhat from servility to patrons, tended to become a kind of culture hero. It is as though aristocratic behavior retreated into the arts. The moneyed minority in America which supports, for example, symphony orchestras and opera companies, keeps this view alive in the face of its rejection by most of the society.

But for generating a sense of belonging to a comfortable elite, or for purposes of upward mobility (which at a certain altitude becomes social climbing), Beethoven or Debussy or Tchaikovsky or anyone else whose music has undergone the metamorphosis into museum pieces will serve much better than a living composer. And Europeans are vastly better than Americans, even if they are still alive, because it is understandable if they are aristocratic. As a result most composers in the U.S.A. are supported by the only widely-acceptable form of subsidy: posts as teachers in college and university music schools.

While the general musical life of the country mirrors the state of the world by reminding us constantly that there are many musics, most music schools still operate as if European music (and mostly that of the eighteenth and nineteenth centuries) were the only music of significance. This hegemony is challenged by jazz programs that transcend the "fun and games" state, and in a few places by performing groups growing out of ethno-musicological programs. Its most serious challenge has come from active groups of composers, who may be bent upon perpetuating

the traditions of concert-making and attendant musical activities, but who are com-
mitted to overcoming the resistance to new repertory and to changing musical performing practices. But this activity only affects the professional world indirectly
except in rare instances. Even the efforts of composers' societies seem to have relatively weak effects.

Sufficiently resourceful people can always create enclaves and cliques, but
how much wider than that will the interested listening public ever grow to be? Just
how long does the cultural lag have to get before we ask ourselves seriously if the
gap will ever close? These questions were raised by Gunther Schuller in an address
to the American Society of University Composers in the spring of 1980. But where I
part company with Schuller is that I heard no hint of a way out of this cul-de-sac in
his address and I have heard none in his music, unless what he proposes to do is to
abandon concert music in the European tradition for jazz or ragtime or some other
more popular music.

These seem to me weighty questions, and the finger pointed at us composers by Schuller to accuse us of having helped to bring about this situation seems
not altogether unjust. Much so-called new music does not really deserve the wider
audience it complains about being denied. If the only alternative to this is the end-
less replay of "the classics" or an attempt to rewrite them or to quote them or even
to parallel them, we have already abandoned the serious effort to keep concert
music alive.

I would be unhappy to see this happen. I would like the tradition of Western concert music to continue to develop among the world's musics in a future in
which its dominance will have ended. But can we possibly regard the present state
of concert music in this country as a state of health?

Questions of this kind assailed me right from the outset of my composing
career, not least because of my contact with Harry Partch. I remember writing to
him soon after I read his book, *Genesis of a Music,* that I had long felt that the very
scale we were using had condemned contemporary composers to an ever-narrowing
effort to exhaust the remaining possibilities in a closed system. Partch's determina-
tion to throw out almost the whole of Western traditions of composing, performing, theorizing, and bringing music to an audience impressed but also alarmed me.
I could see even then how unlikely it would be that his work would even reach a
wide public, let alone precipitate changes of so sweeping a nature.

I have never felt that the tradition of European concert music was either
worthless or hopeless, though I have come more and more to see that we have
allowed it to become an albatross around our necks. How and why it became so
began to interest me extremely.

Among the early strong impressions pushing me toward becoming a
musician was a lecture I heard at the age of twelve at Wesleyan Conservatory of
Music in Macon, Georgia. It concerned the importance of the acoustical findings of

Helmholtz in the development of Debussy's music. The lecturer used a monochord to demonstrate the basic premises of just-tuned intervals and the phenomenon of overtones. I never lost the feeling of mystery and unfolding new possibilities that world of simple mathematical ratios opened to me. Debussy instantly became a figure of importance to me, though I had previously paid his music little attention.

Later, when I studied music theory, it was a disappointment and finally a disillusionment how cavalierly it sidestepped the principles of acoustics. By that time I was determined to master it and to acquire the tradition of European concert music, so I did not reject it, as Partch had done earlier. What happened to me was a gradually strengthening conviction that the tradition had gone awry a long time ago and was in need of rechanneling. This initially gained impetus from the impact of *Genesis of a Music* and subsequently six months' apprenticeship in Partch's studio at Gualala, California, in 1950.

It took me about ten years to digest that experience. When I finally decided to act upon these stimuli I set out to learn electronic studio techniques at Columbia-Princeton Studio while on a Guggenheim Fellowship in 1959–60. I quickly discovered that this medium was not ready for the use I wished to make of it, and that my aptitude for that kind of composing was not high. It gradually became clear that neither that route nor Partch's was the best path for me, but rather the forbidding one of getting traditionally trained performers using conventional instruments to alter their performance practices sufficiently to play just-tuned music elaborated to the point of microtonality. As soon as I returned to Illinois after my sabbatical, in 1960, I set about trying to compose such music.

I was convinced that this freeing of music from the artificial shackles of twelve-tone equal temperament would prove to be a key to why most twentieth-century concert music has seemed intelligible to so limited an audience. I am today more than ever convinced of this. It is a very important change I think composers could make in the unhealthy situation of music today.

Partch's aversion to European musical values originated in a rejection of American education as well as of traditions of "classical music". Since he spent his childhood and early youth in a part of Arizona very near to the Mexican border at a time when the region was only just emerging from the condition of frontier life, the urban culture of America was as exotic to him as a foreign country. When he encountered it he did not identify with it, but rejected it passionately, stubbornly maintaining against it an art and a life-style drawn directly from his early influences. The fact that his parents were apostate Protestant missionaries to China, and maintained something of what they had absorbed of Chinese culture, and the circumstance of living in American Indian country figured importantly in his formation.

Even after he plunged into twentieth-century America in Los Angeles he continued to draw almost all his artistic and cultural sustenance from non-European sources rich in the California environment. He was associated with the earliest artistic community at Big Sur. During this period one of his closest friends was Jaime de Angulo, a radically unconventional anthropologist who was studying California Indian cultures largely by assimilating into them. Thus Partch's sympathies were always with what much later would be called counter-cultures. When you add to this the fact that he chose to live all his life on the economic margin of American culture, surviving mostly on odd jobs, hand-outs and private grants, you can begin to see how his extraordinary independence came to be, and why he seemed to much of the drop-out counter-culture of the sixties a prophetic older brother.

But the culture as a whole has not gone in those directions, and he runs the posthumous risk of becoming a kind of anti-religious patron saint of drop-outs except in the Southwest, where cultural currents of the same kind as those which produced him still generate artists of a unique breed. Without in any way wishing to diminish his large importance in these contexts, I think his significance and potential value are much larger than this.

In several crucial respects Harry Partch offers directions out of the trap our musical culture has gotten itself into. He refused resolutely to be drawn into the concert music world, not even that of "modern music" or its offspring "contemporary music" and "new music". He knew he was not part of it and would never willingly consent to further its aims by affiliating with it. His association with B.M.I. was the creation of Oliver Daniels and Carl Haverlin and amounted to a continuing subsidy of his work almost without strings attached. Partch was grateful and occasionally cooperative, but remained aloof and aggressively independent.

He refused with equal vehemence to have anything more than peripherally to do with the world of commercial music, which has swallowed up almost all the music this continent has spawned. Most of his recordings were produced and distributed privately, and his few commercial record contracts were negotiated with much effort and persuasion from colleagues who saw the importance of getting his work out to a wider public as outweighing even Partch's rejection of the values imposed by commercial and corporate interests. When his work began to attract rock musicians (for instance Frank Zappa) there was always one inevitable barrier between them: the dependence of rock music upon a world of commercial values.

Even Partch's affiliations with universities and colleges were as tenuous and temporary as he could make them, and suspicion on the part of musical conservatives and reactionaries that the institution was harboring a cultural subversive was only marginally over-balanced by the recognition from a determined minority that this was an artist of major importance.

Even more basically, Partch saw the identification of European artistic traditions with wealth, power, and social position in American society, and fought it at every opportunity. He looked to other cultures in the world for sources and influences in his own work, and he looked behind modern European culture to its sources to discover where it went wrong. In his work he set out to correct these errors in cultural, philosophical and artistic values. In his life he stayed as independent of the economic and institutional forces that mold cultural attitudes as he could while still forced to derive his sustenance indirectly from them. It was for that reason that he was willing to accept support from individuals who had demonstrated a belief in his work, but only rarely and with misgivings from corporate entities and institutions.

It must have looked to Partch as if the European heritage in American culture was impervious to change and insensitive to influence, and indeed this is in many respects very nearly true. But there is vastly more in our culture than that one component, and world trends are clearly running counter to a continued dominance of that particular strain. It is in fact a long time since the art music of Europe and its onetime colonies such as the U.S.A. was of anything like the strength or importance either here or in most of the rest of the world as the various popular musics so effectively disseminated by the mass media. It is above all in this respect that the United States holds a position of artistic leadership whether we are leading in a desirable direction or not.

We already face a situation in this culture where the values of "serious music" are threatened economically as well as culturally. If we elect to preserve only the museum aspects of this tradition because of the anachronistic social and economic organization of the main channels of its dissemination, we will ensure its atrophy.

In the face of this prospect, two main problems demand solutions: how can the tradition continue to grow without losing its public, and how can it become a healthy, fruitful and even powerful stimulus to the world's other musics rather than an adulterative and disintegrative influence? If these problems are not addressed successfully the traditions of European concert music will not only wither in this country and elsewhere, but will be displaced successfully by rival traditions of music which reject above all its aristocratic anachronisms.

It begins to look as if serious music needs Harry Partch more than he ever needed it. He addressed problems it is ignoring with far more than tentative success, and he diagnosed many of its most serious ills with uncanny accuracy. The time is long overdue when diagnosis should be followed by prescription and treatment.

In 1946 Circle magazine published an article by Harry Partch entitled "Show Horses in the Concert Ring." It has been republished more recently by Soundings magazine. In it Partch launches an attack on American concert music and proposes his alternatives. Here are some excerpts:

It need hardly be labored that music is a physical art, and that a periodic grouping into the physical, a reaching for an understanding of the physical, is the only basic procedure, the only way a musical era will attain any enduring significance....

The age of specialization has given us an art of sound that denies sound, and a science of sound that denies art ... a music-drama that denies drama, and a drama that—contrary to the practices of all other people of the world—denies music.

One does not fertilize the creative instinct by twenty year plans of practice ... to play music written by others, mostly long dead ... And we permit an industrialization of music on the basis of such parlous degeneracy: issuance of interpretation upon interpretation of the accepted limited repertory by the record companies; facture on an assembly line of the accepted instruments and in whatever asinine notation and implied nomenclature they require—by still other companies, and soon, perennially sporting a bloom of pride over the magnificent spread of our culture. The 'so on' stands for literally thousands of scholarly magazine articles, ... ubiquitous classes in music appreciation, multiplex radio programs, all deliberately calculated to weight us permanently with the incubi and the succubi of an interpretive age: That is, with a factitious, non-creative art. The only real vitality in this entire picture is exuded by the men who are out to make money in the deal.... Value of intrinsic content—value of human beings, of human works and attitudes—never enters the picture....

Some very drastic remedies are called for in order to bring vitality to a body of theory that rejects investigation and a physical poetry that excludes all but purely metaphysical poets. A period of comparative anarchy, with each composer employing his own instrument or instruments, his own scale, his own forms is very necessary for a way out of this malaise.

As a first step, Partch's work can be and must be brought before a wider public and his significance correctly assessed, not diminished to the level of a cultural oddity. As an even more important second step, those of us who can must carry on aspects of his work in directions of which, perhaps, he never dreamed or felt himself ill-equipped to deal with.

During his life I helped Partch to get his work before the public for as long as he permitted. I was responsible for getting him to the University of Illinois, where he produced *The Bewitched, Revelation in the Courthouse Park*, and *Water, Water*, and where he met Danlee Mitchell, his heir. When we came to odds as a result of his delegation to me of choice of choreographer for *The Bewitched* and my subsequent holding together of the production, it was necessary for me to leave to others the active job of carrying out his work. I never ceased to be a supporter.

Since his death I have again tried to help, though I have no direct affiliation with the Harry Partch Foundation or with the ensemble which continues to produce his works.

With the aid of several other people, most particularly Thomas McGeary, a young musicologist from San Diego, I have begun to gather together oral history and other data on his life from people who knew and worked with him. I do not have the intention of producing a biography of Partch, but such materials will be important to anyone who does. More recently, with the aid of a team of young researchers, Glenn Hackbarth, Larry Polansky, Janet Cameron, Mark Culbertson, Mark Behm, and Christopher Granner, I have initiated the preparation of three works of Partch for publication in a notation designed to be as little different from ordinary traditional notation as possible. The works are *Seventeen Lyrics by Li Po*, *Eleven Intrusions*, and *Daphne of the Dunes*. Our aim is to make Partch's scores as accessible as possible to the ordinary musician.

The most significant aspect of my own work as composer is a very extensive development of microtonal just intonation. I have developed a theory in support of this which greatly extends Partch's. Since I am dealing with traditions of performing and with instruments and players which are in the European tradition, I have steeped myself in that music and have studied the techniques and aesthetic attitudes of all its phases of development up through the present. But my purpose has not been to Europeanize Partch's ideas. Rather it has been to alter that tradition so as to render it pervious to his way of thinking.

Lastly, I will not identify myself with Harry Partch. Early on in our association he paid me a compliment I did not recognize as such. He said I would never be a follower of his. Stung a little by what I took to be a rejection, I asked him why not. He said I was too much like him and I would have to find my own way.

10

IN SEARCH OF PARTCH'S *BEWITCHED*
PART ONE: CONCERNING PHYSICALITY

Kenneth Gaburo

Berlin Festival performance of *The Bewitched*, 1979.

A. PREMISE:

HARRY PARTCH'S:
THE BEWITCHED[1]

PROLOGUE: The lost musicians mix magic. The
witch appears and takes command of her chorus, the
band of lost musicians.

SCENES OF WITCHERY: (1) Three undergrads
become transfigured in a Hong Kong Music Hall;
(2) Exercises in harmony and counterpoint are tried
in a court of ancient ritual;
                              (3) The romancing of a
pathological liar comes to an inspired end;
                                        (4) A soul
tormented by contemporary music finds a humaniz-
ing alchemy;
                    (5) Visions fill the eyes of a defeated
basketball team while in the shower room;
                                        (6)
Euphoria descends a Sausalito stairway;
                                    (7) Two
detectives on the trail of a tricky culprit turn in
their badges;
                    (8) A court in its own contempt rises to
a motherly apotheosis;
                        (9) A lost political soul finds
himself among the voteless women of paradise;
                                        (10)
The cognoscenti are plunged into a demonic descent.

EPILOGUE: "Later!", says the witch, and she
vanishes. The lost musicians wander away.

The
underlying
premise
for
my
discussion
of
physicality
in
the
light
of
Partch's
Bewitched
is
observation.[2]

ALL
humans
observe.

The
ACTion
of
observation
at
least
involves:

CAST: lost musicians;
        witch;
        dancers;
        costumes and lighting design;
        stage manager;
        lighting technician;
        house managers;
        stage crew;

Kenneth Gaburo, director;
Lou Blankenburg, choreographer and
                  assistant director;
Danlee Mitchell, music director.[3]

                Observing an entity;
                Describing that entity;
                    and,
                Making sense of that entity.

(An entity can be one's self; another human;
another life-form; another so-called "thing". In what
follows, I shall occasionally refer to life-forms by the
symbol: 'I'; non-life forms by the symbol: 'it'; and to
the interaction between them as follows: I↔I; I↔it).

THE INSTRUMENTS:
Adapted Koto
Spoils of War
Marimba Eroica
Cloud-Chamber Bowls
Chromelodeon I
New Boo I
Bass Clarinet
Piccolo and Flute
Clarinet
Adapted Viola
Kithara II
Diamond Marimba
Bass Marimba
Harmonic Canon II
Surrogate Kithara[4]

Observing an I, it, implicates *PERCEPTION*.
Describing a perceived I, it, implicates language,
(i.e. *NOTATION* in some form), e.g.: notes, words,
gestures.

Notation is always registered (located) somewhere
by way of some instrument-mechanism, (i.e.
'TECHNOLOGY') e.g.: a synapse, paper, "score",
performance, oscillator.

Making sense of a perceived I, it, involves physical,
thinking, cognitive processes which are implicitly
COMPOSITIONAL, (i.e., constructing realities), as
is the observed I, it, 'composed'.[5]

STATEMENT BY PARTCH:

We are all bewitched, and mostly by accident; the accident of form, color, and sex;
of prejudices conditioned from the cradle on up; of the particular ruts we have
found ourselves in or have dug for ourselves because of our individual needs.
Those in a long-tenanted rut enjoy larger comforts of mind and body, and as
compensation it is given to others who are not so easily domesticated to become
mediums for the transmission of perception, more frequently. Among these are
the lost musicians. The present-day musician grows up in a half-world between
"good" music and "not-so-good" music. Even when he has definitely made his
choice between the two, he is still affected by the other, and to that extent he is
dichotomous and disoriented. His head is bathed in an ancient light through a
Gothic window, while his other end swings like a miniature suspension bridge in a
cool right-angle gale. The perception of displaced musicians may germinate,
evolve, and mature in concert, through a developing at-one-ness, through
their beat.

THE BEWITCHED is in the tradition of world-wide ritual theater. It is the
opposite of the specialized. I conceived and wrote it in California in the period
1952-55, following the several performances of my version of Sophocles' OEDIPUS.
In spirit, if not wholly in content, THE BEWITCHED is a satyr-play. It is a
seeking for release – through satire, whimsy, magic, ribaldry – from the catharsis
of tragedy. It is an essay toward a miraculous abeyance of civilized rigidity, in the
feeling that the modern spirit might thereby find some ancient and magical sense
of rebirth. Each of the ten scenes is a theatrical unfolding of nakedness, a psychological strip-tease, or – a diametric reversal, which has the effect of underlining
the complementary character, the strange affinity, of seemingly opposites.[6]

B. PHYSICALITY: (In this section, Physicality is rigorously described,
                                       on the way to discussing Partch's concept of
                                       Corporeality. This is so, because I think one can be
                                       physical without being corporeal, but cannot be
The expression: corporeal without being physical. Moreover,
                                       Corporeality is a *kind* of physicality, and, necessar-
PHYSICALITY,   ily, can be comprehended more fully in its light.)

signifies a phenomenon. It is not a thing in itself. No further self-consciousness

about it could obtain if, in answer to the question: "What is Physicality?",
the answer was merely:

PHYSICALITY IS PHYSICALITY IS PHYSICALITY...n

Even though the "is" in this case acts as-if it refers to a thing, (i.e. Physicality),
neither "is", nor "Physicality" are illuminated by their presence, ...that is, by
their mere *appearance*[7], ...as given. Unless something else happens, the expression
simply allows an observer to be caught up in the redundancy of the expression,
...by the evidence *in* the expression..., without the possibility of its issuing, or an
observer inferring, much further evidence of its nature. But, something could
happen to change this circumstance. For instance, an observer could *wonder*[8]
about it, and ask:

PHYSICALITY IS . . . . WHAT?

The interrogative "WHAT", at least, becomes an expressed desire to search out
some significance[9] for the expression: Physicality Is Physicality Is Physicality,
which, ...as it appears..., is merely 'self '- (it-) referential. However, *that* it appears
is sufficient to trigger a response in the form of an interrogation. To do so would
relieve the expression of its isolation. Clearly, an observer would have to initiate
further ACTion. If left to its 'own' devices, the expression would merely sit here,
...on this page..., as a 'thing in itself', unnoticed or unquestioned.

But, an ACTion *did* happen. Somehow, the expression: Physicality, got on a page.
It did not inscribe itself. Its actual appearance is so, in this case, because I initiated
and carried out some ACTion. For instance, it would not have appeared without:

1. my calling it forth (i.e., from experience),
2. my locating it somewhere (e.g., a page),
3. my entering it in some manner (e.g., inscribing),
4. my need of some mechanism (e.g., a typewriter),
5. my intention (e.g., to discuss Partch);

and, most certainly not without an awareness, ...i.e., my self-consciousness..., of
having done so. I know it was on the page because I put it there, and *observed
myself* doing so. Now it is on *this* page, and something also is *happening*. What is
inscribed here could not be known by you, unless you, too, initiated some ACTion
(e.g., by picking up, and opening this journal), and carried it out (e.g., by reading
this page).

For the moment I shall assume these matters have something to do with the
expression: Physicality. As such, more can be said on the way to making sense of it:

6. The expression: PHYSICALITY, contains,
   ...nested within it..., sub-texts which suggest
   what it could refer to:

(PHYSICALITY)

PARTCH (with respect to playing the Bass Marimba):

COORDINATE FOOTWORK WITH
PLAYING TECHNIQUES! IN FAST
AND DIFFICULT PASSAGES THE BASS
MARIMBA PART ACTUALLY BECOMES A DANCE,
OR A ROUND OF BOXING IN THE FIGHT RING. IN
SOME PASSAGES THE FEET SHOULD PLANT THEMSELVES
WIDE APART (ATLAS CARRYING THE WORLD), SO THAT
THE TWO OUTSIDE BLOCKS MAY BE REACHED ALTERNATELY,
STRONGLY, AND EASILY.[10]

> 7. The expression: PHYSICALITY, expresses itself
>   in a physical manner. Here, I have in mind its
>   letters, dimension, place on the page, et alia. In
>   this respect, it is 'saying' something, even-if
>   merely 'sitting'. Whatever one can know of it, is
>   thought out in its presence.[11] For anything to be
>   said at all, both presences, ...someone and it...,
>   are necessary.

PARTCH (with respect to bowing techniques for the Adapted Viola):

MY FINAL ADVICE TO BOWED STRING
PLAYERS INVOLVED IN MY WORK:
SEIZE THE CONCEPT EVEN THOUGH YOU
DON'T UNDERSTAND IT, CONTEMPLATE, DO
YOGA EXERCISES...THE SCORES THEMSELVES DO NOT
HELP AT ALL; THEY ARE SIMPLY CRYPTIC NOTES, OR
CRYPTIC RATIOS.[12]

> 8. With regard to the observer:
>   a. The ACTion of observing (perceiving) the
>   expression: PHYSICALITY, is, at least,
>   physical, e.g.: presence, location, brain, mind;
>   b. The ACTion of describing (notating) the
>   expression: PHYSICALITY, is, at least,
>   physical, e.g.: speaking, writing; as is (are) the
>   instruments,... (mechanism(s))..., for doing so,
>   e.g.: eyes, ears, pen, typewriter;
>   c. The ACTion of making sense (developing
>   one's self-consciousness) of the expression:
>   PHYSICALITY, is, at least, physical, e.g.:
>   wondering, thinking.

PARTCH (with respect to the Boo):

PREDICTABILITY IN A PIECE OF BAMBOO
IS VERY LOW, AND BECAUSE OF THE EXASPERATION
THIS CAUSES I HAVE EXPERIMENTED WITH LARGE PLASTIC

TUBING. HERE ONE DOES FIND PREDICTABILITY, BUT HE LOSES
THE WARM, RICH TONES OF BAMBOO.
IN THE ORIENT THERE IS UNDOUBTEDLY
TO BE TAPPED – SOMEWHERE – A COMPENDIUM OF INFORMATION
REGARDING VARIETIES OF BAMBOO AND THEIR
PREDICTABLE BEHAVIOUR. IN TIME, I
HOPE, THIS WILL BE KNOWN
ELSEWHERE.[13]

9. The language thus far used to discuss the
   expression: PHYSICALITY, ...e.g.: experience,
   page, typewriter, discuss PARTCH..., exhibits
   certain physical features, namely:

   a. each expression is unique (bound) only to the
      extent that it is not any other one; nor is an
      observer any of these;[14]
   b. each expression is not exclusive (cf. B. 7, page 59);
   c. each expression is subject-dependent, and not
      object-independent.

PARTCH (with respect to the cloud chamber bowls):

MAINTENANCE: HERE IS ONLY THE PROBLEM
OF CUTTING ANOTHER CARBOY WHEN ONE
OF THE BOWLS IS BROKEN. (ONE
ALWAYS HOPES – IT IS GENERALLY FUTILE –
THAT HE WILL GET SOMETHING CLOSE
TO THE TONE OF THE BROKEN PIECE!)[15]

Earlier, each of the expressions: experience, page, inscribing, typewriter, discuss
PARTCH, was referenced to PHYSICALITY. Without all of these, at least, the
expression: PHYSICALITY, could not have appeared on this page. No one, or
some of these would have been sufficient. Each functioned as a unique *part,* but, in
itself, could not have been the *whole* of the ACTion. The presence of each, ...no
longer an exclusive "thing" (object) in itself..., and, the sense of each, was
dependent (contingent) on the presence of the others, and on the observer. Each,
necessarily, *referred* to the other, and to the *subject:* PHYSICALITY. Their
involvement formed part of what I call a referential system. The following
notations express, in one way, the distinctions I make between the parts and the
whole of the ACTion:

(PHYSICALITY) (I) (EXPERIENCE,PAGE,INSCRIBING,TYPEWRITER,DISCUSS) (PARTCH)

(PHYSICALITYINEXPERIENCEPAGEINSCRIBINGT TYPEWRITERDISCUSSPARTCH)

Now, if I experience the expressions: experience, page, inscribing, typewriter,
discuss, PARTCH, each to be physically unique, I cannot conclude 'all that is

physical' resides in only *one* of them. Even though each one somehow is bound to the others because each *is* physical, it follows that each reflects a *difference in kind* within 'all that is physical'. Furthermore, I cannot conclude these constitute all the unique physical expressions there are. Accordingly, if 'all that is physical' cannot merely reside in some of them, and if some of them cannot be 'all that is physical', then what can one call 'all that is physical'?

I call the expression:

PHYSICALITY,

'all that is physical'.

But, suppose one could come to know *all* unique physical expressions, ...that is, to know there are no others...? If so, this order of magnitude could still not go beyond 'all that is physical'. And, since the expression: PHYSICALITY, cannot go beyond 'all that is physical', one could at least theoretically postulate: ALL unique physical expressions equal THE unique expression: physicality.

This postulation raises an historical assumption, namely: THE WHOLE IS EQUAL TO THE SUM OF ITS PARTS. But since the whole has also been perceived differently from its parts, ...particularly because of a sense of its magnitude..., the above postulation has raised another historical assumption, namely: THE WHOLE IS GREATER THAN THE SUM OF ITS PARTS. Because, subsequently, I shall be discussing Partch's concepts of Corporeality and Whole Theater, these assumptions are briefly considered here:

> 10. Because each unique expression exhibits a physical difference in kind, it follows that all unique expressions would exhibit all physical differences in kind. As such, they could not be *equal* to the expression: Physicality, because differences are not equivalent.

> 11. Although the expression: Physicality is distinct, ...in that it negates 'all that is *not* physical' ...; and, although it is also whole, ...in that it signifies 'all that *is* physical' ..., it is expressed (shows up) as those differences in kind, which physical expressions manifest. Thereby, it, too, is distinct, but not exclusively so. Its ACTion is, at least, *distributive*. Because it is, it becomes a member of its own set; a set which *includes* 'all that is physical'. It cannot be "greater" than that.

Now, I hold it is not possible to refer to the expression: PHYSICALITY (as whole), without referring to all its expressions (its parts); AND vice versa. That the above assumptions of parts-whole do not exhibit this perception is primarily so, because they are quantified expressions. They suggest that the parts and the whole can, somehow, be separated from each other; that each is distinct, and somehow,

exclusive; that each, somehow, is merely *relational*. But, as *interactions*, each
exhibits differences in kind of quite another dimension:

> 12. PHYSICALITY (whole, in itself), cannot be
> more than a *part* of any ENTITY:
> and,
> ANY ENTITY (whole, in *it*self), cannot be more
> than a *part* of PHYSICALITY.
>
> e.g., in general notation:

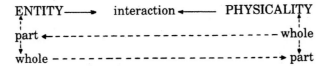

What is implicit in this assumption is neither entity nor physicality can be fully
imbued by the other; neither can become the other. Moreover, the unique
properties which each exhibit are not *lost*, or given up, because the *binding*..., by
way of interactions..., is physical. This is particularly so, because their *kinds* of
physical difference are also unique. It is their necessary, mutual participation in
action, and, thereby, the *influences* which each exert on the other, that renders
each distinct, but *non-exclusive*. They are *included* in each other, but neither can
be *ALL INCLUSIVE*. The expression: PHENOMENON, refers to a state which is
all inclusive:[16]

> 13. ENTITIES AND PHYSICALITY are each, by
> the other, constrained within (bound by) 'All
> that is *inclusively* Physical'.
>
> e.g., in general notation:

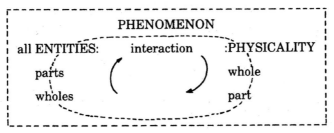

PARTCH: I BELIEVE IN MANY THINGS: IN AN INTONATION AS *JUST* AS I
AM CAPABLE OF MAKING IT; IN MUSICAL INSTRUMENTS ON STAGE,
DYNAMIC IN FORM, VISUALLY EXCITING...I BELIEVE IN DRAMATIC
LIGHTING, REPLETE WITH GELS, TO ENHANCE THEM...I BELIEVE IN
MUSICIANS WHO ARE *TOTAL* CONSTITUENTS OF THE MOMENT...
I BELIEVE IN PLAYERS IN COSTUME...IN SOMETHING, JUST SOME-
THING, THAT WILL REMOVE THEM FROM THE PEDESTRIAN...I BELIEVE

IN BASS MARIMBISTS...WHO MOVE THE TRUNKS OF THEIR BODIES
LIKE ATHLETES...I BELIEVE IN ALL SOUNDS OF THE HUMAN VOICE,
FREE FROM THE BEL-CANTO STRAIT JACKET...I BELIEVE IN A TOTAL
INTEGRATION OF FACTORS, NOT AS SEPARATE AND SEALED SPECIAL-
TIES...SOUND AND SIGHT...VISUALLY DYNAMIC AND DRAMATIC, ALL
CHANNELED INTO A SINGLE, WHOLLY FUSED, AND PURPOSEFUL
DIRECTION. *ALL*.[17]

C. HOW IT IS WITH PARTCH:

To enter any of Partch's work in any capacity,[18] and with any seriousness, is to
be involved in an extraordinarily complex confrontation. I do not know many
20th century works, in or out of music, which approach Partch's demands,
...particularly those of Corporeality and Whole Theater...,[19] nor any which
surpass them.[20]

PARTCH: THE STRINGS IN GENERAL REPRESENT THE SOUL OF MY WORK, AND IF THEY ARE NOT STRONGLY PLAYED IT HAS NO SOUL. PERCUSSION REPRESENTS THE BODILY STRUCTURE, AND IT IS VERY IMPORTANT.[21]

At the outset, I imagine the use of the expression: 'complex', with regard to Partch, might seem inappropriate to some, particularly since so much has been made of his compositional simplicity,[22]...its "directness", "primitiveness", "basicness", et alia.

When one speaks of Partch, one generally refers to him in the light of certain
crucial 'identifying' features, such as: his (non-western) tuning systems; his
(hand-made) instruments; his (political) anti-intellectual, -institutional,
-technological stance;[23] his (stage) language, e.g.: Kabuki, Ritual, Satire,
Expressionism; his so-called (conceptual) link with Dionysus, and Wagner's
Gesamtkunstwerke.[24]

PARTCH: IT IS ALTOGETHER TOO EASY TO FOCUS ON ONE SMALL TECHNICAL FACT AND TO IGNORE A VERITABLE WHIRLWIND OF CREATION BEYOND THAT FACT. IN THE DESCRIPTIONS OF MY WORK IN PUBLIC PRINT MUCH IS MADE OF THE PHRASE, "43 TONES TO THE OCTAVE". THAT PRECISE 43 IS THE *ONE-HALF TRUTH OF THE ONE-FOURTH FACTOR*. THE EMPHASIS HAS NEVER BEEN MINE, BECAUSE THE NUMBER

Certainly, the apprehension of any of these 'features' is no "simple" matter. If not, then what kinds of perception could have generated such less-than-complex assessments?

In my view, following are some:

1. The persistence with which focus has been, and is, directed to one or another of these identifying features, easily suggests they are regarded as self-contained, separate entities; as-if this one or that one constitutes a valid description of what Partch's work stands for:

APPLIES ONLY TO MY INSTRUMENTS OF FIXED PITCH, AND MY SCORES FOR 36 YEARS PAST ARE ELOQUENT TESTIMONY TO THE FACT THAT – BEYOND THE FIXED-PITCH IDEA –, I LIMIT MYSELF IN NO WAY WHATEVER.[25]

"Partch's music speaks…Let…43, and more, irregular meters, klang…the …dissonant contrapuntal fabric, corporeality, phase beating…music… plucked strings, exotic percussion, reed organs, adapted viola, attentive wood-winds…speak…cross accents, timbral juxtaposition, themes…for…the Baroque Concerto Grosso".[26]

2. The persistence with which not much more than a passing reference, and sometimes, outright dismissal, has been given to Corporeality and Whole Theater, …*the essentials*…, which necessarily bind and integrate identifying features:

"It is beyond the scope of this article to deal with Partch's dramatic and theatrical concepts except in passing. The intention is rather to focus attention upon his musical thought, which has not received proper examination by others; *para-musical* issues are eloquently put by Partch himself".[27]

3. The persistence with which a particular perceiver,…a spectator, musician, dancer, choreographer, et alia…, 'adjusts' the whole of a Partchwork to that view, …persuasion…, already held in the mind of that perceiver, e.g.:

from its complexity, dancers and choreographers extract "dance", musicians and critics extract "music", actors and directors extract "theater", stage crews and technicians extract "set, lighting".

4. The persistence with which current-day notions of music, (e.g., with regard to notes, rhythms, forms, tunings), …and similarly in other areas of art…, *despite* abundant evidence to the contrary, have not been sufficiently expanded to include that a human body can function as an instrument; that an instrument (e.g., Partch's Kithara) can function as a 'voice'; that an actor can function as a dancer; that a dancer can function as a musician; that lighting can be more than mere illumination; or set more than mere environmental color.

PARTCH: THE INSTRUMENTS WOULD NOT BE CROWDED INTO A
RESTRICTED SPACE BUT DISPOSED ARCHITECTURALLY AND LAND-
SCAPICALLY, SO THAT THE DANCERS WOULD BE IN, AROUND, AMONG
THEM (AND MIGHT EVEN USE THEM), OCCASIONALLY.[28]

> In the absence of an awareness for how all of these identifying features could be
> made to work as an integrated whole, focus on any particular one, …by any
> description, including actual productions…, becomes reductionist; the parts are
> regarded as-if they are the whole; as-if *ends,* and not *means.* But: one needs to
> constantly ask such questions as: *just intonation* in the light of what?; *music* in
> the light of what?; *acting* in the light of what?; *anti-intellectualism* in the light
> of what? By not so doing, it is easy to see how Partch's work can be rendered
> "simple", and crucially, how certain kinds of violence can be done to it, even
> when one speaks eloquently in his behalf.

PARTCH: IN WRITING THIS OUTLINE I HAVE LET MY MIND WANDER
WITH LITTLE HINDRANCE. MY SUGGESTIONS REGARDING STAGE-SET,
COSTUMES, AND MOVEMENTS ABOUT THE STAGE GO INTO HIGHLY
TECHNICAL AREAS, AND I WOULD LIKE TO INVOKE EXPERIENCES
AND ATTITUDES BEYOND MY OWN. MY STATEMENTS ARE REALLY
QUESTIONS: IS THIS PARTICULAR IDEA A GOOD IDEA? IN COSTUME? IN
SET? IN LIGHTING? IN MOVEMENT? IS WHAT I'M ASKING THROUGHOUT.
THE IMPORTANT THING IS AN AGREED-ON BASIS FOR PERFORMANCE,
SO THAT A TRUE COLLABORATION AND INTEGRATION RESULTS.
AND IF IT RESULTS, A MAJOR STEP MAY HAVE BEEN TAKEN IN
RE-DISCOVERING – IN WESTERN TERMS – AN ANCIENT VALUE.[29]

> Contrarily, with Partch, musical thought *cannot* be separated from corporeal-
> theatrical thought. With Partch, to observe the work as a concrete, ideally
> realized whole, should make it impossible to separate functions. With Partch,
> what is demanded is that *parts* must give up their *partness* in favor of a
> *wholeness* which includes them.
> It is getting at this wholeness, …Partch's omni-present referent…, which
> makes his work complex and confrontive. Concomitant with the work as a
> whole, integrated, 'fused' entity, are the performers, and, ultimately, the
> audience, who have also to be fused; the wholeness of the persona is asked to
> participate in the wholeness of the work, also not ideally separable. The entire
> 'apparatus', so-to-speak, has to be a flexible, giving, ritualistic one.

PARTCH: SATIRE NEED NOT BE HEAVY-HANDED. IT CAN DESCEND
LIGHTLY AND WITH LOVE…IT CAN BRING RE-EVALUATION AND
SELF-PERCEPTION…IT CAN BRING A SPONTANEOUS FEELING FOR
HUMANITY THROUGH ART, A FEELING THAT LIES WITHIN OUR BONES.[30]

> Partch, above all else, is anti-reductionist. His referent, …his bonding…,

resides in the nature of physicality, itself. Certainly it is not overly difficult to formulate a theory and an aesthetic description for his referent. But it is immensely difficult to bring it off as an actual case.

Notation One:

I. PHYSICALITY	II. REALITY	SPACE	MATTER	INTELLECT	INTENTION	AFFECTION
PHYSICAL	EXISTENCE	DIMENSION	FEATURE	DESCRIPTION	NECESSITY	EMOTION
CORPOREAL	EVIDENT	BOUNDARY	SUBSTANCE	INTUITION	POSSESSION	ILLUMINATE
BODY	WHOLE	QUANTITY	ELASTICITY	COMPOSITION	PERFORMANCE	SATISFACTION
ENERGY	FORCE	AGITATION	FRICTION	OBSERVATION	EFFORT	QUIESCENCE
FEELING	CONCRETE	CONTIGUITY	PERCEPTION	INQUIRY	DOING	IMPRESSION
TOUCH	RELATION	INTERVAL	PRESSURE	INFER	RECEIVE	DELICACY
MOVEMENT	MUTABLE	PASSAGE	DENSITY	VENTURE	CONSEQUENCE	EXCITATION
SHAPE	FORM	CONTENT	ASPECT	FOCUS	CONSTRUCT	PLEASURE
GESTURE	SIGN	SITUATION	INTENSITY	EXPRESSION	OFFER	DESIRE
PRESENCE	INSTANCE	INHABIT	EMERGE	MIND	COMMIT	SPECIFY
STATE	CONDITION	STRUCTURE	ATTITUDE	AWARENESS	INTERACTION	FULLNESS
PLACE	PART	CIRCUMSTANCE	INSERTION	ARRANGE	REFER	DISTINCTION
MYSTICAL	LATENCY	DIRECTION	BLURRED	UNCERTAINTY	CHARM	CELEBRATE
MAGIC	APPEARANCE	ATTRACTION	AURA	IMAGINE	INFLUENCE	SEDUCTION
RITE	SYSTEM	DEPTH	VITALITY	CONTEXT	FUNCTION	DEMONSTRATE

III.   IV.

D. ELABORATION: NOTATIONS ONE AND TWO

NOTATION ONE, above, exhibits certain expressions which are sufficient in number and kind to further illuminate physicality, but not to exhaust its nature. For the moment, the expressions have been grouped, weighted, and ordered into 'fixed' rows and columns as follows:

> GROUP I: Physicality
> GROUP II: Domains (6 in number)
> GROUP III: Attributes (15 in number)
> GROUP IV: Modifiers (90 in number)

NOTATION ONE, as given, gives rise to certain comments. Following are some:

> 1. It may be regarded:
>
>> a. as a *simultaneity;* that is, as a whole, but not as 'all that is physical';
>>
>> b. as a *generative grammar;* that is, each expres-

sion signifies a particular kind or state of physicality, but is not-yet action-directed with reference to some specific context;

c. as *allo-referential;* that is, each expression implicitly refers to, and is interactive with, the others.

2. The task of an observer, …always understood to be present…, would be to engage the notation, and to connect those expressions found, in any quantity, and, thereby, to begin the process of interaction with them. Access to the notation may obtain in a variety of ways. In the following approaches, the expression: P, signifies Physical-ity, but may also signify: Perception, Perceiver, Phenomenon, and Partch:

a. expressions are connected by *fixed* row-column constraints:

(1)   P: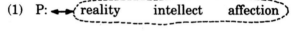

(2)   P: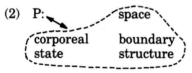

b. expressions are connected by *associations* not constrained by rows and columns:

(1)   P: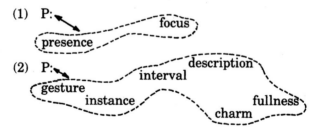

(2)   P:

c. expressions are connected by *exchanges* between, (and among) *fixed* row-column states:

(1)   P: 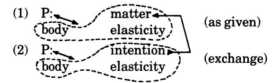   (as given)

(2)   P: (exchange)

3. The *sense* of any particular grouping of expressions is changed, even-if only *one* of them is exchanged for another, e.g.:

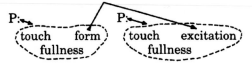

4. Each expression, as inscribed, implies the existence of other grammatical forms of itself, even though these are not shown:

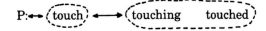

5. The simultaneity, ...although whole..., does not include other expressions which refer to physicality. With regard to MATTER, for instance, the expressions: hardness, dryness, brittleness, are not shown, but could have been. If entered, such expressions would not only *expand* the simultaneity, ...however, always within physicality..., but would also change its quality, e.g.:

(imagine)

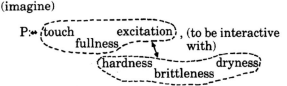

PARTCH: THE OCCASIONAL STATUE-LIKE IMMOBILITY OF THE DANCERS...THIS HAS THE EFFECT OF MAKING MOVEMENT MORE VITAL, MORE UNCERTAIN, THEREFORE MORE TENSIVE TO THE VIEWER...THERE SHOULD BE NO INNATE COMPULSION TO MOVE CONSTANTLY SIMPLY BECAUSE ONE IS ON STAGE...IN A SERIOUS LOVE DUET OR A FIGHT DUET, A DANCER NEVER TOUCHES ANOTHER DANCER, IN GESTURE OF ENDEARMENT OR ANGER. I NOTED, LONG BEFORE I EVER SAW ORIENTAL DANCING, HOW TENSION WAS LIKELY TO DROP THE MOMENT TWO SUCH CHARACTERS BECAME PHYSICALLY EMBROILED.[31]

6. The so-called domains, given in the notation, at least,[32] are always implicit, even-if not shown in a particular sub-grouping (cf. item 5, preceding). Sub-groupings cannot be experienced in context, without an observer's involvement with:

  a. some REALITY (e.g., as in 'being')

  b. some SPACE (e.g., as in 'location')

  c. some MATTER (e.g., as in 'material')

  d. some INTELLECT (e.g., as in 'idea formation')

  e. some INTENTION (e.g., as in 'purpose')

  f. some AFFECTION (e.g., as in 'regard')

7. The notation, as given, is conspicuous by its presences, but also by its absences. I regard the 'presence' of certain "absences" to be a positive value. Absences show that NOTATION ONE is sufficient to illuminate physicality, but not to define its closure.[33] In this sense, NOTATION ONE is bound,... limited..., by its presences, but unbound,... unlimited..., with respect to its absences. Its absences may be described as *knowns* or unknowns, in the following sense:

  a. known by some observer; unknown, *but knowable,*[34] by another observer;

  b. unknown to any observer at the moment, but presumed to be imminent within the Phenomenon of Physicality.[35]

8. Even though NOTATION ONE constitutes an ordering of physical expressions, ...i.e., by weighting, rows, columns..., access to it is *random*. One may enter at any point, travel through it in any direction, group its expressions in any configuration, all the while reorganizing its notational ordering, but not its simultaneousness. Moreover, the particular order of any motion through it, ...however inconsistent with the orderliness of the notation..., does not affect the order in the simultaneity. At once, any expression, ...by an intentional ACTion..., can be connected to any, and all, other(s). Since this is so, I have *unfixed* NOTATION ONE, and have transformed it into a state which I prefer:

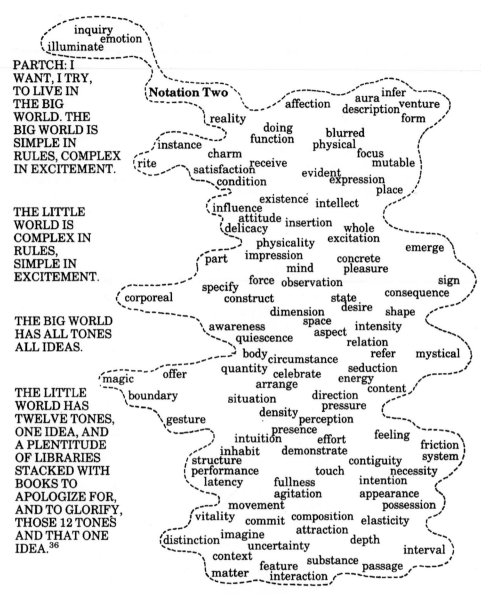

PARTCH: I
WANT, I TRY,
TO LIVE IN
THE BIG
WORLD. THE
BIG WORLD IS
SIMPLE IN
RULES, COMPLEX
IN EXCITEMENT.

THE LITTLE
WORLD IS
COMPLEX IN
RULES,
SIMPLE IN
EXCITEMENT.

THE BIG WORLD
HAS ALL TONES
ALL IDEAS.

THE LITTLE
WORLD HAS
TWELVE TONES,
ONE IDEA, AND
A PLENTITUDE
OF LIBRARIES
STACKED WITH
BOOKS TO
APOLOGIZE FOR,
AND TO GLORIFY,
THOSE 12 TONES
AND THAT ONE
IDEA.[36]

Deeply imbedded in this section's ELABORATION are the Partchean concepts of Corporeality and Whole Theater. It remains to be shown how they apply by describing the specific contextual circumstances of his work in which they are revealed.

E. DEMYSTIFYING PARTCH:

Interactions are states of being between any I ⟷ I, I ⟷ IT relationship. They, too,
comprise *kinds* of physicality, but of a different *dimension* from those distinct,
physical features which entities, per se, exhibit. Interactions refer to those
non-exclusive properties, without which, entities would be rendered 'things
in themselves'.

Any ACTion by an I, which engages another I, IT, is implicitly interactive. In this
state, the *event* of anything physical is the consequence of some kind of interaction:
and, could *not* obtain without interaction.

A state of interaction cannot be held in one I, or one IT, exclusively; states of
interaction, …understood to be infinitely mutable…, can only be held, *each to the
other,* by way of interactions between them. As such, non-exclusive dimensions of
physicality, by way of interactive states, become the carriers for the *specificity* of
an event, provide the *connection* between unique entities comprising the event;
and, thereby, are *contained in the event.* By its nature, interaction cannot be a
'thing in itself':

PARTCH: MY INSTRU-
MENTS NEED A
HOME WHILE I'M
HERE...

I am in this room; Partch's
Marimba Eroica is in this
room. I am not alone. I am
staring at it; wondering
about it. Even though I
can't call what it's doing:
'staring or wondering'
at-about me, its presence is
made clear because it, too,
is present. (We) are each
sitting in the presence of
the other. It 'tells' me
it is here.

...I CAN SLEEP ON
THE GROUND. I'M
USED TO THAT.[37]

Somehow, (We) each got
here and now are facing
each other.

I slowly walk to it, and
touch it. It feels cold. I feel
its coldness, not mine. (I
am not cold). Its coldness is
evident to me, because it
is cold. Even though it
doesn't say 'I am cold'
(in my language)
it *does* say it; (in *my*
language). Now its coldness

PARTCH: BUT
BEFORE THE INSTRU-
MENTS CAN SOUND
COMPETENTLY
UNDER THE HANDS,
AND THUS ALLOW
THE PLAYERS TO
ACT, THEY MUST
BE IN TIP-TOP
CONDITION...

...NOT A SMALL PART
OF THE ELEMENT OF
GOOD CONDITION IS
THE *VISUAL*. I
ENDEAVOR TO KEEP
MY INSTRUMENTS
LOOKING WELL...

resides in me. It didn't
before I touched it. Its coldness is now in both of (us).

I keep my hand there; on
one corner of the largest
block, (#1, with a tone
about 9/5,...cf., below the
lowest A on the piano...,);
remove it, then touch it
again. It is warmer; it says
it. (We) each have some of
my warm. It doesn't say
'thank you', (in my
language), but it has
responded to my touch; it
does say it.

(We) play for a long time.
I give; it responds. I
respond; it gives. (We) are
no longer merely staring
at each other.

I don't know if it knows
me; but I'm beginning to
know it; because it
presents itself to me, and
does something when I
touch it, it lets me know it
is there, and here.

Only once do I strike the
bar vigorously with a hand
slap. It gives me back a
roar which reverberates in
the space for a very
long time.

I don't think what is happening can be called Zen.[39]

...THE INSTRUMENTS
DO NOT MAINTAIN
THEMSELVES...

...WHEN THIS
EFFORT IS NOT
MADE, THE RESULT –
IN ONE YEAR'S TIME
– IS A PILE OF
INCREDIBLE JUNK![38]

However, it is precisely these phenomenal, interactive, dynamic states between
and among entities and physicality, ...each, to be made sense of in the light of the
other..., which frequently gives rise to perceptual, and, hence, conceptual
difficulties. Since distinct entities "appear" to be neither here nor there, ...nor,
this or that..., exclusively; and since the precise fixing of an event, say, "appears"
so elusive, it follows that some other kind of expression would need to be invoked
in order to explain what *is* going on.

Certainly the expression: 'all that is physical' suggests at least one other, namely:

'all that is *not* physical'. By this latter, *Metaphysicality* is generally understood. But, Metaphysicality, …in the allegorical sense…, embraces the *transcendence* of all that is physical; i.e., its concern is with going *beyond* physicality. And so, Physicality and Metaphysicality are distinct phenomena. They do not refer to each other except in the trivial sense that they are mutually exclusive. It follows that the same may be said for those entities contained within each.

This is so, even if I were to argue that Metaphysicality can be *referred* to Physicality only to the extent that the former does not go beyond, …that is, be included within…, the latter. This "appears" to be an outright contradiction.

It is. Nevertheless, neither the distinction, nor the contradiction, (actually they amount to the same thing), have constrained those who *do* connect them, …by way of some "mix" or other…, to Partch's Corporeality and Whole Theater. I hold that the consequence of this "mixing" of phenomena has resulted in vague and elusive descriptions of Partch; has cluttered, …indeed, blocked…, what would otherwise be a clearer apprehension of his work; and has been responsible for an unfortunate, cultish mysticism on the part of some Partch practitioners, and enthusiasts. But, in some ways, the confusion is plausible:

1. The extraordinary emphasis given to certain of his 'identifying' features, as noted above, …in the absence of equally rigorous attention to his concepts of Corporeality and Whole Theater…, has, de facto, rendered the latter seemingly inexplicable on physical grounds alone.

2. Given the notion that *perception precedes conception*, it follows no clear conception of these matters *could* obtain if their perception was either faulty, or insufficiently cultivated. In this regard, the confusion is not so much between the Physical and the Metaphysical, as it is between *conception* and *perception*, with Metaphysicality being inadvertently drawn into the Partchean arena. But, how could this be otherwise? Most of what is known of Partch is by hear/say, abstract discussions, scores (meaningless unless one can decode his notation), recordings (which, however wonderful, only give us his sounds), assorted pictures and films (mostly promotional), and, performances, …which, except for a small-but-elegant-number, fall short of his demands.

3. Partch's verbal language has contributed to the confusion. In Notations One and Two, the expressions: *corporeal, whole, magic, rite,* have been included; partially because Partch persistently used them; partially because I shall show that they can help illuminate Physicality in the Partchean sense.

   The expression: *mystical,* is also included. As far as I know, it has never been used by Partch; but it is given because his writings, speakings, and the verbal language in his scores, (which, parenthetically, enlarge this *kind* of language considerably),[40] convey the "appearance" of a mystical mind. It is understandable that Partch's usage would register "Metaphysical" to those who hold them in its light, and, who, consequently, would attach their significance to his. Now, Partch intended no such thing, and often said so.

PARTCH: AT A PRIVATE AFFAIR SOMEONE
ASKED "WHAT DO YOU THINK ABOUT ZEN
BUDDHISM?" I REPLIED, "I DON'T GIVE A
FUCK ABOUT ZEN BUDDHISM", AND SOME-
ONE AT THE BACK OF THE ROOM MUTTERED,
"THERE'S A TRUE ZEN BUDDHIST."

But, then, why would he   MAYBE YES,
intentionally use such   MAYBE NO.
expressions, if, by their   I DO NOT CARE.

MUSIC IS A TIME ART, AND BY GOD I KNOW
EXACTLY WHAT I WANT DONE IN THAT
TIME, EXACTLY HOW IT IS TO BE DONE,
EXACTLY WHAT TO EXPECT, AND I WILL
WASTE NEITHER MY TIME NOR ANYONE
ELSE'S WITH THE ANYTHING-ANYPLACE-
ANY-SOUND-APPEAR-DON'T-APPEAR-
SYNDROME. TO ME IT'S A DISEASE.[41]

use, conceptual confusion would result? Certainly he knew, ...however conjured-up were his images..., they would have to be *shown* on *stage,* the intended location for most of his made work. He knew perfectly well he could not actually *show* magic, or the mystical.

But, Partch needed to participate in the *liberation* of mundane human existence, in and by his work. In order to get to this, he found it necessary to use a language, ...*musical, verbal, visual...,* which would excite the imagination. Mundane language could not do it. In this light, then, his language can only be regarded as metaphoric.

The problem is that his language has been taken literally. And, if it has been so-taken, it is because the "appearance of things", (e.g., the appearance of *the expression:* "magic"), has also been taken as the *case.* Now to expect *literal* magic, by way of the mere "appearance" of the expression, ...taken as *the case...,* and then to attach both to the Metaphysical, is surely a paradox without resolution. Of course the confusion could easily be resolved simply by asking: "What are those so-called properties of magic, or the mystical, which *so-appear*"?

Metaphoric magic, or the mystical, is quite another matter; each signifies: *as-if* magic, *as-if* mystical; and, *so*-appears. Metaphors *can* be *translated* without going beyond all that is physical. It is precisely in this sense that I have included them in the notations.

4. Partch's music, if seen as "music", has contributed to the confusion. But, the crucial task is realizing a Partchwork on the stage. It is precisely in this location that his concepts of music, and those of Corporeality and Whole theater are challenged, and challenging. It is also here that necessary

distinctions between the Physical and Metaphysical become abundantly
clear. Following is one of numerous writings by Partch which outline the
basic scenario of Bewitched. In particular, it addresses the Prologue to
Scene One:

> (About the Bewitched):[42]
> A group of "lost" musicians wander onto a half-dark
> stage full of strange instruments and begin to play.
> In the enveloping ensemble of sound they momen-
> tarily find a direction, and forget that they are lost.
> Their music becomes a power, and their power a
> vision. Out of a percussive climax an ancient Witch
> materializes, and she takes command of her Chorus
> of Lost Musicians. The Witch and her Chorus then
> proceed to conjure up ten scenes that satirize the
> human situation as we live it.

This expression sits on the page, and resides in my mind as I observe it.
I ask: "How does one get it off the page, ...and out of this (my) mind-state...,
and onto the stage, ...to another (my) mind-state; and to other (performer)
mind-states..., as an ACTion? How are the expressions "lost", "wander",
"direction", "forget", "vision", et alia, to be shown, such that they have some
connection with that which resides on the page?"

But, of course, these expressions are not static; are not frozen "objects". For
instance, "wander" – "play" are somehow to be connected; some transition
has to take place. The space which separates their respective, distinct states,
has to be 'filled' with something. The *some thing*, in general is, at least
physical movement:

> (movement):
> A person (or so-called "thing") cannot be said to
> move from one place to another, unless the person or
> "thing" passes in succession through *every* inter-
> mediate place; hence motion is only such a change of
> place as is *successive*.

Precisely how is the space between "wander-play" to be traversed by
movement?\The possibilities are numerous; but which of these would
translate, ...*vivify*..., into theatrical ACTion, the metaphor Partch had in
mind? Part II of this paper will present a vigorous, detailed discussion of
these matters. But here, I cite two concerns, ...revealed by the above
scenario..., which contribute to the confusion about which I speak, namely: a
typical Partchean *ambiguity,* and an omni-present Partchean *belief:*

THE AMBIGUITY: ...*lost* musicians *wander*
(*cf.* above)   ...*strange instruments...*
                       begin to *play...*

Here, "to play" is to initiate the Prologue to the ten scenes which follow.

NOTE: the musicians have not-yet found a direction, forgotten they are lost, nor had a vision.

But, the music they play is immediately, obviously, complexly virtuosic. It is composed, precise, specific; it has had to be rehearsed. And, every *participant* knows that. No time has been provided in the score, scenario, or by way of Partch's numerous descriptions, for "fumbling" around with these strange instruments; which, if strange, could not, ...*at once*..., be played virtuosically. If the theatrical (metaphoric) implications of the scenario are dismissed, thereby, in favor of the compelling demand of virtuosic music, then one is given *MUSIC*, and *not* Whole Theater;[43] (it won't quite work the other way around since the music's 'real time' precision cannot be dismissed). If in this case, Corporeality and Whole Theater are *assumed*,... e.g., to merely reside in the minds of the performers, and in the minds of the audience (who have been given program notes which "describe" them); to somehow be imbedded in the virtuosic music, set, dance, or costume; to be "all there" merely because everything is on stage..., *BUT* are not *concretely* present, then what results, at best, is magnificent *performance*. All the rest is utter pretense.

But, as performance, ...and not as Corporeal Whole Theater, a Partchwork is distinguished only in *kind* from professional performances of other music(s); performances made up of parts, brought together by a conductor; each distinct, privately held, and moving in *parallel* metaphors. In a Partchwork, it has frequently been thought to be the "mix" of these metaphors, e.g., dance, set, music, which generates the "magic"; which becomes the "whole". However, there can be no such mix without intrinsic interaction of all those expressions which *comprise* the work; mere relationships won't do it; occupying the same space won't do it; nor will mysticism or plausibility. Mostly, the ambiguity of Partch's music, *within* his theater, has never been sufficiently dealt with. To not do so makes any Partch production, anti-Partch.

Linked with this ambiguity is:

THE BELIEF:

In the above scenario, it is clear that *change* has to take place; change from "lost" to "unlost"; from "wander" to "direction", from "power" to "vision", from "materialization" to "command", from "conjure" to "scene". That Partch continually desired change is made clear by the manner in which he lived his life, and what he made during its course. In this, the scenario points to *him,* as well as to Bewitched. He did not merely bring new works to the fore as a consequence of changes in his life, but made resident a *'life of change'* in each work. His ambiguities are not impossibilities, but *actual* difficulties to be resolved in the light of a desire for change.

Partchean change does not signify: change the rhythm, the lights, the scenario; nor did poetic license, self-indulgence, or superficial titillation signify it to him. Partchean change signifies: *intrinsic* change. But from what, and by whom? The 'what' is change from mundane, status-quo existence; the 'whom' is each of us.

PARTCH: TOO OFTEN, IN PEOPLES' MINDS, *DISCIPLINE* MEANS *CON-VENTION*. THIS WAS CLEARLY EVIDENT SOME YEARS AGO IN THE BAROQUE ART OF BALLET, AND, AS A DIRECT RESULT OF THE EQUAT-ING OF DISCIPLINE WITH CONVENTION IN THE MINDS OF BALLET MASTERS, WE NOW HAVE THE SPECTACLE OF BOYS AND GIRLS THROW-ING THEIR ARMS AND THEIR EYES TO HEAVEN IN GESTURES OF ANGUISH AND DESPAIR, IN THE WOMEN'S GYMS OF COLLEGES ALL OVER THE COUNTRY.

THROUGH MODERN DANCE THE INEVITABLE REVOLT, THE DEMONST-RATION, CAME, SEVERAL YEARS AGO, SHOWING THAT DISCIPLINES OUTSIDE THE PURVIEW OF BALLET COULD ALSO CONSTITUTE A DANCE ART. ALAS, LIKE THE PURITANS, WHO – WHEN THEY MOVED ACROSS THE OCEAN AND BECAME MASTERS – FATHERED A PHILOSOPHY JUST AS INTOLERANT AS THAT OF THE EARLIER TORMEN-TORS, MODERN DANCE PROCEEDED TO CONSECRATE THE DOGMAS OF ITS SAINTS AND TO PUT ONE OF ITS DISCIPLES IN EVERY WOMEN'S GYM. THE DOORS THAT CLOSE *BECAUSE* OF EDUCATION ARE THE SADDEST DOORS THAT HUMANITY NEVER WALKED THROUGH.

OBVIOUSLY, ANY FINE ART INVOLVES A DISCIPLINE, BUT IT MUST BE A FORCE THAT CUTS ITS OWN WAY, THROUGH A VERITABLE JUNGLE OF POSSIBILITIES. IT MAY HAVE ONLY THE MOST TENUOUS CONNECTION WITH MOMENTARY CONVENTION. WHEN A CONCEPT IS A SO-CALLED PIONEERING EFFORT ESPECIALLY, IT MUST CREATE ITS OWN DISCIPLINES.[44]

Now, of course, Partch's desire for change is not necessarily another's. Where it does not exist, his is simply viewed as plausible, and his work, perhaps as curiously amusing. Nevertheless, on stage, change has to be shown. It doesn't just happen. And it is the responsibility of the production, taken as a whole, to show it; and, at least, to provide the *occasion* for change in others.

Lou Blankenburg has expressed this necessity clearly and beautifully:

> "The Bewitched dancers, musicians, and Witch
> must *experience,* not merely *indicate* change."[45]

To achieve *this* state is no easy matter. But, when it occurs, …and, it *has* occurred…, one observes significant change of such intensity and focus, and of such perceivable wholeness, that the mundane, in fact, has been transcended, thereby. This is what Partch intended. He did not intend the transcendence of Physicality.

F. PARTCH'S THEATER: THE ULTIMATE, DESIRED, INTEGRATION:[46]

In all of the foregoing, focus, necessarily, has been directed to Physicality, and its sine qua non attendant, human perception. I have assumed that one can attend to the physical, but not necessarily, ...at least not self-consciously..., to corporeality. I have approached corporeality indirectly; firstly, because I have intended to demystify it; secondly, because I think one can be physical without being corporeal, but cannot be corporeal without being physical.

As perceptions take place, so do *desires* to connect with that which is perceived take place. I hold making connections, ...between and among 'entities' perceived..., to be a fundamental, human, ...indeed, living organismic..., biological, necessity. As such, the 'desire to connect', exhibits, ...at once..., the properties of non-exclusiveness, and potential 'changes of state'.

However, a desire to connect is merely implicit until some ACTion is initiated. Once an ACTion is, a desire becomes explicit, and, is observable as a physical, mind-body *interaction;* i.e., a connection has taken place. Now, of course, "things", (i.e., non-living physical matter), such as sand-storms, can initiate, or be the consequence of, ACTion; but, by no stretch of my imagination, can I attribute to their ACTion, a 'desire to connect'. Here, my premise holds only for I↔I, I↔IT connections. In each of these, at least one 'I' is always present:

> (Partch: in reference to his Cloud-Chamber bowls)
> "I said above that bowls were broken only by
> right hands (i.e., by right-handed players; ed.).
> One bowl was broken, or broke, because the
> Marimba Eroica was struck when it was close by,
> and one bowl simply disintegrated. *Now, Bowls
> are never placed close to the Eroica, on stage,
> or in studio.*"[47]

A perceiving human *is* the connecting link, and the *connector* between another 'I', or 'IT' relationship. This is so for all humans. Without human presence, no connections one could know of, would take place. It is the actual state of observable interaction, by participants in the action, which provides the *occasion* for experience; for making sense of "things"; for developing conscious-ness; for change. Because interactions, experience, making sense, consciousness, and change are mutable, they, too, cannot be held, exclusively, as "things" in themselves.

But, of course, all of this is mere theoretical speculation unless a given, participating, human is *aware* of her, his need to interact; and, by its process, to be involved in changing, and change.[48] If one is not aware of this need, mere participation is: simply that; change remains imminent, ...locked, in states of interaction..., but is not perceived by that perceiver who holds it imminently.

It is precisely the absence of awareness which I consider to be the formative groundwork for the mundane; for the status-quo. Awareness, if only by way of the intuitive, has to be developed cognitively. Mere unobserved, anti-intellectual, body-no-mind action won't do it. How mind-body awareness, and therefore, a kind of corporeality, can be developed, cognitively, is an essential difficulty. This is so, in general, but becomes *the* particular difficulty when embracing Partch and his work. Surely, *he* held mind-body awareness to a magnificent degree. It is observable in the attention he gave to the most minute detail:

> (e.g., with regard to the maintenance and repair of his Harmonic Canons):

> "a bad tone always results when the lip of the groove at one end of the nuts is not decisive. The groove should climb at an angle to the lip, and there should be an acute drop *at* the lip. If the lip groove is too wide, or if it is fuzzy, the string tends to vibrate *in* the groove, which causes the bad tone. Use a small triangular file and cut the groove (in the oak ends) at an angle, *delicately*, ..."[49]

and, to the 'mass' of his audience:

> (statement on *THE BEWITCHED* program notes, premiere performance):

> "I prefer to follow a policy of confidence in my audience. The Bewitched germinated in a dramatic-satiric idea in which words – with their characteristic talents and limitations – played a very large part, and I believe that an audience has a right to know what the verbal ingredient in that idea is. It is exactly because the talents of words are different from those of music and dance that they can be valuable in a complementary way. I am quite agreeable to alterations, editing, and shortening, if these changes can be accomplished without destroying the flavor, animation, and integrity of the verbal concept. The notes might antagonize some listeners, possibly even some who would respond to the music, though I am inclined to doubt this. The basic idea – The Bewitched – demands immediate explanation, and the scenes likewise. Without explanation the scene titles especially seem unnecessarily tricky, perhaps even precious..."[50]

Between these two examples, taken as an arbitrary boundary, lies a vast space. Partch, caught up in a motion which spanned such extremes, ...traversing every step between them..., engaged continually in acts of connecting what he found in the external world to his inner one, and, out again.

It is no wonder that his perceptions led him to connect Corporeality with Theater: theater, because its nature is interactive, ...i.e., as between kinds of materials and kinds of artists...; and, because its participants need to develop acute awareness of those unending, intimate states of interaction between mind and body, without which theater wouldn't be theater. To be sure, it was a political act for Partch to conspire to get musicians out of the orchestra pit and onto the stage. But, having done so, then what? Obviously, all of those physical actions which attend to performance, such as gesture and spatial proximity, ...suppressed in the pit, in favor of the sound itself..., become visible on stage. Here, ...for Partch..., there could no longer be pretense, nor a kind of hiding of self, behind the acoustical screen (mask) of the music.

PARTCH: AT NO TIME ARE THE PLAYERS OF MY INSTRUMENTS TO BE UNAWARE THAT THEY ARE ON STAGE, *IN THE ACT*. THERE CAN BE NO HUMDRUM PLAYING OF NOTES, IN THE BORED BELIEF THAT BECAUSE THEY ARE "GOOD" MUSICIANS THEIR PERFORMANCE IS IPSO FACTO "MASTERLY". WHEN A PLAYER FAILS TO TAKE FULL ADVANTAGE OF HIS ROLE IN A VISUAL OR ACTING SENSE, HE IS MUFFING HIS PART – IN MY TERMS – AS THOROUGHLY AS IF HE BUNGLED EVERY NOTE IN THE SCORE.[51]

In theater, even the most minute motion is registered as significant. This is what Partch had in mind, and he did everything he could to subvert the tendency of performers to revert to type when on stage; and to distract audiences from giving undue attention to one aspect or another. He made elegant, visually beautiful instruments; he formulated non-verbal, metaphoric plots; he poked his nose in all aspects of stagecraft; he intimately involved non-musicians ..., dancers, tumblers, acrobats...; he fashioned gorgeous, seductive sounds; all to be integrated into a complex of bodily movement, and action. When Partch said "All", he signified *ALL*!

Partch has to have assumed that participants in his work, e.g., performers, audience, could either be sensitive to it or not. If the former, then he hoped self-group awareness would occur: hence, corporeal theater; corporeality-as-ritual. If the latter, then he hoped interactions would at least trigger self-awareness: hence, corporeal growth.

His desire to elicit either of these responses, ...responses which would *signal* change..., is expressed in a particular way: each work is uniquely imbued with a kind of physical *seduction;* ...a kind of *sensuality*...; (here, I do *not* intend sexuality). As has been mentioned, awareness of the whole with respect to its parts, is the consequence of one's perception. If one assumes: "The whole is only to be profoundly enough comprehended, as the inner experience is *connected* to the outer,"[52] then, in Partch, one can assume intrinsic interaction, ...and, therefore, a kind of *bonding*..., can take place by way of an awareness of physical sensuality. I, for one, *do* assume that; (I did touch the Marimba Eroica, and *it* felt wonder/full).

In my interaction *with* my own makings; and *with* numerous individuals; and *with* small groups; and (so-to-speak) *with* non-human physical matter; and twice *with* Partch productions; and, sometimes *with* audiences, I have experienced physical sensuality. In these experiences I am aware of having given up, ...even-if, for a moment..., something of my sense of distinctness (exclusiveness), in favor of another kind of distinction: one in which I am *included* in the ACTion of others, as they become included in mine. And, because of this, a

heightened sense of awareness, intimacy, and (by current language) *validation,*
obtains. *I call these senses Corporeal, and also Whole.* I have every reason to
believe this is what Partch intended.

Now, it is one matter to speak of Corporeality and Whole 'Theater' when the
experience of interaction involves one, or a small number of others. It is quite
another when the Corporeality desired is in the magnitude of Bewitched. In the
following, the expression: IT, refers to Bewitched:

> (for the composer): ...it is in one sense to wonder it;
> in another to think it;
> in another to say it;
> in another to do it;
> in another to feel it;
> in another to show it;
> in another to be seduced by it; AND:

> (for the performers
> and stage crew): ...it is in another sense to wonder it;
> in another to think it;
> in another to say it;
> in another to do it;
> in another to feel it;
> in another to show it;
> in another to be seduced by it; AND:

> (for the audience): ...it is yet in another sense to wonder it;
> in another to think it;
> in another to say it;
> in another to do it;
> in another to feel it;
> in another to show it;
> in another to be seduced by it;

These conditions, each evidenced in a multiplicity of ways, states, and dimensions,
have, somehow, to be gathered up into a coherent, integrated wholeness, if all of
its participants are to experience Corporeality. It is not a condition that the
experience be uniformly the same. It would be rather impossible to know
that anyway. It is a condition that the experience of being included in the
validating, sensuous action of give-take, between and among all of the constituency, is evident (felt) by each member in the constituency. As the observable
state of the entire corporeal presence manifests itself, so does each member come
to know it. Thus, Corporeality and Whole Theater require a particular state of
being together. Of course, as in any 'made' theater, the best a maker can do is to
provide a circumstance, ...an occasion..., for change; and thereby, to *provoke* it.
Its actuation, however, is up to the participants. But, when it happens there can
be no question about it. No one is where they were when they came in.
In this sense, the Theater is no longer merely *on stage*. It is everywhere, as is the

Corporeal state. When integration of this kind obtains, I am unable to discern any significant difference between Corporeality and Whole Theater. Now, of course, this experience is in another order of magnitude from Partch's *desire*. *This is a Parchean dream, ...a vision..., perhaps even a seemingly unattainable nightmare!* But dreams, visions, and nightmares, too, can be translated within Physicality.

PARTCH: IN DANCE ESTHETICS, THE HUMAN BODY HAS A SACRED, MYSTERIOUS IDENTITY WHICH CAN BE EASILY AND SHOCKINGLY DAMAGED, AND THE BODY'S PRESERVED SACREDNESS TENDS TO ILLUMINE THE TERRIBLE FACT OF EVERY PERSON'S ALONENESS.[53]

Early in 1979, the 'Berlin' Bewitched was set in motion. There were numerous meetings, castings, private discussions with all parties concerned. On July 28, 1979, the group as a whole convened for the first time. It was the beginning of a six month effort. Among various statements offered, was the following:

I imagine a work: ...of continual, persistent energies & energizings, ...here, there, everywhere, ...coming from the entire space, from each and everyone, ...energies coming and going in diverse shapes, forms, mood, action, colors, intensities in each micro-existence of the work's existence; ...energies coming and going in large and small locations, in tiny pockets and massive densities.

I imagine a work in which I have been invited to be, to act as so-called director; ...in which I am responsible for the concept and shaping of the work as a whole, and for the shaping of its parts. I imagine a work in which nothing is imposed by virtue of ego, or self-advancement, but is inferred from that which resides IN the work, and can be drawn from it.

I imagine a work in which the many words and discussions which necessarily will flow in order to fulfill the work, will eventually vanish as the work assumes its FORCE; ...a force which I see as essentially PHYSICAL. I imagine the physicality of sounds, and vocal utterance; of sculptures and physical bodies; of movement, and arresting, electric, physical energy. I imagine these to be necessary conditions for a work which wants to put forth "MAGIC" in a day of indifference, cynicism, and tired bodies. I imagine such to be only one expression for the work; others will come sometime; others, as yet to be discovered by the collected sensibilities of our being together, and working together.

I imagine a work in which we are all participants, all necessary, all significant; ...I imagine a work where, except for certain "natural" phenomena caused by the vissisitudes of birth, such as size, weight, age, there are *no* political partitions by role, or function, such as: I, the director; you, the dancers; they, the musicians. Contrarily, I imagine a work which is not-yet yours or mine; but one which can become ours.

I imagine a work: Call the work Bewitched; call the maker HARRY PARTCH.

I imagine in such a work that it may be said: LET HARRY SPEAK FOR
HIMSELF as completely as possible; and, that it may ultimately be said,
(perhaps for once): WE LET HIM speak as completely as possible; for, without
us, Bewitched, ...if left to its own devices, would reside only on paper and in our
heads. But *with* us, and *by* us, ITS incredible action will have been initiated
and released.

5.28.79   (end Part One)
San Diego

Footnotes

[1] ref.: the Berlin Production, Akademie der Kunste; 1980 Berlin Festival; January 20-23

[2] H. Maturana: *Neurophysiology of Cognition* (1970); Collection Two Catalogue; published by Lingua Press

[3] program notes: Berlin Production

[4] ibid.

[5] H. Von Foerster: *On Constructing A Reality;* in *Allos* (Other Language), ed. Kenneth Gaburo; published by Lingua Press, 1980

[6] program notes: Berlin Production

[7] Below I discuss "appearance" in some detail. Here, I note it is one of the conceptual building blocks of Relativism. Also see: A. Schopenhauer, *Selected Writings*, pp. 1-32; ed. R. Taylor; Anchor Books

[8] ibid.

[9] i.e., "making sense"; also see: K. Gaburo, *Whole Language Language* (1978); pub. by Lingua Press

[10] Partch: *Manual: On The Maintenance and repairs of – And The Musical and Attitudinal Techniques for – some Putative Musical Instruments*, pp. 24-5; 1963; MS, Lingua Press

[11] Formally, I refer to 'presence' as any I↔I, I↔IT relation. The sense of any IT↔IT is currently being explored;

[12] Partch: *Manual*, p. 6; cf. fn. 10

[13] Partch: *Manual*, p. 21; cf. fn. 10

[14] K. Gaburo: *Concerning Commonness and Other Conceptual Dysfunctions* (1981); MS in preparation; Lingua Press

[15] Partch: *Manual*, p. 25; cf. fn. 10

[16] K. Gaburo: *C-----IS;* Pub. Lingua Press

[17] Partch: *Collected Papers;* MS, Lingua Press; *extract*, 1968; San Diego

[18] e.g., as performer, director, technician, observer;

[19] Partch: *Genesis of A Music;* U. Wisconsin Press, 1949; re-issued, Da Capo Press.

[20] e.g., including the immensely significant work of Jerzy Grotowski, and Samuel Beckett;

[21] Partch: *Manual*, p. 2-4; cf. fn. 10

[22] even "naivete"

[23] see Partch: *Life In the Houses of Technitution*, 1953; in *Allos* (Other Language), ed. K. Gaburo; published by Lingua Press, 1980

[24] B. Johnston: *Corporealism of Harry Partch;* Perspectives of New Music, spring-summer, 1975; p. 90

[25] Partch: *Collected Papers; extract*, 1968, San Diego; cf. fn. 17

[26] Danlee Mitchell, mus. director; Program notes: Berlin Production;

[27] P. Earls: *Harry Partch: Verses in Preparation for "Delusion of the Fury";* Inter-American Institute for Musical Research; p. 2, V. 3, 1967; Tulana University;

[28] Partch: *Collected Papers; extract* 1959, Urbana; cf. fn. 17;

[29] ibid., *scenario*, p. 58; (1958, Urbana);

[30] ibid.

[31] ibid., p. 59

[32] cf. Notation Two, where arbitrary categories vanish;

[33] Notation One is not a model for Physicality;

[34] e.g., "fusion", (cf. Nuclear Development);

[35] Current speculations regarding the nature of the Proton;

[36] Partch: *Collected Papers; extract* 1968, San Diego; cf. fn. 17

[37] Expressed to this writer; Urbana, 1957;

[38] Partch: *Manual*, p. 2-3; cf. fn. 10;

[39] From my diary: (dated) 4.13.79;

[40] e.g.: "ancient light", "miraculous"; "soul", "vision", "sacred";

[41] Partch: *Collected Papers, extract* 1972, San Diego; cf. fn. 17;

[42] Program notes: Berlin Production;

[43] There is nothing in Partch's writings which indicates he had in mind, the conventions, pretenses, & mannerisms of Music Drama, or Opera. In Partch, theater unfolds in ontological, not psychological time.

[44] Bewitched *scenario*, p. 55; cf. fn. 17;

[45] Statement by the Choreographer; Program Notes: Berlin Production;

[46] In effect, an introduction to Part II of this paper, which will follow, subsequently;

[47] Partch: *Manual*, p. 35; cf. fn. 10

[48] Dunn-Gaburo: *Collaboration Two: Publishing As Eco-System (1983);* pub. Lingua Press, P.O. Box 481, Ramona, CA., 92065;

[49] Partch: *Manual*, p. 7; cf. fn. 10

[50] Extraordinary difficulties with Alwin Nikolais, Choreographer for the Bewitched premiere, University of Illinois, led Partch to publicly denounce the changes in scene titles, et alia, which Nikolais made.

[51] Partch: *Manual*, p. 2; cf. fn. 10

[52] A. Schopenhauer, p. 26; cf. fn. 7

[53] Bewitched *scenario*, p. 59; cf. fn. 17

Berlin Festival performance of *The Bewitched*, 1979.

11

THE UMBILICAL CORD STILL VIBRATES

Harry Partch

A dispassionate and therefore disembodied observer might find the contemporary scene in the creative arts tantalizing beyond his understanding: that Americans require and will pay for *new* plays, *new* books, *new* architecture, even *new* art now and then, but require only *old* music, or "new" music that sounds like *old* music. ("It has to sound like *some*thing, doesn't it—Haydn, Mendelssohn, Gershwin—in order to *mean* anything?")

If our observer equates creative ferment with youth, and living in the past with age, he would take one look at the concert-interpretation industry, another at the recording repertory, and conclude that the American culture of "serious" music was born old and is staying old—that the old boy has been wheezing in a wheelchair throughout his entire life. And he might note, finally, that the business of staying old is profitable, and consequently might go on forever.

The old soldiers of the concert hall neither die *nor* fade away. They begin life over constantly; they are electronically regenerated, and the promise of their discographic future fills the Western world with a vibration that leaves room for little else of its general type. Obviously, this must continue just so long as discophiles are drawn into arguments over the "fidelity of recording" and the "felicity of interpretation" of Tweedledee *versus* Tweedledum in old-soldier recordings. From among dozens of examples one might choose a favorite piece for interpretative contention among those devoted to the grand piano and its variously celebrated concert minions, Beethoven's *Emperor* Concerto, of which there have been no less than twenty-one editions, an average of about one and a third a year, in the last sixteen years.[*]

Despite an exceptional and occasional Procrustes-slayer like Stokowski or Mitropoulis, American practices and attitudes in serious music contrast sharply

---

[*] F. F. Clough and G. J. Cuming. *The World's Encyclopaedia of Recorded Music.* The London Gramophone Corp. in association with Sidegwick and Jackson Ltd. 1952.

Also: W. Schwann. *Long Playing Record Catalog.* Cambridge, Mass. October, 1952.

with those of any other imaginative art. In order to get a focus, let us take them as a standard and run a parallel to them in plays: in almost any large city we would find Shakespeare being performed in at least one commercial theater or school theater (more likely in several), perhaps Marlowe at another across the street, or at the university, Racine at the one down the block, and perhaps Goethe and Schiller at a couple of neighborhood playhouses—at various times or even simultaneously.

Carrying this hypothesis to its logical end, we would find an Ibsen or a Shaw introduced once in a while as a sop to "modern" taste (or—if the counterpart of Mitropoulis is operative—even a T. S. Eliot), only to result in a chorus of offside exclamation: "I never *will* understand modern drama!" And where would Eugene O'Neill, Arthur Miller, and Tennessee Williams be? Why of course! Doing one-night stands for the students of girls' colleges dedicated to progressive education, if lucky.

It is the humorists and comedy playwrights who seem to stand apart and smile at us, and weep for us. So it was in the ancient world: one of the sinews of the mind, according to a Greek comic poet, is to "remember to disbelieve," and to learn that the line was often quoted in antiquity is highly illuminating. In order to emphasize the point one might paraphrase the Wilde play title as *The Importance of Being Irreverent*, for it appears to be a historic fact that those who give their lives to an exclusively specialized analysis of the work of past ages accomplish little or nothing toward vitalizing their own. (It would seem futile for any musician to protest his irreverence. Why talk to yourself?) In the realm of creative accomplishment they stand helpless before the strength of their own awareness. And—they tend to sterilize their own culture, for when they are sufficiently powerful they see to it that everyone around them is helpless also.

This pattern of intimidation before the classic might of the past—this helplessness—seems to run with few exceptions through the entire musical gentry, starting with teachers and continuing with students, professional musicians, conductors, critics, and ending—finally—with business executives (in concert bureaus and recording and publishing companies) and the musicians' union. These last two supply the nut and the lock-washer to keep everything and everybody in place and tightly screwed down. But the history of the imaginative arts would suggest that they can grow and expand only when there is some freedom of choice, when the creative individual who in the last analysis is the basic constituent of the aggregate we call *glory* can produce; in short, when everything and everybody is at least slightly *un*screwed.

Human beings have put imaginative creativity into three rough categories—art, literature, music—that are generally regarded as capable of enduring value and capable of transmission in a fairly exact form. The historical period of art, dating from the first that is widely seen and reproduced, is about four thousand years, of literature about twenty-five hundred years, of music only about three hundred years. Thus, by the *classic* yardstick, the rather gruesome classroom sense of the best first, music is the youngest of these arts by at least two thousand years.

New, wild dreams! These are ordinarily considered synonymous with youth. What do we have in music, this baby of the arts? Continuing development of new instruments? of new musical forms and concepts? of new weddings of music with other arts? No, but we *do* have some *new* interpretations, of Schubert's *Unfinished*, for example. (No less than forty-five record editions in the last sixteen years—nearly three a year. Twenty-six pages of the cited encyclopedia are required to list this composer's recorded works.)

And we *do* have youth and vigor—yes indeed; we even have rules for youth and vigor, A.D.1600–1900, with a center of gravity at about 1800 in the middle of Germany. Further, we can feel reassured that the student learns these rules for youth and vigor when we know that the record companies are always ready with new copies of the same examples. (No less than thirty-three editions of Beethoven's *Fifth* in the cited sixteen-year period.)

Nineteenth-century philosophers of the law were fond of noting the beauty and symmetry of the *corpus juris*; how thrilled they would be could they but behold in all its authoritarian symmetry the *corpus musicum*! The piano scale—no other; the piano and the European-dictated instruments of the symphony orchestra—no others; to be played in exactly the way they were played in Beethoven's day (or Berlioz' at the latest)—no others; the European usages and prototypes of harmonic progession, counterpoint, modulation—only slight "individualistic" deviations permitted. Finally, the concert forms: oratorio, cantata, quartet, symphony, concerto, opera (what bold soul will call it drama?), which may vary materially but must conform spiritually (for "*good*" *music* and *concert* are virtually synonymous).

Lawyers might wonder just how musical malefactors are dealt with, and here the *symmetry* beats anything. No trial by jury, no referee, no cross-examination, no pleading at the podium. The eccentric who (if he dares) sends in some incredible thing that grows straight out of the soil on which he stands, or something—to pin down an alternative—that more approaches a dithyrambic dance to Dionysus than the oratorio, symphony, or quartet exactly screwed down in the announcement of the prize competition is treated to a "symmetrical" silence that is simply magnificent.

What sentence could be more dreaded by the murderer, or the rapist, or the defrauder of widows, than that he should be ignored thenceforth and forever? The musical malefactor, the pioneer, becomes one with idiots, criminals, and other deviates, and—being a philosopher—this is an identification that he must circumstantially consider natural and valid, and perhaps should even welcome, because with these there is at least a possibility that he can feel at home.

The sentence of silence goes straight up to heaven, for there is no appeal. In the mind of the cultivated and professional layman—the editor, the physicist, the lawyer, the novelist, the professor of humanities, the men who might constitute a board of appeal—"good" music (meaning, of course, European music of about 1650–1900) is the most sacred of sacred things. The belief in "good" music is synonymous with the belief in Toscanini, home, mother, and free enterprise. The novelist introduces a character humming a symphonic fragment from Brahms and this is all in the world he has to do in order to make the man sympathetic, righteous, and wholly superior.

One can tear Shakespeare to pieces, and get an audience—it has been done; one can advance argument over the impact of the teachings of Jesus Christ, and get into print. But to question in any facet the Great-Wall-of-China reverence for John Sebastian Bach!

The Greek comic poet come suddenly among us could easily mistake large groups of American musicians for modern *maenads*—spending their walking hours awaiting, and preparing for, the *B Minor Mass* and the yearly ritual of the Bach Festival, to "go mad" about Bach. (The recorded works of Bach fill more than thirty-six full pages of the cited encyclopedia, and if the sampling of two pages is any indication these thirty-six list at least two thousand recordings of the composer's works in the fifteen-year period 1936–1951.)

Is this not wholly natural, considering that the American heritage is European? Perhaps, but—again—how does music compare? In at least one avenue of intellectual organization we scrutinized the European bequest with fierce honesty, and with monumental seriousness we built an edifice with our own stamp. In government, from the beginning, we developed an articulate attitude of irreverent reverence. Finally, we jumped into the shaggy lion's military enclosure and chased him into his den, thus assuming the lion's attributes. Other peoples could question our sanity if they wanted to; we could think for ourselves and told the world so.

Outbursts of passionate irreverence even sound forth once in a while from the special precincts of our art and architecture, and our literature is rich with them. But music? Judged by the synthesized curricula of our music schools only one thing is really important: the learning, the teaching, the repeating—generation upon generation—of classic European dogma. One example, the one that was bandied around Europe for a probable two hundred years before Americans somehow got wind of it: that the science of tone—acoustics, has nothing to do with the art of tone—music. If a writer were to assert that the meaning of words has nothing to do with sentences we would probably elevate him to the position of an eccentric celebrity, but the musician who aggressively asserts what is as close to a musical equivalent as one can get is likely to become an obscure pillar of society and a secure teacher of harmony.

The haughty pronouncement that Beethoven got along without acoustics overlooks the fact that Beethoven was not contemporary with the Bell Laboratories and Western Electric, this entirely aside from the fact that it is not strictly true anyhow. Parenthetically it might be observed that Beethoven was neither afraid of his own age nor intimidated by past ages. Times change—but not the average American professor of counterpoint. (Nor the record repertory: in the sixteen-year period 1936–1952 no less than thirty-two editions of Beethoven's *Eroica*. Twenty full pages of the cited encyclopedia are used to list this composer's recorded music.)

We sometimes point with pride to the popular and jazzy side of the contemporary music dichotomy, just as though we had brought the seeds of it over on the Mayflower, and as evidence that we aren't afraid of our age and are giving it suitable expression. But how much pride are we really entitled to? Aside from observing that it excites a mass and folksy kind of temporary rhythmic animality, and therefore "endures" as something terribly fascinating to the human animal, temporarily, there is as yet neither time nor palpable basis for connecting it to the idea of enduring value. The task of picking out any one popular-music concept as such is singularly ungratifying. A rhythmic pattern may endure, but who can or even wants to remember *On the Trail of the Lonesome Pine* unless it also happens to recall a piece of ancient amorous luck?

There is obviously more than one way of seeking some continuation of oneself beyond death; most people automatically beget children and let it go at that. Others there are who have insane compulsions about a kind of art that may extend their spirits beyond the moments of their mortal bodies. The human race has always bred these sports apparently, and has never seemed sorry, once they were dead.

The American public cries New! New! New! And so we get a *new* recording of—say, Tschaikowsky's *Pathétique* (no less than thirty editions in the cited sixteen-year period), in our continuing obsession with the enduring values provided by *another* people and *another* age. One might conclude, from the current emphasis on one small segment of the world's music, that there are three kinds of emphasis: ordinary emphasis, wellnigh irresistible emphasis, and—finally—recording companies. We are encouraged, universally, to center our musical tastes in the past because this ensures a maximum percentage in the gamble of profit in the present. To tumble down a few cultural rungs, why gamble on any *new* art when *Washington Crossing the Delaware* is already so popular? Also, it is easier for teachers to reiterate the technical dogma involved in painting people who look like Washington than to sympathize with the excitement of discovering Li'l Abner.

The chain of cooperation that crystallizes this situation into an archetypical *status quo* is smooth and beautiful, and has neither beginning nor end. The schools inculcate, the music and record critics pontificate, the concert and record industries magnificate, and the schools re-inculcate—a genuine musical *perpetuum mobile*. Cadmus sowed the dragon's teeth and raised an army; about twenty-five years ago some concert hall dilettante must have mislaid his false choppers in a publications office, because a whole line of record critics has arisen and has been chewing over *his* meat ever since. (No less than twenty-seven editions of Tschaikowsky's *Fifth* in the cited period. The listing of Tschaikowsky's recorded music takes nearly seventeen pages in the aforementioned encyclopedia.)

And why shouldn't the critics follow the crowd, especially when it is the *Washington-Crossing-the-Delaware* boys who carry the financial lubricant, and assert the moment? It has been said that a competent review will include a description, an exposition, and will convey something of the force of an actual hearing. One might at least wonder whether a review should not also—occasionally—introduce the philosophic question of our entire direction. What is our basis for belief in ourselves and our work, our *own* creative vitality, relative to past ages that were vital and productive by the evidence of history? Does the aggregate of our artistic leadership provide a climate for the free exercise of integrity in any area more human than the rhetorical vacuum?

One might justifiably maintain—after observing and analyzing music schools, entrepreneurs, critics, and audiences—that nine-tenths of the people interested in imaginative creativity are ahead of nine-tenths of their leaders in the perception of enduring values, and there is surely no one who wouldn't forgive him if in California he changes that fractional 9 to 999 at both ends. As audiences we do not consciously undertake to assess enduring value, yet a few of us remember some occasions with poignant awareness, or perhaps we remember being upset—we hardly know why, and these memories are not unrelated to enduring value. (There are others of us who can't remember the musicals and spectacles of ten years ago that we then sought seats for in a kind of orgasmic desperation—a slight suggestion of popular-music transience?)

Were we to take the longest period of historical awareness, the art span of about four thousand years—which is itself figuratively a fraction of a second in the conjectured history of man's evolution—and think of it in terms of one day (time is significant only in relation to time), ten years would be one and eight-tenths minutes and a hundred years would be only eighteen minutes. This telescoping of time tends to point up and render ridiculous any reluctance we may have to think for ourselves, to wait for the morning edition. It also suggests that it might be a good idea to examine the value of those whom we have allowed by default to take over the job of examining value, that may endure, say, for one and eight-tenths minutes. And let us invoke a lofty precedent: what is sauce for the President-of-the-United-States' daughter is presidential sauce for the music critic.

On the very rare occasions when he is faced with new work the music critic must think not only of his present public but rather especially of his future publics, at least half-consciously, and a frightening thought it is! But he has compensations, for he fits easily into a cosmopolitan society where nearly everyone likes to show an ugly side once in a while—like children at Hallowe'en—only because he is really not ugly, and can, with one gesture, exclaim: "See how handsome I really am!"

With books, plays, art, the respective critics are almost wholly concerned with an at least superficial resemblance to *new* work, while in music a rough guess of ninety-nine per cent of the critics' comments are perforce on the level of "stylistic" execution; whether so-and-so's A# wasn't too flat or her Bb too sharp in that Brahms *lied*; or whether the trumpets weren't a bit groggy on their entrances. One might therefore be intrigued into the assumption that music critics are hired for, are an essential part of, live, move, and have their only excuse for being in the concert industry.

Further assuming that this vocation of hashing over the minutiae of execution and interpretation was chosen willingly, can they lay any claim, by the very fact of this choice, to a predisposition toward even partially new ideas, new work, that remaining one per cent of their time? Let us try to be rational: if they can it is a case of personal triumph over the mutually exclusive, and Gian-Carlo Menotti's request for drama—not music—critics to listen to his new operas was among the most rational of human acts. Truly, the creative and realistic person must shudder with the dismay of probable future nothingness if his work is applauded by contemporary music critics.

Even when one is exceptionally qualified it is quite an overwhelming challenge to rush from the hall and bang out judgements on a typewriter in time for the next edition, while a voice over the shoulder whispers, anywhere from ten to a hundred years (or one and eight-tenths to eighteen minutes) in the future: "You're wrong!" There is probably not a critic in the arts who doesn't secretly long to be a sports writer; in the 100-yard dash you can *see* who comes in first.

What would you and I do, were we suddenly instituted as card-carrying critics? Would we be miserable and want company, that is to say—victims? Would we, overnight, talk like oracles, deign to notice or not notice, feel that even a caustic review is a personal favor in this damn-me-praise-me-so-long-as-you-notice-me world, throw our weight around, and consider this gift of power as a kind of divine fore-compensation for sure damnation in the future? The chances are: yes.

Other reverent specialists in this European culture that America has klieglighted sometimes have a by-line in the magazines of opinion or the magazines of what-have-you. From their infrequency, however, we can assume that music in this country—outside of the largely archeological contention of its own journals—is virtually beyond the purview of opinion. This would astonish an ancient Greek, who was ready to tear anybody's musical hair out at a moment's notice. Let us contemplate, then, this level of twentieth-century A.D. "opinion": what the impresario Umpty said to the celebrated conductor Humpty on the occasion of Dumpty's premiere as soloist.

Creativity? Something to charge the musical imagination and to set it running with curiosity and wonder? No. Rather, more chit-chat for the incipient record collector in the O-dear-me-nothing-*modern*! School of the Status Quo. (No less than twenty-five editions of Brahms' *First* in the last sixteen years. Nineteen pages of the cited encyclopedia are required to list Brahms' recorded music.)

Recently, four pages and the lead article of a nationally circulated magazine of opinion were devoted to the recording of Beethoven's *Ninth* (no less than thirteen editions in the last sixteen years) by Toscanini. This probably startled no one, a probability which in itself is startling, at least to a comic poet. More to the point, however, is the author's word and idea preoccupation (hardly unexpected in a disc reviewer), his reverent phrasing—a type of emotional pathology that seems to inter the conductor in a mausoleum somewhat prematurely. Our poet might also be startled by this, and suggest that not even an orchestra conductor enjoys being buried alive.

We have abounding admiration for the man who has become a musical institution housing the Beethoven symphonies, through a long life of artistry as master of the orchestra. And so—through the devoted eyes of the record critic—we see his movements as though he were a solitary figure in a drama—the number of steps he took (*five*) into the hall, and the number of stairs he mounted (*thirteen*) to his dressing room, on the occasion of his entrance for this recording. These details are doubtless avidly digested by the musically literate public, and when it is stated as a fact that the studio of the Italian interpreter of an early nineteenth-century German composer is the *sanctum sanctorum of musical America* few will be so presumptuous as to doubt it. Would it be chauvinistic to wish for some editorial guts in those among our writers who are privileged to appear in widely circulated journals? Let's run the risk: perhaps this *is* the Valley Forge of American musical vitality, for—despite a great deal of effort by at least a few rebellious American musical thinkers and creators—it could hardly show a more convincing symptom of devitalized inadequacy.

Creativity? A living, dynamic music in the ferment and flux of generation?

No, the umbilical cord attached to the old European music is as taut but unbroken as ever even with the ancient child in a wheelchair, and vibrates in classic patterns of oscillation (with electronic amplification of course) in the soul of every well-inculcated record collector. (No less than twenty-eight editions of Wagner's *Liebestod* in the aforementioned period. Twenty-one pages, in the cited encyclopedia, are needed to list the same composer's recorded music. One has to look hard to find the recorded music of a contemporary American composer that fills half a page.)

Now and then someone comes forth with a blast about politics, or about art, architecture, or playwriting that is distinguished by candor and perception, and jars us out of our comfortably boring ruts. He speaks from a position that commands attention and in a way that makes it a pleasure to get up in the morning. Who knows? Little children might be alive right now who will live to see the day when one of these privileged prophets will emerge from the protective cloak of his particular modern specialty and discover that humanity has more than one music!

NOTES ON CONTRIBUTORS

Elaine Barkin joined the UCLA music faculty in 1974. In prior years she taught at Queens College, Sarah Lawrence College, the University of Michigan, and Princeton University. She has been the recipient of various commissioning & recording grants and composer residencies, and from 1964–84, with crony-colleague Benjamin Boretz, was editorially associated with *Perspectives of New Music*. More recently she has: continued to compose sound and text; been involved in collaborative endeavors ranging from autonomous group improvisation sessions to work with dancers; been assembling tape collages and graphic-text collections; joined UCLA's Javanese Gamelan Ensemble.

Henry Brant has been the most ambitious explorer of "spatial" composition in the 20th century. His large catalogue is comprised of works of extremely diverse instrumentation and innovative design, including the exploration of heterogeneous juxtapositions between separate ensembles and radically different kinds of music. In addition to an active career as a composer and orchestrator in New York City, he taught composition, orchestration and conducting at Bennington College in Vermont. He currently resides in Santa Barbara, California.

David Dunn is an experimental composer, author, and interdisciplinary theorist. In addition to having been an assistant to Harry Partch, he was active as a performer of Partch's music for approximately ten years. His music and writings have appeared in many international forums, concerts, broadcasts, exhibitions, and publications. For many years his work has explored the interrelationships between a variety of geophysical phenomena, environmental sound, and music. The connection of this work to many non-musical disciplines such as linguistics, cognitive ethology, cybernetics, and systems philosophy has expanded his creative activities to include philosophical writings within a broad domain. Currently he is on the faculty of the Contemporary Music Program at the College of Santa Fe, New Mexico.

Paul Earls was born in Springfield, Missouri, 1934, educated at Southwest Missouri State College, the Eastman School of Music and the University of Rochester: B.M. *cum laude*, M.M., Ph.D. (Composition/Musicology). Academic appointments at S.M.S, Duke University, Chabot College, University of Lowell, Massachusetts

College of Art, Massachusetts Institute of Technology and has been a Fellow of the Center for Advanced Visual Studies since 1970. His major works include four operas and numerous large laser/music installations. He met Harry Partch while teaching at the University of Oregon; worked with him for two years, conducting his music, playing Boo, Kitharas, and the Canons. With Partch's help he built a copy of one of the Canons. Awards: Fulbright to Turkey, 1964–65; Guggenheim Fellowship in Music Composition, 1970; two NEA Composers Awards, DAAD invitational fellowship to West Berlin, 1984.

Kenneth Gaburo was internationally recognized for his innovative work including 110 experimental compositions, and numerous philosophical, aesthetic, sociopolitical writings. He founded New Music Choral Ensemble in 1960 (200 new works performed); Lingua Press in 1974 (115 distinguished publications by 71 authors); and honors included Guggenheim, UNESCO, Thorne, Fromm, Rockefeller, Koussevitsky. In 1980 Gaburo staged the first urtext production of Partch's *Bewitched* (Berlin Festival). He died in 1993.

Glenn Hackbarth was born in 1949 in Milwaukee, Wisconsin. Following an early training in jazz, he received degrees in music from the University of Wisconsin and the University of Illinois, where he studied composition with Herbert Brun, Ben Johnston and Edwin London. In 1976 he moved to Phoenix to join the faculty at Arizona State University and is currently the director of the New Music Ensemble and the Electronic Music Studios at that institution. The recipient of grants and awards for musical composition from ASCAP, the Arizona Arts Commission and the National Endowment for the Arts, he has composed for a large variety of instrumental combinations in both the acoustical and electronic mediums. Available recordings of his work include the *Double Concerto* for Trumpet, tuba and large ensemble on Crystal Records, *Le Cheval Aile* for Flute, contrabass, piano, percussion and tape on Access Records, and *Metropolis* for also saxophone and chamber ensemble on Orion Records.

Lou Harrison's compositional career not only spans six decades but an amazingly diverse array of musical styles, materials and cultures. As one of the most quintessential of West coast composers, his work and thinking have been a profound influence upon the California and American musical communities. As a dynamic champion of other composers works, he has been closely associated with many of the major figures of 20th century American music including Charles Ives, Henry Cowell, Arnold Schoenberg, Carl Ruggles, John Cage, and Harry Partch. In fact, Partch considered Harrison to be the only living composer for which he had full enthusiasm. Not only has Lou Harrison been the most comprehensive explorer of non-Western musics among American composers, he has pursued this exploration experientially as a whole musician: composer, theorist, instrument-builder, writer, and humanist.

Ben Johnston has been one of the most comprehensive explorers of extended just intonation and microtonal theory in the United States. In addition to studies with Darius Milhaud and John Cage, among others, he worked closely with Harry Partch as an apprentice in his Gualala, California studio. Rather than following in Partch's footsteps by building new acoustical instruments, he has composed in extended just intonation for ordinary instruments and traditionally trained performers. In addition to his distinguished career as a composer, he has been a Professor of Music at the University of Illinois, Champaign-Urbana, and concurrently at Northwestern University in Evanston, Illinois. His *String Quartet No. 8* was priemered at the Kennedy Center by the Kronos Quartet.

Danlee Mitchell became associated with Harry Partch in 1956 at the University of Illinois and worked closely with him until his death. Mitchell is the world's leading authority on the performance of Partch's music and has directed performances in Los Angeles, San Francisco, San Diego and other West coast cities, New York, the Aspen and Berlin Festivals, West German Radio Cologne, on CBS, CRI, and New World recordings. He is Professor of Music at San Diego State University and curator of the Harry Partch Instrument Collection and Archive.

Harry Partch was one of the major visionaries of 20th Century music. He was born in 1901 in Oakland, California, and spent most of his life in California and the Southwest. With no formal academic training he set about to revitalize the inherited traditions of Western music through an interrogation of its theoretical, material, and philosophical assumptions. Included in this exploration was one of the most comprehensive examinations of intonation and tuning theory attempted during his generation. His experiments in extended just intonation led to the construction of a unique ensemble of musical instruments created to realize his original musical ideas. These concepts were principally dedicated to the creation of a unique form of musical drama. Partch used the term *Corporeality* to embody the totality of his work: The visual beauty of his instruments, the sonic resources of his tuning system, and the physical presence and participation of musicians in the ritual action were all intrinsic parts of an inseparable whole. Throughout his life Partch stressed that his work had to be regarded as a whole effort which could not be reduced to isolated factors. The inability of most critics, composers and theorists to respect this demand was a continuous source of despair. Despite this frustration he remained a profoundly creative and non-compromising figure who deeply inspired subsequent generations. He died in San Diego, California in 1974.

Rudolf Rasch (b. 1945) is a Dutch musicologist specializing in such subjects as tuning and temperament and Dutch music history. He has written several books and articles on these subjects, including annotated reprints of early texts on tuning and temperament (e.g. by Werckmeister, Huygens, Sauveur and Bosanquet). He is employed by the Department of Musicology of the University of Utrecht (Netherlands). He runs a small specialized publishing house, the Diapason Press, which issues, among others, a series of microtonal music.

INDEX

CONTENTS OF THE ACCOMPANYING CD

1. An unedited interview with Harry Partch by Edwin Gordon. Recorded at the University of California, Los Angeles after a dress rehearsal of *Delusion of the Fury*. The interview was intended for eventual Voice of America broadcast in Europe.
2. The day the Kithara fell. Final edited broadcast of a somewhat sensationalized accident on the set of *Delusion of the Fury*, one day before the premiere.

Other titles in the Contemporary Music Studies series:

This book is part of a series. The publisher will accept continuation orders which may be cancelled at any time and which provide for automatic billing and shipping of each title in the series upon publication. Please write for details.